UNCLE ABNER
Master of Mysteries

UNCLE ABNER
Master of Mysteries

Uncle Abner has long been recognised in America as a major classic of detective fiction. Ellery Queen has ranked it with the work of Edgar Allan Poe, G. K. Chesterton and Conan Doyle. But, strangely enough, it has never been published in Britain until now. Only odd stories have appeared in anthologies to whet the appetite of British readers.

Now here at last is *Uncle Abner*, complete.

And a marvellous book it is. We are taken back to the hills of Virginia in the early days of the American republic, when there were no police and remote communities had to find their own justice. Abner, seen through the eyes of his young nephew, and accompanied usually by Squire Randolph as a kind of Watson, protects the innocent and exposes the evil-doer with a combination of shrewd deductive skill and an Old Testament moral grandeur which makes him seem, at times, to be the authentic voice of the Lord.

He shows how a murderer came through a closed window without so much as disturbing the cobwebs; how thieves crept through a keyhole to steal a horde of gold; how a dead man and his horse were made to vanish. He causes a judge to be tried in his own courtroom and reasons a lynching party into shame.

As Edmund Crispin says, in a specially written new introduction Davisson Post gives Abner some wonderfully fine puzzles to work on. But, in the end, it is the character of Abner himself, and the strong simple community around him, which stick in the mind unforgettably. In the whole of detective literature there is no other book quite like *Uncle Abner*.

UNCLE ABNER
Master of Mysteries

by

Melville Davisson Post

TOM STACEY

This edition published 1972 by
Tom Stacey Reprints Ltd
28–29 Maiden Lane, London, WC2E 7JP
England

ISBN 0 85468 131 0

Printed in Great Britain
C. Tinling & Co. Ltd.
Prescot and London

To

MY FATHER

Whose unfailing faith in an ultimate justice behind
the moving of events has been to the writer
a wonder and an inspiration

Introduction

The Uncle Abner stories remain undated to this day, chiefly because they are an early, and a very distinguished, corpus of historical detective fiction. We are in the Virginia of Jefferson's time. Davisson Post, writing mostly in the few years before the First World War, may indeed have mistaken that Virginia. Nowadays, however, it seems a great deal more like the truth than what subsequent fictional and film treatments have accustomed us to—the Palladian-style white-painted mansion, the sprightly girls in sprig muslin, the men too ready with their duelling pistols, and the impeccably groomed negro slaves handing round mint juleps on silver salvers.

Uncle Abner's Virginia—virtually cut off from the state capital by the Alleghenies—is something else again: a crude, primitive community of cattlemen and rivermen in which fine linen and a silk stock are eccentricities; in which the stink of horses is omnipresent; in which a blight on a crop may bankrupt a squire; in which legalism runs riot, and the taste of Old Testament doctrine permeates the land.

From these roots, as their representative, comes Uncle Abner, bearded, sinewy and huge in stature. His Bible is always in his pocket—and from one of the stories we learn that out of the fight which resulted when he was mocked for reading the Book by a tavern fire, only Abner, at the last, was able to stride his horse. It would be a mistake, nevertheless, to regard Abner as either Calvinist or Manichaean. Seeing the works of the Devil, he still believes implicitly in the justice of God. Moreover, men, he thinks, though they may send themselves to Hell in their own way, will never by predestination be forced to it. Some of Abner's actions seem odd—for example, his freeing of the inexcusable murderer Dix. To be sure, "Vengeance is mine, saith the Lord"; but Abner, unexpectedly, is not a retributive man. His Bible reading has sophisticated him, teaching him many things. If he were to be set down in our permissive society he would despise it, but would scarcely be surprised; in Scripture, permissive societies abound.

Abner, then, is a great deal less naïve than we might expect. For him, God is no reasoning Being: knowing all, God has no need of reason. But to find truth, man has need of it—and Abner is a superb reasoner. Like all great detectives, he reasons from observation of physical facts ("The edges fit!"). Davisson Post gives him wonderfully fine puzzles to reason from (gives him, also, that love of the apparently paradoxical statement which we remember from Sherlock Holmes and from Father Brown). Yet it is, in the long run, the character of Abner and the backdrop against which we see him that give his mastery of mysteries a special dimension. He is not the sort of figure much to be found in contemporary fiction of any kind. Strict with himself, he would pity our laxity. Therefore he stands out as a figure not merely notable but nowadays entirely fresh: the good man and the reasoning man splendidly combined in one.

EDMUND CRISPIN

Contents

A*

Chapter 1

The Doomdorf Mystery

THE PIONEER was not the only man in the great mountains behind Virginia. Strange aliens drifted in after the Colonial wars. All foreign armies are sprinkled with a cockle of adventurers that take root and remain. They were with Braddock and La Salle, and they rode north out of Mexico after her many empires went to pieces.

I think Doomdorf crossed the seas with Iturbide when that ill-starred adventurer returned to be shot against a wall; but there was no Southern blood in him. He came from some European race remote and barbaric. The evidences were all about him. He was a huge figure of a man, with a black spade beard, broad, thick hands, and square, flat fingers.

He had found a wedge of land between the Crown's grant to Daniel Davisson and a Washington survey. It was an uncovered triangle not worth the running of the lines; and so, no doubt, was left out, a sheer rock standing up out of the river for a base, and a peak of the mountain rising northward behind it for an apex.

Doomdorf squatted on the rock. He must have brought a belt of gold pieces when he took to his horse, for he hired old Robert Steuart's slaves and built a stone house on the rock, and he brought the furnishings overland from a frigate in the Chesapeake; and then in the handfuls of earth, wherever a root would hold, he planted the mountain behind his house with peach trees. The gold gave out; but the devil is fertile in resources. Doomdorf built a log still and turned the first fruits of the garden into a hell-brew. The idle and the vicious came with their stone jugs, and violence and riot flowed out.

The government of Virginia was remote and its arm short and feeble; but the men who held the lands west of the mountains against the savages under grants from George, and after

13

that held them against George himself, were efficient and expeditious. They had long patience, but when that failed they
went up from their fields and drove the thing before them out
of the land, like a scourge of God.

There came a day, then, when my Uncle Abner and Squire
Randolph rode through the gap of the mountains to have the
thing out with Doomdorf. The work of this brew, which had
the odors of Eden and the impulses of the devil in it, could be
borne no longer. The drunken Negroes had shot old Duncan's
cattle and burned his haystacks, and the land was on its feet.

They rode alone, but they were worth an army of little men.
Randolph was vain and pompous and given over to extravagance of words, but he was a gentleman beneath it, and fear
was an alien and a stranger to him. And Abner was the right
hand of the land.

It was a day in early summer and the sun lay hot. They
crossed through the broken spine of the mountains and trailed
along the river in the shade of the great chestnut trees. The
road was only a path and the horses went one before the other.
It left the river when the rock began to rise and, making a detour through the grove of peach trees, reached the house on
the mountain side. Randolph and Abner got down, unsaddled
their horses and turned them out to graze, for their business
with Doomdorf would not be over in an hour. Then they took
a steep path that brought them out on the mountain side of
the house.

A man sat on a big red-roan horse in the paved court before
the door. He was a gaunt old man. He sat bare-headed, the
palms of his hands resting on the pommel of his saddle, his
chin sunk in his black stock, his face in retrospection, the wind
moving gently his great shock of voluminous white hair.
Under him the huge red horse stood with his legs spread out
like a horse of stone.

There was no sound. The door to the house was closed; insects moved in the sun; a shadow crept out from the motionless figure, and swarms of yellow butterflies maneuvered like
an army.

Abner and Randolph stopped. They knew the tragic figure
—a circuit rider of the hills who preached the invective of

Isaiah as though he were the mouthpiece of a militant and avenging overlord; as though the government of Virginia were the awful theocracy of the Book of Kings. The horse was dripping with sweat and the man bore the dust and the evidences of a journey on him.

"Bronson," said Abner, "where is Doomdorf?"

The old man lifted his head and looked down at Abner over the pommel of the saddle.

" 'Surely,' " he said, " 'he covereth his feet in his summer chamber.' "

Abner went over and knocked on the closed door, and presently the white, frightened face of a woman looked out at him. She was a little, faded woman, with fair hair, a broad foreign face, but with the delicate evidences of gentle blood.

Abner repeated his question.

"Where is Doomdorf?"

"Oh, sir," she answered with a queer lisping accent, "he went to lie down in his south room after his midday meal, as his custom is; and I went to the orchard to gather any fruit that might be ripened." She hesitated and her voice lisped into a whisper: "He is not come out and I cannot wake him."

The two men followed her through the hall and up the stairway to the door.

"It is always bolted," she said, "when he goes to lie down." And she knocked feebly with the tips of her fingers.

There was no answer and Randolph rattled the doorknob.

"Come out, Doomdorf!" he called in his big, bellowing voice.

There was only silence and the echoes of the words among the rafters. Then Randolph set his shoulder to the door and burst it open.

They went in. The room was flooded with sun from the tall south windows. Doomdorf lay on a couch in a little offset of the room, a great scarlet patch on his bosom and a pool of scarlet on the floor.

The woman stood for a moment staring; then she cried out:

"At last I have killed him!" And she ran like a frightened hare.

The two men closed the door and went over to the couch.

Doomdorf had been shot to death. There was a great ragged hole in his waistcoat. They began to look about for the weapon with which the deed had been accomplished, and in a moment found it—a fowling piece lying in two dogwood forks against the wall. The gun had just been fired; there was a freshly exploded paper cap under the hammer.

There was little else in the room—a loom-woven rag carpet on the floor; wooden shutters flung back from the windows; a great oak table, and on it a big, round, glass water bottle, filled to its glass stopper with raw liquor from the still. The stuff was limpid and clear as spring water; and, but for its pungent odor, one would have taken it for God's brew instead of Doomdorf's. The sun lay on it and against the wall where hung the weapon that had ejected the dead man out of life.

"Abner," said Randolf, "this is murder! The woman took that gun down from the wall and shot Doomdorf while he slept."

Abner was standing by the table, his fingers round his chin.

"Randolph," he replied, "what brought Bronson here?"

"The same outrages that brought us," said Randolph. "The mad old circuit rider has been preaching a crusade against Doomdorf far and wide in the hills."

Abner answered, without taking his fingers from about his chin:

"You think this woman killed Doomdorf? Well, let us go and ask Bronson who killed him."

They closed the door, leaving the dead man on his couch, and went down into the court.

The old circuit rider had put away his horse and got an ax. He had taken off his coat and pushed his shirtsleeves up over his long elbows. He was on his way to the still to destroy the barrels of liquor. He stopped when the two men came out, and Abner called to him.

"Bronson," he said, "who killed Doomdorf?"

"I killed him," replied the old man, and went on toward the still.

Randolph swore under his breath. "By the Almighty," he said, "everybody couldn't kill him!"

"Who can tell how many had a hand in it?" replied Abner.

"Two have confessed!" cried Randolph. "Was there perhaps a third? Did you kill him, Abner? And I too? Man, the thing is impossible!"

"The impossible," replied Abner, "looks here like the truth. Come with me, Randolph, and I will show you a thing more impossible than this."

They returned through the house and up the stairs to the room. Abner closed the door behind them.

"Look at this bolt," he said; "it is on the inside and not connected with the lock. How did the one who killed Doomdorf get into this room, since the door was bolted?"

"Through the windows," replied Randolph.

There were but two windows, facing the south, through which the sun entered. Abner led Randolph to them.

"Look!" he said. "The wall of the house is plumb with the sheer face of the rock. It is a hundred feet to the river and the rock is as smooth as a sheet of glass. But that is not all. Look at these window frames; they are cemented into their casement with dust and they are bound along their edges with cobwebs. These windows have not been opened. How did the assassin enter?"

"The answer is evident," said Randolph: "The one who killed Doomdorf hid in the room until he was asleep; then he shot him and went out."

"The explanation is excellent but for one thing," replied Abner: "How did the assassin bolt the door behind him on the inside of this room after he had gone out?"

Randolph flung out his arms with a hopeless gesture.

"Who knows?" he cried. "Maybe Doomdorf killed himself."

Abner laughed.

"And after firing a handful of shot into his heart he got up and put the gun back carefully into the forks against the wall!"

"Well," cried Randolph, "there is one open road out of this mystery. Bronson and this woman say they killed Doomdorf, and if they killed him they surely know how they did it. Let us go down and ask them."

"In the law court," replied Abner, "that procedure would be considered sound sense; but we are in God's court and things are managed there in a somewhat stranger way. Before we go

let us find out, if we can, at what hour it was that Doomdorf died."

He went over and took a big silver watch out of the dead man's pocket. It was broken by a shot and the hands lay at one hour after noon. He stood for a moment fingering his chin.

"At one o'clock," he said. "Bronson, I think, was on the road to this place, and the woman was on the mountain among the peach trees."

Randolph threw back his shoulders.

"Why waste time in a speculation about it, Abner?" he said. "We know who did this thing. Let us go and get the story of it out of their own mouths. Doomdorf died by the hands of either Bronson or this woman."

"I could better believe it," replied Abner, "but for the running of a certain awful law."

"What law?" said Randolph. "Is it a statute of Virginia?"

"It is a statute," replied Abner, "of an authority somewhat higher. Mark the language of it: 'He that killeth with the sword must be killed with the sword.' "

He came over and took Randolph by the arm.

"Must! Randolph, did you mark particularly the word 'must'? It is a mandatory law. There is no room in it for the vicissitudes of chance or fortune. There is no way round that word. Thus, we reap what we sow and nothing else; thus, we receive what we give and nothing else. It is the weapon in our own hands that finally destroys us. You are looking at it now." And he turned him about so that the table and the weapon and the dead man were before him. " 'He that killeth with the sword must be killed with the sword.' And now," he said, "let us go and try the method of the law courts. Your faith is in the wisdom of their ways."

They found the old circuit rider at work in the still, staving in Doomdorf's liquor casks, splitting the oak heads with his ax.

"Bronson," said Randolph, "how did you kill Doomdorf?"

The old man stopped and stood leaning on his ax.

"I killed him," replied the old man, "as Elijah killed the captains of Ahaziah and their fifties. But not by the hand of any man did I pray the Lord God to destroy Doomdorf, but with fire from heaven to destroy him."

He stood up and extended his arms.

"His hands were full of blood," he said. "With his abomination from these groves of Baal he stirred up the people to contention, to strife and murder. The widow and the orphan cried to heaven against him. 'I will surely hear their cry,' is the promise written in the Book. The land was weary of him; and I prayed the Lord God to destroy him with fire from heaven, as he destroyed the Princes of Gomorrah in their palaces!"

Randolph made a gesture as of one who dismisses the impossible, but Abner's face took on a deep, strange look.

"With fire from heaven!" he repeated slowly to himself. Then he asked a question. "A little while ago," he said, "when we came, I asked you where Doomdorf was, and you answered me in the language of the third chapter of the Book of Judges. Why did you answer me like that, Bronson?—'Surely he covereth his feet in his summer chamber.' "

"The woman told me that he had not come down from the room where he had gone up to sleep," replied the old man, "and that the door was locked. And then I knew that he was dead in his summer chamber like Eglon, King of Moab."

He extended his arm toward the south.

"I came here from the Great Valley," he said, "to cut down these groves of Baal and to empty out this abomination; but I did not know that the Lord had heard my prayer and visited His wrath on Doomdorf until I was come up into these mountains to his door. When the woman spoke I knew it." And he went away to his horse, leaving the ax among the ruined barrels.

Randolph interrupted.

"Come, Abner," he said; "this is wasted time. Bronson did not kill Doomdorf."

Abner answered slowly in his deep, level voice:

"Do you realize, Randolph, how Doomdorf died?"

"Not by fire from heaven, at any rate," said Randolph.

"Randolph," replied Abner, "are you sure?"

"Abner," cried Randolph, "you are pleased to jest, but I am in deadly earnest. A crime has been done here against the state. I am an officer of justice and I propose to discover the assassin if I can."

He walked away toward the house and Abner followed, his hands behind him and his great shoulders thrown loosely forward, with a grim smile about his mouth.

"It is no use to talk with the mad old preacher," Randolph went on. "Let him empty out the liquor and ride away. I won't issue a warrant against him. Prayer may be a handy implement to do a murder with, Abner, but it is not a deadly weapon under the statutes of Virginia. Doomdorf was dead when old Bronson got here with his Scriptural jargon. This woman killed Doomdorf. I shall put her to an inquisition."

"As you like," replied Abner. "Your faith remains in the methods of the law courts."

"Do you know of any better methods?" said Randolph.

"Perhaps," replied Abner, "when you have finished."

Night had entered the valley. The two men went into the house and set about preparing the corpse for burial. They got candles, and made a coffin, and put Doomdorf in it, and straightened out his limbs, and folded his arms across his shot-out heart. Then they set the coffin on benches in the hall.

They kindled a fire in the dining room and sat down before it, with the door open and the red firelight shining through on the dead man's narrow, everlasting house. The woman had put some cold meat, a golden cheese and a loaf on the table. They did not see her, but they heard her moving about the house; and finally, on the gravel court outside, her step and the whinny of a horse. Then she came in, dressed as for a journey. Randolph sprang up.

"Where are you going?" he said.

"To the sea and a ship," replied the woman. Then she indicated the hall with a gesture. "He is dead and I am free."

There was a sudden illumination in her face. Randolph took a step toward her. His voice was big and harsh.

"Who killed Doomdorf?" he cried.

"I killed him," replied the woman. "It was fair!"

"Fair!" echoed the justice. "What do you mean by that?"

The woman shrugged her shoulders and put out her hands with a foreign gesture.

"I remember an old, old man sitting against a sunny wall, and a little girl, and one who came and talked a long time with the old man, while the little girl plucked yellow flowers out of the grass and put them into her hair. Then finally the stranger gave the old man a gold chain and took the little girl away." She flung out her hands. "Oh, it was fair to kill him!" She looked up with a queer, pathetic smile.

"The old man will be gone by now," she said; "but I shall perhaps find the wall there, with the sun on it, and the yellow flowers in the grass. And now, may I go?"

It is a law of the story-teller's art that he does not tell a story. It is the listener who tells it. The story-teller does but provide him with the stimuli.

Randolph got up and walked about the floor. He was a justice of the peace in a day when that office was filled only by the landed gentry, after the English fashion; and the obligations of the law were strong on him. If he should take liberties with the letter of it, how could the weak and the evil be made to hold it in respect? Here was this woman before him a confessed assassin. Could he let her go?

Abner sat unmoving by the hearth, his elbow on the arm of his chair, his palm propping up his jaw, his face clouded in deep lines. Randolph was consumed with vanity and the weakness of ostentation, but he shouldered his duties for himself. Presently he stopped and looked at the woman, wan, faded like some prisoner of legend escaped out of fabled dungeons into the sun.

The firelight flickered past her to the box on the benches in the hall, and the vast, inscrutable justice of heaven entered and overcame him.

"Yes," he said. "Go! There is no jury in Virginia that would hold a woman for shooting a beast like that." And he thrust out his arm, with the fingers extended toward the dead man.

The woman made a little awkward curtsy.

"I thank you, sir." Then she hesitated and lisped, "But I have not shoot him."

"Not shoot him!" cried Randolph. "Why, the man's heart is riddled!"

"Yes, sir," she said simply, like a child. "I kill him, but have not shoot him."

Randolph took two long strides toward the woman.

"Not shoot him!" he repeated. "How then, in the name of heaven, did you kill Doomdorf?" And his big voice filled the empty places of the room.

"I will show you, sir," she said.

She turned and went away into the house. Presently she returned with something folded up in a linen towel. She put it on the table between the loaf of bread and the yellow cheese.

Randolph stood over the table, and the woman's deft fingers undid the towel from round its deadly contents; and presently the thing lay there uncovered.

It was a little crude model of a human figure done in wax with a needle thrust through the bosom.

Randolph stood up with a great intake of the breath.

"Magic! By the eternal!"

"Yes, sir," the woman explained, in her voice and manner of a child. "I have try to kill him many times—oh, very many times!—with witch words which I have remember; but always they fail. Then, at last, I make him in wax, and I put a needle through his heart; and I kill him very quickly."

It was as clear as daylight, even to Randolph, that the woman was innocent. Her little harmless magic was the pathetic effort of a child to kill a dragon. He hesitated a moment before he spoke, and then he decided like the gentleman he was. If it helped the child to believe that her enchanted straw had slain the monster—well, he would let her believe it.

"And now, sir, may I go?"

Randolph looked at the woman in a sort of wonder.

"Are you not afraid," he said, "of the night and the mountains, and the long road?"

"Oh no, sir," she replied simply. "The good God will be everywhere now."

It was an awful commentary on the dead man—that this strange half-child believed that all the evil in the world had gone out with him; that now that he was dead, the sunlight of heaven would fill every nook and corner.

It was not a faith that either of the two men wished to shatter, and they let her go. It would be daylight presently and the road through the mountains to the Chesapeake was open.

Randolph came back to the fireside after he had helped her into the saddle, and sat down. He tapped on the hearth for some time idly with the iron poker; and then finally he spoke.

"This is the strangest thing that ever happened," he said. "Here's a mad old preacher who thinks that he killed Doomdorf with fire from Heaven, like Elijah the Tishbite; and here is a simple child of a woman who thinks she killed him with a piece of magic of the Middle Ages—each as innocent of his death as I am. And, yet, by the eternal, the beast is dead!"

He drummed on the hearth with the poker, lifting it up and letting it drop through the hollow of his fingers.

"Somebody shot Doomdorf. But who? And how did he get into and out of that shut-up room? The assassin that killed Doomdorf must have gotten into the room to kill him. Now, how did he get in?" He spoke as to himself; but my uncle sitting across the hearth replied:

"Through the window."

"Through the window!" echoed Randolph. "Why, man, you yourself showed me that the window had not been opened, and the precipice below it a fly could hardly climb. Do you tell me now that the window was opened?"

"No," said Abner, "it was never opened."

Randolph got on his feet.

"Abner," he cried, "are you saying that the one who killed Doomdorf climbed the sheer wall and got in through a closed window, without disturbing the dust or the cobwebs on the window frame?"

My uncle looked Randolph in the face.

"The murderer of Doomdorf did even more," he said. "That assassin not only climbed the face of that precipice and got in through the closed window, but he shot Doomdorf to death and got out again through the closed window without leaving a single track or trace behind, and without disturbing a grain of dust or a thread of a cobweb."

Randolph swore a great oath.

"The thing is impossible!" he cried. "Men are not killed today in Virginia by black art or a curse of God."

"By black art, no," replied Abner; "but by the curse of God, yes. I think they are."

Randolph drove his clenched right hand into the palm of his left.

"By the eternal!" he cried. "I would like to see the assassin who could do a murder like this, whether he be an imp from the pit or an angel out of Heaven."

"Very well," replied Abner, undisturbed. "When he comes back tomorrow I will show you the assassin who killed Doomdorf."

When day broke they dug a grave and buried the dead man against the mountain among his peach trees. It was noon when that work was ended. Abner threw down his spade and looked up at the sun.

"Randolph," he said, "let us go and lay an ambush for this assassin. He is on the way here."

And it was a strange ambush that he laid. When they were come again into the chamber where Doomdorf died he bolted the door; then he loaded the fowling piece and put it carefully back on its rack against the wall. After that he did another curious thing: He took the blood-stained coat, which they had stripped off the dead man when they had prepared his body for the earth, put a pillow in it and laid it on the couch precisely where Doomdorf had slept. And while he did these things Randolph stood in wonder and Abner talked:

"Look you, Randolph. . . . We will trick the murderer. . . . We will catch him in the act."

Then he went over and took the puzzled justice by the arm.

"Watch!" he said. "The assassin is coming along the wall!"

But Randolph heard nothing, saw nothing. Only the sun entered. Abner's hand tightened on his arm.

"It is here! Look!" And he pointed to the wall.

Randolph, following the extended finger, saw a tiny brilliant disk of light moving slowly up the wall toward the lock of the fowling piece. Abner's hand became a vise and his voice rang as over metal.

" 'He that killeth with the sword must be killed with the sword.' It is the water bottle, full of Doomdorf's liquid, focusing the sun. . . . And look, Randolph, how Bronson's prayer was answered!"

The tiny disk of light traveled on the plate of the lock.

"It is fire from heaven!"

The words rang above the roar of the fowling piece, and Randolph saw the dead man's coat leap up on the couch, riddled by the shot. The gun, in its natural position on the rack, pointed to the couch standing at the end of the chamber, beyond the offset of the wall, and the focused sun had exploded the percussion cap.

Randolph made a great gesture, with his arm extended.

"It is a world," he said, "filled with the mysterious joinder of accident!"

"It is a world," replied Abner, "filled with the mysterious justice of God!"

Chapter 2

The Wrong Hand

ABNER NEVER WOULD have taken me into that house if he could have helped it. He was on a desperate mission and a child was the last company he wished; but he had to do it. It was an evening of early winter—raw and cold. A chilling rain was beginning to fall; night was descending and I could not go on. I had been into the upcountry and had taken this short cut through the hills that lay here against the mountains. I would have been home by now, but a broken shoe had delayed me.

I did not see Abner's horse until I approached the crossroads, but I think he had seen me from a distance. His great chestnut stood in the grassplot between the roads, and Abner sat upon him like a man of stone. He had made his decision when I got to him.

The very aspect of the land was sinister. The house stood on a hill; round its base, through the sodded meadows, the river ran—dark, swift and silent; stretching westward was a forest and for background the great mountains stood into the sky. The house was very old. The high windows were of little panes of glass and on the ancient white door the paint was seamed and cracked with age.

The name of the man who lived here was a byword in the hills. He was a hunchback, who sat his great roan as though he were a spider in the saddle. He had been married more than once; but one wife had gone mad, and my Uncle Abner's drovers had found the other on a summer morning swinging to the limb of a great elm that stood before the door, a bridle-rein knotted around her throat and her bare feet scattering the yellow pollen of the ragweed. That elm was to us a duletree. One could not ride beneath it for the swinging of this ghost.

The estate, undivided, belonged to Gaul and his brother.

27

This brother lived beyond the mountains. He never came until he came that last time. Gaul rendered some accounting and they managed in that way. It was said the brother believed himself defrauded and had come finally to divide the lands; but this was gossip. Gaul said his brother came upon a visit and out of love for him.

One did not know where the truth lay between these stories. Why he came we could not be certain; but why he remained was beyond a doubt.

One morning Gaul came to my Uncle Abner, clinging to the pommel of his saddle while his great horse galloped, to say that he had found his brother dead, and asking Abner to go with some others and look upon the man before one touched his body—and then to get him buried.

The hunchback sniveled and cried out that his nerves were gone with grief and the terror of finding his brother's throat cut open and the blood upon him as he lay ghastly in his bed. He did not know a detail. He had looked in at the door—and fled. His brother had not got up and he had gone to call him. Why his brother had done this thing he could not imagine—he was in perfect health and he slept beneath his roof in love. The hunchback had blinked his red-lidded eyes and twisted his big, hairy hands, and presented the aspect of grief. It looked grotesque and loathsome; but—how else could a toad look in his extremity?

Abner had gone with my father and Elnathan Stone. They had found the man as Gaul said—the razor by his hand and the marks of his fingers and his struggle on him and about the bed. And the country had gone to see him buried. The hills had been afire with talk, but Abner and my father and Elnathan Stone were silent. They came silent from Gaul's house; they stood silent before the body when it was laid out for burial; and, bareheaded, they were silent when the earth received it.

A little later, however, when Gaul brought forth a will, leaving the brother's share of the estate to the hunchback, with certain loving words, and a mean allowance to the man's children, the three had met together and Abner had walked about all night.

As we turned in toward the house Abner asked me if I had got my supper. I told him "Yes"; and at the ford he stopped and sat a moment in the saddle.

"Martin," he said, "get down and drink. It is God's river and the water clean in it."

Then he extended his great arm toward the shadowy house.

"We shall go in," he said; "but we shall not eat nor drink there, for we do not come in peace."

I do not know much about that house, for I saw only one room in it; that was empty, cluttered with dust and rubbish, and preëmpted by the spider. Long double windows of little panes of glass looked out over the dark, silent river slipping past without a sound, and the rain driving into the forest and the loom of the mountains. There was a fire—the trunk of an apple tree burning, with one end in the fireplace. There were some old chairs with black hair-cloth seats, and a sofa—all very old. These the hunchback did not sit on, for the dust appeared when they were touched. He had a chair beside the hearth, and he sat in that—a high-backed chair, made like a settee and padded—the arms padded too; but there the padding was worn out and ragged, where his hands had plucked it.

He wore a blue coat, made with little capes to hide his hump, and he sat tapping the burning tree with his cane. There was a gold piece set into the head of this black stick. He had it put there, the gossips said, that his fingers might be always on the thing he loved. His gray hair lay along his face and the draft of the chimney moved it.

He wondered why we came, and his eyes declared how the thing disturbed him; they flared up and burned down—now gleaming in his head as he looked us over, and now dull as he considered what he saw.

The man was misshapen and doubled up, but there was strength and vigor in him. He had a great, cavernous mouth, and his voice was a sort of bellow. One has seen an oak tree, dwarfed and stunted into knots, but with the toughness and vigor of a great oak in it. Gaul was a thing like that.

He cried out when he saw Abner. He was taken by surprise; and he wished to know if we came by chance or upon some errand.

"Abner," he said, "come in. It's a devil's night—rain and the driving wind."

"The weather," said Abner, "is in God's hand."

"God!" cried Gaul. "I would shoestrap* such a God! The autumn is not half over and here is winter come, and no pasture left and the cattle to be fed."

Then he saw me, with my scared white face—and he was certain that we came by chance. He craned his thick neck and looked.

"Bub," he said, "come in and warm your fingers. I will not hurt you. I did not twist my body up like this to frighten children—it was Abner's God."

We entered and sat down by the fire. The apple tree blazed and crackled; the wind outside increased; the rain turned to a kind of sleet that rattled on the window-glass like shot. The room was lighted by two candles in tall brass candlesticks. They stood at each end of the mantelpiece, smeared with tallow. The wind whooped and spat into the chimney; and now and then a puff of wood-smoke blew out and mounted up along the blackened fireboard.

Abner and the hunchback talked of the price of cattle, of the "blackleg" among yearlings—that fatal disease that we had so much trouble with—and of the "lump-jaw."

Gaul said that if calves were kept in small lots and not all together the "blackleg" was not so apt to strike them; and he thought the "lump-jaw" was a germ. Fatten the bullock with green corn and put it in a car, he said, when the lump begins to come. The Dutch would eat it—and what poison could hurt the Dutch! But Abner said the creature should be shot.

"And lose the purchase money and a summer's grazing?" cried Gaul. "Not I! I ship the beast."

"Then," said Abner, "the inspector in the market ought to have it shot and you fined to boot."

"The inspector in the market!" And Gaul laughed. "Why, I slip him a greenback—thus!"—and he set his thumb against his palm. "And he is glad to see me. 'Gaul, bring in all you can,' said one; 'it means a little something to us both.' " And the hunchback's laugh clucked and chuckled in his throat.

And they talked of renters, and men to harvest the hay and

---

* Referring to the custom of flogging a slave with a shoemaker's strap.

feed the cattle in the winter. And on this topic Gaul did not laugh; he cursed. Labor was a lost art and the breed of men run out. This new set were worthless—they had hours—and his oaths filled all the rafters. Hours! Why, under his father men worked from dawn until dark and cleaned their horses by a lantern. . . . These were decadent times that we were on. In the good days one bought a man for two hundred eagles; but now the creature was a citizen and voted at the polls—and could not be kicked. And if one took his cane and drubbed him he was straightway sued at law, in an action of trespass on the case, for damages. . . . Men had gone mad with these new-fangled notions, and the earth was likely to grow up with weeds!

Abner said there was a certain truth in this—and that truth was that men were idler than their fathers. Certain preachers preached that labor was a curse and backed it up with Scripture; but he had read the Scriptures for himself and the curse was idleness. Labor and God's Book would save the world; they were two wings that a man could get his soul to Heaven on.

"They can all go to hell, for me," said Gaul, "and so I have my day's work first."

And he tapped the tree with his great stick and cried out that his workhands robbed him. He had to sit his horse and watch or they hung their scythes up; and he must put sulphur in his cattle's meal or they stole it from him; and they milked his cows to feed their scurvy babies. He would have their hides off if it were not for these tender laws.

Abner said that, while one saw to his day's work done, he must see to something more; that a man was his brother's keeper in spite of Cain's denial—and he must keep him; that the elder had his right to the day's work, but the younger had also his right to the benefits of his brother's guardianship. The fiduciary had One to settle with. It would go hard if he should shirk the trust.

"I do not recognize your trust," said Gaul. "I live here for myself."

"For yourself!" cried Abner. "And would you know what God thinks of you?"

"And would you know what I think of God?" cried Gaul.

"What do you think of Him?" said Abner.

"I think He's a scarecrow," said Gaul. "And I think, Abner, that I am a wiser bird than you are. I have not sat cawing in a tree, afraid of this thing. I have seen its wooden spine under its patched jacket, and the crosspiece peeping from the sleeves, and its dangling legs. And I have gone down into its field and taken what I liked in spite of its flapping coattails. . . . Why, Abner, this thing your God depends on is a thing called fear; and I do not have it."

Abner looked at him hard, but he did not answer. He turned, instead, to me.

"Martin," he said, "you must go to sleep, lad." And he wrapped me in his greatcoat and put me to bed on the sofa— behind him in the corner. I was snug and warm there and I could have slept like Saul, but I was curious to know what Abner came for and I peeped out through a buttonhole of the greatcoat.

Abner sat for a long time, his elbows on his knees, his hands together and his eyes looking into the fire. The hunch-back watched him, his big, hairy hands moving on the padded arms of his chair and his sharp eyes twinkling like specks of glass. Finally Abner spoke—I judged he believed me now asleep.

"And so, Gaul," he said, "you think God is a scarecrow?"

"I do," said Gaul.

"And you have taken what you liked?"

"I have," said Gaul.

"Well," said Abner, "I have come to ask you to return what you have taken—and something besides, for usury."

He got a folded paper out of his pocket and handed it across the hearth to Gaul.

The hunchback took it, leaned back in his chair, unfolded it at his leisure and at his leisure read it through.

"A deed in fee," he said, "for all these lands . . . to my brother's children. The legal terms are right: 'Doth grant, with covenants of general warranty.' . . . It is well drawn, Abner; but I am not pleased to 'grant.' "

"Gaul," said Abner, "there are certain reasons that may move you."

The hunchback smiled.

"They must be very excellent to move a man to alienate his lands."

"Excellent they are," said Abner. "I shall mention the best one first."

"Do," said Gaul, and his grotesque face was merry.

"It is this," said Abner: "You have no heirs. Your brother's son is now a man; he should marry a wife and rear up children to possess these lands. And, as he is thus called upon to do what you cannot do, Gaul, he should have the things you have, to use."

"That's a very pretty reason, Abner," said the hunchback, "and it does you honor; but I know a better."

"What is it, Gaul?" said Abner.

The hunchback grinned. "Let us say, my pleasure!"

Then he struck his bootleg with his great black stick.

"And now," he cried, "who's back of this tomfoolery?"

"I am," said Abner.

The hunchback's heavy brows shot down. He was not disturbed, but he knew that Abner moved on no fool's errand.

"Abner," he said, "you have some reason for this thing. What is it?"

"I have several reasons for it," replied Abner, "and I gave you the best one first."

"Then the rest are not worth the words to say them in," cried Gaul.

"You are mistaken there," replied Abner; "I said that I would give you the best reason, not the strongest. . . . Think of the reason I have given. We do not have our possessions in fee in this world, Gaul, but upon lease and for a certain term of service. And when we make default in that service the lease abates and a new man can take the title."

Gaul did not understand and he was wary.

"I carry out my brother's will," he said.

"But the dead," replied Abner, "cannot retain dominion over things. There can be no tenure beyond a life estate. These lands and chattels are for the uses of men as they arrive. The needs of the living overrule the devises of the dead."

Gaul was watching Abner closely. He knew that this was

some digression, but he met it with equanimity. He put his big, hairy fingers together and spoke with a judicial air.

"Your argument," he said, "is without a leg to stand on. It is the dead who govern. Look you, man, how they work their will upon us! Who have made the laws? The dead! Who have made the customs that we obey and that form and shape our lives? The dead! And the titles to our lands—have not the dead devised them? . . . If a surveyor runs a line he begins at some corner that the dead set up; and if one goes to law upon a question the judge looks backward through his books until he finds out how the dead have settled it—and he follows that. And all the writers, when they would give weight and authority to their opinions, quote the dead; and the orators and all those who preach and lecture—are not their mouths filled with words that the dead have spoken? Why, man, our lives follow grooves that the dead have run out with their thumbnails!"

He got on his feet and looked at Abner.

"What my brother has written in his will I will obey," he said. "Have you seen that paper, Abner?"

"I have not," said Abner, "but I have read the copy in the county clerk's book. It bequeathed these lands to you."

The hunchback went over to an old secretary standing against the wall. He pulled it open, got out the will and a pack of letters and brought them to the fire. He laid the letters on the table beside Abner's deed and held out the will.

Abner took the testament and read it.

"Do you know my brother's writing?" said Gaul.

"I do," said Abner.

"Then you know he wrote that will."

"He did," said Abner. "It is in Enoch's hand." Then he added: "But the date is a month before your brother came here."

"Yes," said Gaul; "it was not written in this house. My brother sent it to me. See—here is the envelope that it came in, postmarked on that date."

Abner took the envelope and compared the date. "It is the very day," he said, "and the address is in Enoch's hand."

"It is," said Gaul; "when my brother had set his signature to this will he addressed that cover. He told me of it." The hunchback sucked in his cheeks and drew down his eyelids. "Ah, yes," he said, "my brother loved me!"

"He must have loved you greatly," replied Abner, "to thus disinherit his own flesh and blood."

"And am not I of his own flesh and blood too?" cried the hunchback. "The strain of blood in my brother runs pure in me; in these children it is diluted. Shall not one love his own blood first?"

"Love!" echoed Abner. "You speak the word, Gaul—but do you understand it?"

"I do," said Gaul; "for it bound my brother to me."

"And did it bind you to him?" said Abner.

I could see the hunchback's great white eyelids drooping and his lengthened face.

"We were like David and Jonathan," he said. "I would have given my right arm for Enoch and he would have died for me."

"He did!" said Abner.

I saw the hunchback start, and, to conceal the gesture, he stooped and thrust the trunk of the apple tree a little farther into the fireplace. A cloud of sparks sprang up. A gust of wind caught the loose sash in the casement behind us and shook it as one, barred out and angry, shakes a door. When the hunchback rose Abner had gone on.

"If you loved your brother like that," he said, "you will do him this service—you will sign this deed."

"But, Abner," replied Gaul, "such was not my brother's will. By the law, these children will inherit at my death. Can they not wait?"

"Did you wait?" said Abner.

The hunchback flung up his head.

"Abner," he cried, "what do you mean by that?" And he searched my uncle's face for some indicatory sign; but there was no sign there—the face was stern and quiet.

"I mean," said Abner, "that one ought not to have an interest in another's death."

"Why not?" said Gaul.

"Because," replied Abner, "one may be tempted to step in before the providence of God and do its work for it."

Gaul turned the innuendo with a cunning twist.

B

"You mean," he said, "that these children may come to seek my death?"

I was astonished at Abner's answer.

"Yes," he said; "that is what I mean."

"Man," cried the hunchback, "you make me laugh!"

"Laugh as you like," replied Abner; "but I am sure that these children will not look at this thing as we have looked at it."

"As who have looked at it?" said Gaul.

"As my brother Rufus and Elnathan Stone and I," said Abner.

"And so," said the hunchback, "you gentlemen have considered how to save my life. I am much obliged to you." He made a grotesque, mocking bow. "And how have you meant to save it?"

"By the signing of that deed," said Abner.

"I thank you!" cried the hunchback. "But I am not pleased to save my life that way."

I thought Abner would give some biting answer; but, instead, he spoke slowly and with a certain hesitation.

"There is no other way," he said. "We have believed that the stigma of your death and the odium on the name and all the scandal would in the end wrong these children more than the loss of this estate during the term of your natural life; but it is clear to me that they will not so regard it. And we are bound to lay it before them if you do not sign this deed. It is not for my brother Rufus and Elnathan Stone and me to decide this question."

"To decide what question?" said Gaul.

"Whether you are to live or die!" said Abner.

The hunchback's face grew stern and resolute. He sat down in his chair, put his stick between his knees and looked my uncle in the eyes.

"Abner," he said, "you are talking in some riddle. . . . Say the thing out plain. Do you think I forged that will?"

"I do not," said Abner.

"Nor could any man!" cried the hunchback. "It is in my brother's hand—every word of it; and, besides, there is neither ink nor paper in this house. I figure on a slate; and when I have a thing to say I go and tell it."

"And yet," said Abner, "the day before your brother's death you bought some sheets of foolscap of the postmaster."

"I did," said Gaul—"and for my brother. Enoch wished to make some calculations with his pencil. I have the paper with his figures on it."

He went to his desk and brought back some sheets.

"And yet," said Abner, "this will is written on a page of foolscap."

"And why not?" said Gaul. "Is it not sold in every store to Mexico?"

It was the truth—and Abner drummed on the table.

"And now," said Gaul, "we have laid one suspicion by looking it squarely in the face; let us lay the other. What did you find about my brother's death to moon over?"

"Why," said Abner, "should he take his own life in this house?"

"I do not know that," said Gaul.

"I will tell you," said Abner; "we found a bloody hand-print on your brother!"

"Is that all that you found on him?"

"That is all," said Abner.

"Well," cried Gaul, "does that prove that I killed him? Let me look your ugly suspicion in the face. Were not my brother's hands covered with his blood and was not the bed covered with his finger-prints, where he had clutched about it in his death-struggle?"

"Yes," said Abner; "that is all true."

"And was there any mark or sign in that print," said Gaul, "by which you could know that it was made by any certain hand"—and he spread out his fingers—"as, for instance, my hand?"

"No," said Abner.

There was victory in Gaul's face.

He had now learned all that Abner knew and he no longer feared him. There was no evidence against him—even I saw that.

"And now," he cried, "will you get out of my house? I will have no more words with you. Begone!"

Abner did not move. For the last five minutes he had been at work at something, but I could not see what it was, for

his back was toward me. Now he turned to the table beside
Gaul and I saw what he had been doing. He had been making
a pen out of a goosequill! He laid the pen down on the table
and beside it a horn of ink. He opened out the deed that he
had brought, put his finger on a line, dipped the quill into
the ink and held it out to Gaul.

"Sign there!" he said.

The hunchback got on his feet, with an oath.

"Begone with your damned paper!" he cried.

Abner did not move.

"When you have signed," he said.

"Signed!" cried the hunchback. "I will see you and your
brother Rufus, and Elnathan Stone, and all the kit and kittle
of you in hell!"

"Gaul," said Abner, "you will surely see all who are to be
seen in hell!"

By Abner's manner I knew that the end of the business had
arrived. He seized the will and the envelope that Gaul had
brought from his secretary and held them out before him.

"You tell me," he said, "that these papers were written at
one sitting! Look! The hand that wrote that envelope was
calm and steady, but the hand that wrote this will shook. See
how the letters wave and jerk! I will explain it. You have kept
that envelope from some old letter; but this paper was written
in this house—in fear! And it was written on the morning that
your brother died. . . . Listen! When Elnathan Stone stepped
back from your brother's bed he stumbled over a piece of
carpet. The under side of that carpet was smeared with ink,
where a bottle had been broken. I put my finger on it and it
was wet."

The hunchback began to howl and bellow like a beast
penned in a corner. I crouched under Abner's coat in terror.
The creature's cries filled the great, empty house. They rose
a hellish crescendo on the voices of the wind; and for accom-
paniment the sleet played shrill notes on the windowpanes,
and the loose shingles clattered a staccato, and the chimney
whistled—like weird instruments under a devil's fingers.

And all the time Abner stood looking down at the man—
an implacable, avenging Nemesis—and his voice, deep and
level, did not change.

"But, before that, we knew that you had killed your brother! We knew it when we stood before his bed. 'Look there,' said Rufus—'at that bloody handprint!' . . . We looked. . . . And we knew that Enoch's hand had not made that print. Do you know how we knew that, Gaul? . . . I will tell you. . . . The bloody print on your brother's right hand was the print of a right hand!"

Gaul signed the deed, and at dawn we rode away, with the hunchback's promise that he would come that afternoon before a notary and acknowledge what he had signed; but he did not come—neither on that day nor on any day after that.

When Abner went to fetch him he found him swinging from his elm tree.

Chapter 3

The Angel of the Lord

I ALWAYS THOUGHT my father took a long chance, but somebody had to take it and certainly I was the one least likely to be suspected. It was a wild country. There were no banks. We had to pay for the cattle, and somebody had to carry the money. My father and my uncle were always being watched. My father was right, I think.

"Abner," he said, "I'm going to send Martin. No one will ever suppose that we would trust this money to a child."

My uncle drummed on the table and rapped his heels on the floor. He was a bachelor, stern and silent. But he could talk . . . and when he did, he began at the beginning and you heard him through; and what he said—well, he stood behind it.

"To stop Martin," my father went on, "would be only to lose the money; but to stop you would be to get somebody killed."

I knew what my father meant. He meant that no one would undertake to rob Abner until after he had shot him to death.

I ought to say a word about my Uncle Abner. He was one of those austere, deeply religious men who were the product of the Reformation. He always carried a Bible in his pocket and he read it where he pleased. Once the crowd at Roy's Tavern tried to make sport of him when he got his book out by the fire; but they never tried it again. When the fight was over Abner paid Roy eighteen silver dollars for the broken chairs and the table—and he was the only man in the tavern who could ride a horse. Abner belonged to the church militant, and his God was a war lord.

So that is how they came to send me. The money was in greenbacks in packages. They wrapped it up in newspaper and put it into a pair of saddle-bags, and I set out. I was about

41

nine years old. No, it was not as bad as you think. I could ride a horse all day when I was nine years old—most any kind of a horse. I was tough as whit'-leather, and I knew the country I was going into. You must not picture a little boy rolling a hoop in the park.

It was an afternoon in early autumn. The clay roads froze in the night; they thawed out in the day and they were a bit sticky. I was to stop at Roy's Tavern, south of the river, and go on in the morning. Now and then I passed some cattle driver, but no one overtook me on the road until almost sundown; then I heard a horse behind me and a man came up. I knew him. He was a cattleman named Dix. He had once been a shipper, but he had come in for a good deal of bad luck. His partner, Alkire, had absconded with a big sum of money due the grazers. This had ruined Dix; he had given up his land, which wasn't very much, to the grazers. After that he had gone over the mountain to his people, got together a pretty big sum of money and bought a large tract of grazing land. Foreign claimants had sued him in the courts on some old title and he had lost the whole tract and the money that he had paid for it. He had married a remote cousin of ours and he had always lived on her lands, adjoining those of my Uncle Abner.

Dix seemed surprised to see me on the road.

"So it's you, Martin," he said; "I thought Abner would be going into the upcountry."

One gets to be a pretty cunning youngster, even at this age, and I told no one what I was about.

"Father wants the cattle over the river to run a month," I returned easily, "and I'm going up there to give his orders to the grazers."

He looked me over, then he rapped the saddlebags with his knuckles. "You carry a good deal of baggage, my lad."

I laughed. "Horse feed," I said. "You know my father! A horse must be fed at dinner time, but a man can go till he gets it."

One was always glad of any company on the road, and we fell into an idle talk. Dix said he was going out into the Ten Mile country; and I have always thought that was, in fact, his intention. The road turned south about a mile our side of the tavern. I never liked Dix; he was of an apologetic manner, with a cunning, irresolute face .

A little later a man passed us at a gallop. He was a drover named Marks, who lived beyond my Uncle Abner, and he was riding hard to get in before night. He hailed us, but he did not stop; we got a shower of mud and Dix cursed him. I have never seen a more evil face. I suppose it was because Dix usually had a grin about his mouth, and when that sort of face gets twisted there's nothing like it.

After that he was silent. He rode with his head down and his fingers plucking at his jaw, like a man in some perplexity. At the crossroads he stopped and sat for some time in the saddle, looking before him. I left him there, but at the bridge he overtook me. He said he had concluded to get some supper and go on after that.

Roy's Tavern consisted of a single big room, with a loft above it for sleeping quarters. A narrow covered way connected this room with the house in which Roy and his family lived. We used to hang our saddles on wooden pegs in this covered way. I have seen that wall so hung with saddles that you could not find a place for another stirrup. But tonight Dix and I were alone in the tavern. He looked cunningly at me when I took the saddle-bags with me into the big room and when I went with them up the ladder into the loft. But he said nothing—in fact, he had scarcely spoken. It was cold; the road had begun to freeze when we got in. Roy had lighted a big fire. I left Dix before it. I did not take off my clothes, because Roy's beds were mattresses of wheat straw covered with heifer skins—good enough for summer but pretty cold on such a night, even with the heavy, hand-woven coverlet in big white and black checks.

I put the saddle-bags under my head and lay down. I went at once to sleep, but I suddenly awaked. I thought there was a candle in the loft, but it was a gleam of light from the fire below, shining through a crack in the floor. I lay and watched it, the coverlet pulled up to my chin. Then I began to wonder why the fire burned so brightly. Dix ought to be on his way some time and it was a custom for the last man to rake out the fire. There was not a sound. The light streamed steadily through the crack.

Presently it occurred to me that Dix had forgotten the fire and that I ought to go down and rake it out. Roy always warned us about the fire when he went to bed. I got up, wrapped the great coverlet around me, went over to the gleam of light and looked down through the crack in the floor. I had to lie out at full length to get my eye against the board. The hickory logs had turned to great embers and glowed like a furnace of red coals.

Before this fire stood Dix. He was holding out his hands and turning himself about as though he were cold to the marrow; but with all that chill upon him, when the man's face came into the light I saw it covered with a sprinkling of sweat.

I shall carry the memory of that face. The grin was there at the mouth, but it was pulled about; the eyelids were drawn in; the teeth were clamped together. I have seen a dog poisoned with strychnine look like that.

I lay there and watched the thing. It was as though something potent and evil dwelling within the man were in travail to re-form his face upon its image. You cannot realize how that devilish labor held me—the face worked as though it were some plastic stuff, and the sweat oozed through. And all the time the man was cold; and he was crowding into the fire and turning himself about and putting out his hands. And it was as though the heat would no more enter in and warm him than it will enter in and warm the ice.

It seemed to scorch him and leave him cold—and he was fearfully and desperately cold! I could smell the singe of the fire on him, but it had no power against this diabolic chill. I began myself to shiver, although I had the heavy coverlet wrapped around me.

The thing was a fascinating horror; I seemed to be looking down into the chamber of some abominable maternity. The room was filled with the steady red light of the fire. Not a shadow moved in it. And there was silence. The man had taken off his boots and he twisted before the fire without a sound. It was like the shuddering tales of possession or transformation by a drug. I thought the man would burn himself to death. His clothes smoked. How could he be so cold?

Then, finally, the thing was over! I did not see it for his face was in the fire. But suddenly he grew composed and stepped back into the room. I tell you I was afraid to look! I do not know what thing I expected to see there, but I did not think it would be Dix.

Well, it was Dix; but not the Dix that any of us knew. There was a certain apology, a certain indecision, a certain servility in that other Dix, and these things showed about his face. But there was none of these weaknesses in this man.

His face had been pulled into planes of firmness and decision; the slack in his features had been taken up; the furtive moving of the eye was gone. He stood now squarely on his feet and he was full of courage. But I was afraid of him as I have never been afraid of any human creature in this world! Something that had been servile in him, that had skulked behind disguises, that had worn the habiliments of subterfuge, had now come forth; and it had molded the features of the man to its abominable courage.

Presently he began to move swiftly about the room. He looked out at the window and he listened at the door; then he went softly into the covered way. I thought he was going on his journey; but then he could not be going with his boots there beside the fire. In a moment he returned with a saddle blanket in his hand and came softly across the room to the ladder.

Then I understood the thing that he intended, and I was motionless with fear. I tried to get up, but I could not. I could only lie there with my eye strained to the crack in the floor. His foot was on the ladder, and I could already feel his hand on my throat and that blanket on my face, and the suffocation of death in me, when far away on the hard road I heard a horse!

He heard it, too, for he stopped on the ladder and turned his evil face about toward the door. The horse was on the long hill beyond the bridge, and he was coming as though the devil rode in his saddle. It was a hard, dark night. The frozen road was like flint; I could hear the iron of the shoes ring. Whoever rode that horse rode for his life or for something more than his life, or he was mad. I heard the horse strike the bridge and thunder across it. And all the while Dix hung there on the ladder by his hands and listened. Now he sprang softly down, pulled on his boots and stood up before the fire, his face—this new face—gleaming with its evil courage. The next moment the horse stopped.

I could hear him plunge under the bit, his iron shoes ripping the frozen road; then the door leaped back and my Uncle Abner was in the room. I was so glad that my heart almost choked me and for a moment I could hardly see—everything was in a sort of mist.

Abner swept the room in a glance, then he stopped.

"Thank God!" he said; "I'm in time." And he drew his hand down over his face with the fingers hard and close as though he pulled something away.

"In time for what?" said Dix.

Abner looked him over. And I could see the muscles of his big shoulders stiffen as he looked. And again he looked him over. Then he spoke and his voice was strange.

"Dix," he said, "is it you?"

"Who would it be but me?" said Dix.

"It might be the devil," said Abner. "Do you know what your face looks like?"

"No matter what it looks like!" said Dix.

"And so," said Abner, "we have got courage with this new face."

Dix threw up his head.

"Now, look here, Abner," he said, "I've had about enough of your big manner. You ride a horse to death and you come plunging in here; what the devil's wrong with you?"

"There's nothing wrong with me," replied Abner, and his voice was low. "But there's something damnably wrong with you, Dix."

"The devil take you," said Dix, and I saw him measure Abner with his eye. It was not fear that held him back; fear was gone out of the creature; I think it was a kind of prudence.

Abner's eyes kindled, but his voice remained low and steady.

"Those are big words," he said.

"Well," cried Dix, "get out of the door then and let me pass!"

"Not just yet," said Abner; "I have something to say to you."

"Say it then," cried Dix, "and get out of the door."

"Why hurry?" said Abner. "It's a long time until daylight, and I have a good deal to say."

"You'll not say it to me," said Dix. "I've got a trip to make tonight; get out of the door."

Abner did not move. "You've got a longer trip to make tonight than you think, Dix," he said; "but you're going to hear what I have to say before you set out on it."

I saw Dix rise on his toes and I knew what he wished for. He wished for a weapon; and he wished for the bulk of bone and muscle that would have a chance against Abner. But he had neither the one nor the other. And he stood there on his toes and began to curse—low, vicious, withering oaths, that were like the swish of a knife.

Abner was looking at the man with a curious interest.

"It is strange," he said, as though speaking to himself, "but it explains the thing. While one is the servant of neither, one has the courage of neither; but when he finally makes his choice he gets what his master has to give him."

Then he spoke to Dix.

"Sit down!" he said; and it was in that deep, level voice that Abner used when he was standing close behind his words. Every man in the hills knew that voice; one had only a moment to decide after he heard it. Dix knew that, and yet for one instant he hung there on his toes, his eyes shimmering like a weasel's, his mouth twisting. He was not afraid! If he had had the ghost of a chance against Abner he would have taken it. But he knew he had not, and with an oath he threw the saddle blanket into a corner and sat down by the fire.

Abner came away from the door then. He took off his great coat. He put a log on the fire and he sat down across the hearth from Dix. The new hickory sprang crackling into flames. For a good while there was silence; the two men sat at either end of the hearth without a word. Abner seemed to have fallen into a study of the man before him. Finally he spoke:

"Dix," he said, "do you believe in the providence of God?" Dix flung up his head.

"Abner," he cried, "if you are going to talk nonsense I promise you upon my oath that I will not stay to listen."

Abner did not at once reply. He seemed to begin now at another point.

"Dix," he said, "you've had a good deal of bad luck. . . . Perhaps you wish it put that way."

"Now, Abner," he cried, "you speak the truth; I have had hell's luck."

"Hell's luck you have had," replied Abner. "It is a good word. I accept it. Your partner disappeared with all the money of the grazers on the other side of the river; you lost the land in your lawsuit; and you are to-night without a dollar. That was a big tract of land to lose. Where did you get so great a sum of money?"

"I have told you a hundred times," replied Dix. "I got it from my people over the mountains. You know where I got it."

"Yes," said Abner. "I know where you got it, Dix. And I know another thing. But first I want to show you this," and he took a little penknife out of his pocket. "And I want to tell you that I believe in the providence of God, Dix."

"I don't care a fiddler's damn what you believe in," said Dix.

"But you do care what I know," replied Abner.

"What do you know?" said Dix.

"I know where your partner is," replied Abner.

I was uncertain about what Dix was going to do, but finally he answered with a sneer.

"Then you know something that nobody else knows."

"Yes," replied Abner, "there is another man who knows."

"Who?" said Dix.

"You," said Abner.

Dix leaned over in his chair and looked at Abner closely.

"Abner," he cried, "you are talking nonsense. Nobody knows where Alkire is. If I knew I'd go after him."

"Dix," Abner answered, and it was again in that deep, level voice, "if I had got here five minutes later you would have gone after him. I can promise you that, Dix.

"Now, listen! I was in the upcountry when I got your word about the partnership; and I was on my way back when at Big Run I broke a stirrup-leather. I had no knife and I went into the store and bought this one; then the store-keeper told me that Alkire had gone to see you. I didn't want to interfere with him and I turned back. . . . So I did not become your partner. And so I did not disappear. . . . What was it that prevented? The broken stirrup-leather? The knife? In old times, Dix, men were so blind that God had to open their eyes before they could see His angel in the way before them. . . . They are still blind, but they ought not to be that blind. . . . Well, on the night that Alkire disappeared I met him on his way to your house. It was out there at the bridge. He had broken a stirrup-leather and he was trying to fasten it with a nail. He asked me if I had a knife, and I gave him this one. It was beginning to rain and I went on, leaving him there in the road with the knife in his hand."

Abner paused; the muscles of his great iron jaw contracted.

"God forgive me," he said; "it was His angel again! I never saw Alkire after that."

"Nobody ever saw him after that," said Dix. "He got out of the hills that night."

"No," replied Abner; "it was not in the night when Alkire started on his journey; it was in the day."

"Abner," said Dix, "you talk like a fool. If Alkire had traveled the road in the day somebody would have seen him."

"Nobody could see him on the road he traveled," replied Abner.

"What road?" said Dix.

"Dix," replied Abner, "you will learn that soon enough." Abner looked hard at the man.

"You saw Alkire when he started on his journey," he continued; "but did you see who it was that went with him?"

"Nobody went with him," replied Dix; "Alkire rode alone."

"Not alone," said Abner; "there was another."

"I didn't see him," said Dix.

"And yet," continued Abner, "you made Alkire go with him."

I saw cunning enter Dix's face. He was puzzled, but he thought Abner off the scent.

"And I made Alkire go with somebody, did I? Well, who was it? Did you see him?"

"Nobody ever saw him."

"He must be a stranger."

"No," replied Abner, "he rode the hills before we came into them."

"Indeed!" said Dix. "And what kind of a horse did he ride?"

"White!" said Abner.

Dix got some inkling of what Abner meant now, and his face grew livid.

"What are you driving at?" he cried. "You sit here beating around the bush. If you know anything, say it out; let's hear it. What is it?"

Abner put out his big sinewy hand as though to thrust Dix back into his chair.

"Listen!" he said. "Two days after that I wanted to get out into the Ten Mile country and I went through your lands; I rode a path through the narrow valley west of your house. At a point on the path where there is an apple tree something caught my eye and I stopped. Five minutes later I knew exactly what had happened under that apple tree. . . . Some-one had ridden there; he had stopped under that tree; then something happened and the horse had run away—I knew that by the tracks of a horse on this path. I knew that the horse had a rider and that it had stopped under this tree, because there was a limb cut from the tree at a certain height. I knew the horse had remained there, because the small twigs of the apple limb had been pared off, and they lay in a heap on the path. I knew that something had frightened the horse and that it had run away, because the sod was torn up where it had jumped. . . . Ten minutes later I knew that the rider had not been in the saddle when the horse jumped; I knew what it was that had frightened the horse; and I knew that the thing had occurred the day before. Now, how did I know that?

"Listen! I put my horse into the tracks of that other horse under the tree and studied the ground. Immediately I saw where the weeds beside the path had been crushed, as though some animal had been lying down there, and in the very center of that bed I saw a little heap of fresh earth. That was strange, Dix, that fresh earth where the animal had been lying down! It had come there after the animal had got up, or else it would have been pressed flat. But where had it come from?

"I got off and walked around the apple tree, moving out from it in an ever-widening circle. Finally I found an ant heap, the top of which had been scraped away as though one had taken up the loose earth in his hands. Then I went back and plucked up some of the earth. The under clods of it were colored as with red paint. . . . No, it wasn't paint.

"There was a brush fence some fifty yards away. I went over to it and followed it down.

"Opposite the apple tree the weeds were again crushed as though some animal had lain there. I sat down in that place and drew a line with my eye across a log of the fence to a limb of the apple tree. Then I got on my horse and again put him in the tracks of that other horse under the tree; the imaginary line passed through the pit of my stomach! . . . I am four inches taller than Alkire."

It was then that Dix began to curse. I had seen his face work while Abner was speaking and that spray of sweat had reappeared. But he kept the courage he had got.

"Lord Almighty, man!" he cried. "How prettily you sum it up! We shall presently have Lawyer Abner with his brief. Because my renters have killed a calf; because one of their horses frightened at the blood has bolted, and because they cover the blood with earth so the other horses traveling the path may not do the like; straightway I have shot Alkire out of his saddle. . . . Man! What a mare's nest! And now, Lawyer Abner, with your neat little conclusions, what did I do with Alkire after I had killed him? Did I cause him to vanish into the air with a smell of sulphur or did I cause the earth to yawn and Alkire to descend into its bowels?"

"Dix," replied Abner, "your words move somewhat near the truth."

"Upon my soul," cried Dix, "you compliment me. If I had that trick of magic, believe me, you would be already some distance down."

Abner remained a moment silent.

"Dix," he said, "what does it mean when one finds a plot of earth resodded?"

"Is that a riddle?" cried Dix. "Well, confound me, if I don't answer it! You charge me with murder and then you fling in this neat conundrum. Now, what could be the answer to that riddle, Abner? If one had done a murder this sod would overlie a grave and Alkire would be in it in his bloody shirt. Do I give the answer?"

"You do not," replied Abner.

"No!" cried Dix. "Your sodded plot no grave, and Alkire not within it waiting for the trump of Gabriel! Why, man, where are your little damned conclusions?"

"Dix," said Abner, "you do not deceive me in the least; Alkire is not sleeping in a grave."

"Then in the air," sneered Dix, "with the smell of sulphur?"

"Nor in the air," said Abner.

"Then consumed with fire, like the priests of Baal?"

"Nor with fire," said Abner.

Dix had got back the quiet of his face; this banter had put him where he was when Abner entered. "This is all fools' talk," he said; "if I had killed Alkire, what could I have done with the body? And the horse! What could I have done with the horse? Remember, no man has ever seen Alkire's horse any more than he has seen Alkire—and for the reason that Alkire rode him out of the hills that night. Now, look here, Abner, you have asked me a good many questions. I will ask you one. Among your little conclusions do you find that I did this thing alone or with the aid of others?"

"Dix," replied Abner, "I will answer that upon my own belief you had no accomplice."

"Then," said Dix, "how could I have carried off the horse? Alkire I might carry; but his horse weighed thirteen hundred pounds!"

"Dix," said Abner, "no man helped you do this thing; but there were men who helped you to conceal it."

"And now," cried Dix, "the man is going mad! Who could I trust with such work, I ask you? Have I a renter that would not tell it when he moved on to another's land, or when he got a quart of cider in him? Where are the men who helped me?"

"Dix," said Abner, "they have been dead these fifty years."

I heard Dix laugh then, and his evil face lighted as though a candle were behind it. And, in truth, I thought he had got Abner silenced.

"In the name of Heaven!" he cried. "With such proofs it is a wonder that you did not have me hanged."

"And hanged you should have been," said Abner.

"Well," cried Dix, "go and tell the sheriff, and mind you lay before him those little, neat conclusions: How from a horse track and the place where a calf was butchered you have reasoned on Alkire's murder, and to conceal the body and the horse you have reasoned on the aid of men who were rotting in their graves when I was born; and see how he will receive you!"

Abner gave no attention to the man's flippant speech. He got his great silver watch out of his pocket, pressed the stem and looked. Then he spoke in his deep, even voice.

"Dix," he said, "it is nearly midnight; in an hour you must be on your journey, and I have something more to say. Listen! I knew this thing had been done the previous day because it had rained on the night that I met Alkire, and the earth of this ant heap had been disturbed after that. Moreover, this earth had been frozen, and that showed a night had passed since it had been placed there. And I knew the rider of that horse was Alkire because, beside the path near the severed twigs lay my knife, where it had fallen from his hand. This much I learned in some fifteen minutes; the rest took somewhat longer.

"I followed the track of the horse until it stopped in the

little valley below. It was easy to follow while the horse ran, because the sod was torn; but when it ceased to run there was no track that I could follow. There was a little stream threading the valley, and I began at the wood and came slowly up to see if I could find where the horse had crossed. Finally I found a horse track and there was also a man's track, which meant that you had caught the horse and were leading it away. But where?

"On the rising ground above there was an old orchard where there had once been a house. The work about that house had been done a hundred years. It was rotted down now. You had opened this orchard into the pasture. I rode all over the face of this hill and finally I entered this orchard. There was a great, flat, moss-covered stone lying a few steps from where the house had stood. As I looked I noticed that the moss growing from it into the earth had been broken along the edges of the stone, and then I noticed that for a few feet about the stone the ground had been resodded. I got down and lifted up some of this new sod. Under it the earth had been soaked with that . . . red paint.

"It was clever of you, Dix, to resod the ground; that took only a little time and it effectually concealed the place where you had killed the horse; but it was foolish of you to forget that the broken moss around the edges of the great flat stone could not be mended."

"Abner!" cried Dix. "Stop!" And I saw that spray of sweat, and his face working like kneaded bread, and the shiver of that abominable chill on him.

Abner was silent for a moment and then he went on, but from another quarter.

"Twice," said Abner, "the Angel of the Lord stood before me and I did not know it; but the third time I knew it. It is not in the cry of the wind, nor in the voice of many waters that His presence is made known to us. That man in Israel had only the sign that the beast under him would not go on. Twice I had as good a sign, and tonight, when Marks broke a stirrup-leather before my house and called me to the door and asked me for a knife to mend it, I saw and I came!"

The log that Abner had thrown on was burned down, and

the fire was again a mass of embers; the room was filled with
that dull red light. Dix had got on to his feet, and he stood
now twisting before the fire, his hands reaching out to it, and
that cold creeping in his bones, and the smell of the fire on
him.

Abner rose. And when he spoke his voice was like a thing
that has dimensions and weight.

"Dix," he said, "you robbed the grazers; you shot Alkire
out of his saddle; and a child you would have murdered!"

And I saw the sleeve of Abner's coat begin to move, then
it stopped. He stood staring at something against the wall.
I looked to see what the thing was, but I did not see it.
Abner was looking beyond the wall, as though it had been
moved away.

And all the time Dix had been shaking with that hellish
cold, and twisting on the hearth and crowding into the fire.
Then he fell back, and he was the Dix I knew—his face was
slack; his eye was furtive; and he was full of terror.

It was his weak whine that awakened Abner. He put up
his hand and brought the fingers hard down over his face,
and then he looked at this new creature, cringing and beset
with fears.

"Dix," he said, "Alkire was a just man; he sleeps as peace-
fully in that abandoned well under his horse as he would sleep
in the churchyard. My hand has been held back; you may go.
Vengeance is mine, I will repay, saith the Lord."

"But where shall I go, Abner?" the creature wailed; "I have
no money and I am cold."

Abner took out his leather wallet and flung it toward the
door.

"There is money," he said—"a hundred dollars—and there
is my coat. Go! But if I find you in the hills to-morrow, or if
I ever find you, I warn you in the name of the living God
that I will stamp you out of life!"

I saw the loathsome thing writhe into Abner's coat and
seize the wallet and slip out through the door; and a moment
later I heard a horse. And I crept back on to Roy's heifer skin.

When I came down at daylight my Uncle Abner was reading by the fire.

Chapter 4

An Act of God

IT WAS THE last day of the County Fair, and I stood beside my Uncle Abner, on the edge of the crowd, watching the performance of a mountebank.

On a raised platform, before a little house on wheels, stood a girl dressed like a gypsy, with her arms extended, while an old man out in the crowd, standing on a chair, was throwing great knives that hemmed her in with a steel hedge. The girl was very young, scarcely more than a child, and the man was old, but he was hale and powerful. He wore wooden shoes, travel-worn purple velvet trousers, a red sash, and a white blouse of a shirt open at the throat.

I was watching the man, whose marvelous skill fascinated me. He seemed to be looking always at the crowd of faces that passed between him and the wagon, and yet the great knife fell to a hair on the target, grazing the body of the girl.

But while the old man with his sheaf of knives held my attention, it was the girl that Abner looked at. He stood studying her face with a strange rapt attention. Sometimes he lifted his head and looked vacantly over the crowd with the eyelids narrowed, like one searching for a memory that eluded him, then he came back to the face in its cluster of dark ringlets, framed in knives that stood quivering in the poplar board.

It was thus that my father found us when he came up.

"Have you noticed Blackford about?" he said; "I want to see him."

"No," replied Abner, "but he should be here, I think; he is at every frolic."

"I sent him the money for his cattle last night," my father went on, "and I wish to know if he got it."

Abner turned upon him at that.

57

"You will always take a chance with that scoundrel, Rufus," he said, "and some day you will be robbed. His lands are covered with a deed of trust."

"Well," replied my father, with his hearty laugh, "I shall not be robbed this time. I have Blackford's request over his signature for the money, with the statement that the letter is to be evidence of its payment."

And he took an envelope out of his pocket and handed it to Abner.

My uncle read the letter to the end, and then his great fingers tightened on the sheet, and he read it carefully again, and yet again, with his eyes narrowed and his jaw protruding. Finally he looked my father in the face.

"Blackford did not write this letter!" he said.

"Not write it!" my father cried. "Why, man, I know the deaf mute's writing like a book. I know every line and slant of his letters, and every crook and twist of his signature."

But my uncle shook his head.

My father was annoyed.

"Nonsense!" he said. "I can call a hundred men on these fair grounds who will swear that Blackford made every stroke of the pen in that letter, even against his denial, and though he bring Moses and the prophets to support him."

Abner looked my father steadily in the face.

"That is true, Rufus," he said; "the thing is perfect. There is no letter or line or stroke or twist of the pen that varies from Blackford's hand, and every grazer in the hills, to a man, will swear upon the Bible that he wrote it. Blackford himself cannot tell this writing from his own, nor can any other living man; and yet the deaf mute did not write it."

"Well," said my father, "yonder is Blackford now; we will ask him."

But they never did.

I saw the tall deaf mute swagger up and enter the crowd before the mountebank's wagon. And then a thing happened. The chair upon which the old man stood broke under him. He fell and the great knife in his hand swerved downward and went through the deaf mute's body, as though it were a cheese. The man was dead when we picked him up; the knife blade stood out between his shoulders, and the haft was jammed against his bloody coat.

We carried him into the Agricultural Hall among the prize apples and the pumpkins, summoned Squire Randolph from the cattle pens, and brought the mountebank before him.

Randolph came in his big blustering manner and sat down as though he were the judge of all the world. He heard the evidence, and upon the word of every witness the tragedy was an accident clean through. But it was an accident that made one shudder. It came swift and deadly and unforeseen, like a vengeance of God in the Book of Kings. One passing among his fellows, in no apprehension, had been smitten out of life. There was terror in the mystery of selection that had thus claimed Blackford in this crowd for death. It brought our voices to a whisper to feel how unprotected a man was in this life, and how little we could see.

And yet the thing had the aspect of design and moved with our stern Scriptural beliefs. In the pulpit this deaf mute had been an example and a warning. His life was profligate and loose. He was a cattle shipper who knew the abominations indexed by the Psalmist. He was an Ishmaelite in more ways than his affliction. He had no wife nor child, nor any next of kin. He had been predestined to an evil end by every good housewife in the hills. He would go swiftly and by violence into hell, the preachers said; and swiftly and by violence he had gone on this autumn morning when the world was like an Eden.

He lay there among the sheaves of corn and the fruits and cereals of the earth, so fully come to the end predestined that those who had cried the prophecy the loudest were the most amazed. With all their vaporings, they could not believe that God would be so expeditious, and they spoke in whispers and crowded about on tiptoe, as though the Angel of the Lord stood at the entrance of this little festal hall, as before the threshing floor of Araunah the Jebusite.

Randolph could do nothing but find the thing an accident, and let the old man go. But he thundered from behind his table on the dangers of such a trade as this. And all the time the mountebank stood stupidly before him like a man dazed, and the little girl wept and clung to the big peasant's hand. Randolph pointed to the girl and told the old man that he would kill her some day, and with the gestures and authority of omnipotence forbade his trade. The old mountebank promised to cast his knives into the river and get at something else. Randolph spoke upon the law of accidents sententiously for some thirty minutes, quoted Lord Blackstone and Mr. Chitty, called the thing an act of God, within a certain definition of the law, and rose.

My Uncle Abner had been standing near the door, looking on with a grave, undecipherable face. He had gone through the crowd to the chair when the old man fell, had drawn the knife out of Blackford's body, but he had not helped to carry him in, and he had remained by the door, his big shoulders towering above the audience. Randolph stopped beside him as he went out, took a pinch of snuff, and trumpeted in his big, many-colored handkerchief.

"Ah, Abner," he said, "do you concur in my decision?"

"You called the thing an act of God," replied Abner, "and I concur in that."

"And so it is," said Randolph, with judicial pomp; "the writers on the law, in their disquisitions upon torts, include within that term those inscrutable injuries that no human intelligence can foresee; for instance, floods, earthquakes and tornadoes."

"Now, that is very stupid in the writers on the law," replied Abner; "I should call such injuries acts of the devil. It would not occur to me to believe that God would use the agency of the elements in order to injure the innocent."

"Well," said Randolph, "the writers upon the law have not been theologians, although Mr. Greenleaf was devout, and Chitty with a proper reverence, and my lords Coke and Blackstone and Sir Matthew Hale in respectable submission to the established church. They have grouped and catalogued injuries with delicate and nice distinctions with respect to their being actionable at law, and they found certain injuries to be acts of God, but I do not read that they found any injury to be an act of the devil. The law does not recognize the sovereignty and dominion of the devil."

"Then," replied Abner, "with great fitness is the law represented blindfold. I have not entered any jurisdiction where his writs have failed to run."

There was a smile about the door that would have broken into laughter but for the dead man inside.

Randolph blustered, consulted his snuffbox, and turned the conversation into a neighboring channel.

"Do you think, Abner," he said, "that this old showman will give up his dangerous practice as he promised me?"

"Yes," replied Abner, "he will give it up, but not because he promised you."

And he walked away to my father, took him by the arm, and led him aside.

"Rufus," he said, "I have learned something. Your receipt is valid."

"Of course it is valid," replied my father; "it is in Blackford's hand."

"Well," said Abner, "he cannot come back to deny it, and I will not be a witness for him."

"What do you mean, Abner?" my father said. "You say that Blackford did not write this letter, and now you say that it is valid."

"I mean," replied Abner, "that when the one entitled to a debt receives it, that is enough."

Then he walked away into the crowd, his head lifted and his fingers locked behind his massive back.

The County Fair closed that evening in much gossip and many idle comments on Blackford's end. The chimney corner lawyers, riding out with the homing crowd, vapored upon Mr. Jefferson's Statute of Descents, and how Blackford's property would escheat to the state since there was no next of kin, and were met with the information that his lands and his cattle would precisely pay his debts, with an eagle or two beyond for a coffin. And, after the manner of lawyers, were not silenced, but laid down what the law would be if only the facts were agreeable to their premise. And the prophets, sitting in their wagons, assembled their witnesses and established the dates at which they had been prophetically delivered.

Evening descended, and the fair grounds were mostly de-

serted. Those who lived at no great distance had moved their
live stock with the crowd and had given up their pens and
stalls. But my father, who always brought a drove of prize
cattle to these fairs, gave orders that we should remain until
the morning. The distance home was too great and the roads
were filled. My father's cattle were no less sacred than the
bulls of Egypt, and not to be crowded by a wagon wheel or
ridden into by a shouting drunkard.

The night fell. There was no moon, but the earth was not
in darkness. The sky was clear and sown with stars like a
seeded field. I did not go to bed in the cattle stall filled with
clover hay under a handwoven blanket, as I was intended to
do. A youngster at a certain age is a sort of jackal and loves
nothing in this world so much as to prowl over the ground
where a crowd of people has encamped. Besides, I wished to
know what had become of the old mountebank, and it was a
thing I soon discovered.

His wagon stood on the edge of the ground among the
trees near the river, with the door closed. His horse, tethered
to a wheel, was nosing an armful of hay. The light of the
stars filtered through the treetops, filled the wheels with
shadows and threw one side of the wagon into the blackness
of the pit. I went down to the fringe of trees; there I sat
squatted on the earth until I heard a footstep and saw my
Uncle Abner coming toward the wagon. He walked as I had
seen him walking in the crowd, his hands behind him and his
face lifted as though he considered something that perplexed
him. He came to the steps, knocked with his clenched hand
on the door, and when a voice replied, entered.

Curiosity overcame me. I scurried up to the dark side of
the wagon. There a piece of fortune awaited me; a gilded
panel had cracked with some jolt upon the road, and by
perching myself upon the wheel I could see inside. The old
man had been seated behind a table made by letting down
a board hinged to the wall. His knives were lying on the floor
beside him, bound together in a sheaf with a twine string.
There were some packets of old letters on the table and a
candle. The little girl lay asleep in a sort of bunk at the end
of the wagon. The old man stood up when my uncle entered,

and his face, that had been dull and stupid before the justice
of the peace, was now keen and bright.

"Monsieur does me an honor," he said. The words were
an interrogation with no welcome in them.

"No honor," replied my uncle, standing with his hat on;
"but possibly a service."

"That would be strange," the mountebank said dryly, "for
I have received no service from any man here."

"You have a short memory," replied Abner; "the justice of
the peace rendered you a great service on this day. Do you
put no value on your life?"

"My life has not been in danger, monsieur," he said.

"I think it has," replied Abner.

"Then monsieur questions the decision?"

"No," said Abner; "I think it was the very wisest decision
that Randolph ever made."

"Then why does monsieur say that my life was in danger?"

"Well," replied my uncle, "are not the lives of all men in
danger? Is there any day or hour of a day in which they are
secure, or any tract or parcel of this earth where danger is
not? And can a man say when he awakes at daylight in his
bed, on this day I shall go into danger, or I shall not? In the
light it is, and in the darkness it is, and where one looks to
find it, and where he does not. Did Blackford believe himself
in danger today when he passed before you?"

"Ah, monsieur," replied the man, "that was a terrible
accident!"

My uncle picked up a stool, placed it by the table and
sat down. He took off his hat and set it on his knees, then
he spoke, looking at the floor.

"Do you believe in God?"

I saw the old man rub his forehead with his hand and the
ball of his first finger make a cross.

"Yes, monsieur," he said, "I do."

"Then," replied Abner, "you can hardly believe that things
happen out of chance."

"We call it chance, monsieur," said the man, "when we do
not understand it."

"Sometimes we use a better term," replied Abner. "Now,

today Randolph did not understand this death of Blackford, and yet he called it an act of God."

"Who knows," said the man; "are not the ways of God past finding out?"

"Not always," replied my uncle.

He gathered his chin into his hand and sat for some time motionless, then he continued:

"I have found out something about this one."

The old mountebank moved to his stool beyond the table and sat down.

"And what is that, monsieur?" he said.

"That you are in danger of your life—for one thing."

"In what danger?"

"Do you come from the south of Europe," replied Abner, "and forget that when a man is killed there are others to threaten his assassin?"

"But this Blackford has no kin to carry a blood feud," said the mountebank.

"And so," cried Abner, "you knew that before you killed him. And yet, in spite of that precaution, there stood a man in the crowd before the justice of the peace who held your life in his hand. He had but to speak."

"And why did he not speak—this man?" said the mountebank, looking at Abner across the table.

"I will tell you that," replied Abner. "He feared that the justice of the law might contravene the justice of God. It is a fabric woven from many threads—this justice of God. I saw three of these threads today stretching into the great loom, and I feared to touch them lest I disturb the weaver at his work. I saw men see a murder and not know it. I saw a child see its father and not know it, and I saw a letter in the handwriting of a man who did not write it."

The face of the old mountebank did not whiten, but instead it grew stern and resolute, and the muscles came out in it so that it seemed a thing of cords under the tanned skin.

"The proofs," he said.

"They are all here," replied Abner.

He stooped, lifted the sheaf of knives, broke the string

and spread them on the table. He selected the one from which Blackford's blood had been wiped off.

"Randolph examined this knife," he continued, "but not the others; he assumed that they are all alike. Well, they are not. The others are dull, but this one has the edge of a razor."

And he plucked a piece of paper from the table and sheared it in two. Then he put the knife down on the board and looked toward the far end of the wagon.

"And the child's face," he said—"I was not certain of that until I saw Blackford's ironed out under the hand of death, and then I knew. And the letter——"

But the old man was on his feet straining over the table, his features twitching like a taut rope.

"Hush! Hush!" he said.

There came a little gust of wind that whispered in the dry grass and blew the dead leaves against the wagon and about my face. They fluttered like a presence, these dead leaves, and pecked and clawed at the gilded panel like the nails of some feeble hand. I began to be assailed with fear as I sat there alone in the darkness looking in upon this tragedy.

My Uncle Abner sat down, and the old man remained with the palms of his hands pressed against the table. Finally he spoke.

"Monsieur," he said, "shall a man lead another into hell and escape the pit himself? Yes, she is his daughter, and her mother was mine, and I have killed him. He could not speak, but with those letters he persuaded her."

The man paused and turned over the packet of yellow envelopes tied up with faded ribbon.

"And she believed what a woman will always believe. What would you have done, monsieur? Go to the law—your English law that gives the woman a pittance and puts her out of the court-house door for the ribald to laugh at! Diable! Monsieur, that is not the law. I know the law, as my father and my father's father, and your father and your father's father knew it. I would have killed him then, when she died, but for this child. I would have followed him into these hills, day after day, like his shadow behind him, until I got a knife into him and ripped him up like a butchered pig. But I could not go to the hangman and leave this child, and so I waited."

He sat down.

"We can wait, monsieur. That is one thing we have in my country—patience. And when I was ready I killed him."

The old man paused and put out his hand, palm upward, on the table. It was a wonderful hand, like a live thing.

"You have eyes, monsieur, but the others are as blind men. Did they think that hand could have failed me? Cunning men have made machinery so accurate that you marvel at them; but there was never a machine with the accuracy of the human hand when it is trained as we train it. Monsieur, I could scratch a line on the door behind you with a needle, and with my eyes closed set a knife point into every twist and turn of it. Why, monsieur, there was a straw clinging to Blackford's coat—a straw that had fallen on him as he passed some horse stall. I marked it as he came up through the crowd, and I split it with the knife.

"And now, monsieur?"

But my uncle stopped him. "Not yet," he said. "I am concerned about the living and not the dead. If I had thought of the dead only, I should have spoken this day; but I have thought also of the living. What have you done for the child?"

There came a great tenderness into the old man's face.

"I have brought it up in love," he said, "and in honor, and I have got its inheritance for it."

He stopped and indicated the pack of letters.

"I was about to burn these when you came in, monsieur, for they have served their purpose. I thought I might need to know Blackford's hand and I set out to learn it. Not in a day, monsieur, nor a week, like your common forger, and with an untried hand—but in a year, and years—with a hand that obeys me, I went over and over every letter of every word until I could write the man's hand, not an imitation of it, monsieur, not that, but the very hand itself—the very hand that Blackford writes with his own fingers. And it was well, for I was able to get the child all that Blackford had, beyond his debts, by a letter that no man could know that Blackford did not write."

"I knew that he did not write it," said Abner.

The old man smiled.

"You jest, monsieur," he said; "Blackford himself could not tell the writing from his own. I could not, nor can any living man."

"That is true," replied Abner; "the letter is in Blackford's hand, as he would have written it with his own fingers. It is no imitation, as you say; it is the very writing of the man, and yet he did not write it, and when I saw it I knew that he did not."

The old man's face was incredulous.

"How could you know that, monsieur?" he said.

My uncle took the letter which my father had received out of his pocket and spread it out on the table.

"I will tell you," he said, "how I knew that Blackford did not write this letter, although it is in his very hand. When my brother Rufus showed me this letter, and I read it, I noticed that there were words misspelled in it. Well, that of itself was nothing for the deaf mute did not always spell correctly. It was the manner in which the words were misspelled. Under the old system, when a deaf mute was taught to write he was taught by the eye; consequently, he writes words as he remembers them to look, and not as he remembers them to sound. His mistakes, then, are mistakes of the eye and not of the ear. And in this he differs from every man who can hear; for the man who can hear, when he is uncertain about the spelling of a word, spells it as it sounds phonetically, using not a letter that looks like the correct one, but a letter that sounds like it —using 's' for 'c' and 'o' for 'u'—a thing no deaf mute would ever do in this world, because he does not know what letters sound like. Consequently, when I saw the words in this letter misspelled by sound—when I saw that the person who had written this letter remembered his word as a sound, and by the arrangement of the letters in it was endeavoring to indicate that sound—I knew he could hear."

The old man did not reply, but he rose and stood before my

c

uncle. He stood straight and fearless, his long white hair thrown back, his bronzed throat exposed, his face lifted, and his eyes calm and level, like some ancient druid among his sacred oak trees.

And I crowded my face against the cracked panel, straining to hear what he would say.

"Monsieur," he said, "I have done an act of justice, not as men do it, but as the providence of God does it. With care and with patience I have accomplished every act, so that to the eyes of men it bore the relation and aspect of God's providence. And all who saw were content but you. You have pried and ferreted behind these things, and now you must bear the obligations of your knowledge."

He spread out his hands toward the sleeping girl.

"Shall this child grow up to honor in ignorance, or in knowledge go down to hell? Shall she know what her mother was, and what her father was, and what I am, and be fouled by the knowledge of it, and shall she be stripped of her inheritance and left not only outlawed, but paupered? And shall I go to the hangman, and she to the street? These are things for you to decide, since you would search out what was hidden and reveal what was covered! I leave it in your hands."

"And I," replied Abner, rising, "leave it in God's."

Chapter 5

The Treasure Hunter

I REMEMBER VERY WELL when the sailor came to Highfield. It was the return of the prodigal—a belated return. The hospitalities of the parable did not await him. Old Thorndike Madison was dead. And Charlie Madison, in possession as sole heir, was not pleased to see a lost brother land from a river boat after twenty years of silence.

The law presumes death after seven years, and for twenty Dabney Madison had been counted out of life—counted out by old Thorndike when he left his estate to pass by operation of law to the surviving son; and counted out by Charlie when he received the title.

The imagination of every lad in the Hills was fired by the romantic properties of this event. The Negroes carried every detail, and they would have colored it to suit the fancy had not the thing happened in ample color.

The estate had gone to rack with Charlie drunk from dawn until midnight. Old Clayborne and Mariah kept the Negro quarters, half a mile from the house. Clayborne would put Charlie to bed and then go home to his cabin. In the morning Mariah would come to get his coffee. So Charlie lived after old Thorndike, at ninety, had gone to the graveyard.

It was a witch's night when the thing happened—rain and a high wind that wailed and whooped round the pillars and chimneys of the house. The house was set on a high bank above the river, where the swift water, running like a flood, made a sharp bend. It caught the full force of wind and rain. It was old and the timbers creaked.

Charlie was drunk. He cried out when he saw the lost brother and got unsteadily on his legs.

"You are not Dabney!" he said. "You are a picture out of a

storybook!" And he laughed in a sort of half terror, like a child before a homemade ghost. "Look at your earrings!"

It was a good comment for a man in liquor; for if ever a character stepped out of the pages of a pirate tale, here it was.

Dabney had lifted the latch and entered without warning. He had the big frame and the hawk nose of his race. He was in sea-stained sailor clothes, his face white as plaster, a red cloth wound tightly round his head, huge half-moon rings in his ears; and he carried a seaman's chest on his shoulder.

Old Clayborne told the story.

Dabney put down his chest carefully, as though it had something precious in it. Then he spoke.

"Are you glad to see me, brother?"

Charlie was holding on to the table with both hands, his eyes bleared, his mouth gaping.

"I don't see you," he quavered. Then he turned his head, with a curious duck of the chin, toward the old Negro. "I don't see anything—do I?"

Dabney came over to the table then; he took up the flask of liquor and a glass.

"Clabe," he said, "is this apple whiskey?"

I have heard the ancient Negro tell the story a thousand times. He gave a great shout of recognition. Those words—those five words—settled it. He used to sing this part in a long, nasal chant when he reached it in his tale: "Marse Dabney! Oh, my Lord! How many times ain't I heard 'im say dem words—jis' lak dat: 'Clabe, is dis apple whisky?' Dem outlandish clo's couldn't fool dis nigger! I'd 'a' knowed Marse Dabney after dat if he'd been 'parisoned in de garments ob Israel!"

But the old Negro had Satan's time with Charlie, who held on to the table and cursed.

"You're not Dabney!" he cried. ". . . I know you! You're old Lafitte, the Pirate, who helped General Jackson thrash the British at New Orleans. Grandfather used to tell about you!"

He began to cry and blame his grandfather for so vividly impressing the figure that it came up now in his liquor to annoy him. Then he would get his courage and shake a trembling fist across the table.

"You can't frighten me, Lafitte—curse you! I've seen worse things than you over there. I've seen the devil, with a spade, digging a grave; and a horsefly, as big as a buzzard, perched on the highboy, looking at me and calling out to the devil: 'Dig it deep! We'll bury old Charlie deep'!"

Clayborne finally got him to realize that Dabney was a figure in life, in spite of the chalk face under the red headcloth.

And then Charlie went into a drunken mania of resentment. Dabney was dead—or if he was not dead he ought to be; and he started to the highboy for a dueling pistol. His fury and his drunken curses filled the house. The place belonged to him! He would not divide it.

It was the devil's night. About daybreak the ancient Negro got Charlie into bed and the sailor installed in old Thorndike's room, with a fire and all the attentions of a guest.

After that Charlie was strangely quiet. He suffered the intrusion of the sailor with no word. Dabney might have been always in the house for any indication in Charlie's manner. There was peace; but one was impressed that it was a sort of armistice.

Dabney went over the old estate pretty carefully, but he did not interfere with Charlie's possession. He laid no claim that anybody heard of. Charlie seemed to watch him. He kept the drink in hand and he grew silent.

There seemed no overt reason, old Clayborne said, but presently Dabney began to act like a man in fear. He made friends with the dog, a big old bearhound. He got a fowling piece and set it up by the head of his bed, and finally took the dog into the room with him at night. He kept out of the house by day.

One could see him, with a mariner's glass, striding across the high fields above the river, or perched in the fork of a tree. He wore the sailor clothes, and the red cloth wound round his head.

I am sure my uncle Abner saw him more than once. I know of one time. He was riding home from a sitting of the county justices. Dabney was walking through the deep broom sedge in the high field beyond the old house. Abner called and he came down to the road. He had the mariner's glass, the sailor clothes and the headcloth.

He was not pleased to see my uncle. He seemed nervous, like a man under some restraint. While my uncle talked he would take three steps straight ahead and then turn back. Abner marked it, with a query.

"Dabney," he said, "why do you turn about like that?"

The man stopped in his tracks; for a moment he seemed in a sort of frenzied terror. Then he cursed:

"Habit—damme, Abner!"

"And where did you get a habit like that?" said my uncle.

"In a ship," replied the man.

"What sort of ship?" said my uncle.

The sailor hesitated for a moment.

"Now, Abner," he cried finally, "what sort of ships are they that sail the Caribbee and rendezvous on the Dry Tortugas?" His voice took a strained, wild note. "Have they spacious cabins, or does one take three steps thus in the narrow pen of their hold?"

My uncle gathered his chin into his big fingers and looked steadily at the man.

"Strange quarters, Dabney," he said, "for a son of Thorndike Madison."

"Well, Abner!" cried the man, "what would you have? It was that or the plank. It's all very nice to be a gentleman and the son of a gentleman under the protection of Virginia; but off the Bermudas, with the muzzle of a musket pressed into your back and the sea boiling below you—what then?"

My uncle watched the man closely and with a strange expression.

"A clean death," he said, "would be better than God's vengeance to follow on one's heels."

The sailor swore a great oath.

"God's vengeance!" And he laughed. "I should not care how that followed on my heels. It's the vengeance of old Jules le Noir and the damned Britisher, Barrett, following on a man's heels, that puts ice in the blood. God's vengeance! Why, Abner, a preacher could pray that off in a meeting-house; but can he pray the half-breed off? Or the broken-nosed Englishman?"

The man seemed caught in a current of passion that whirled

him headlong into indiscretions from which a saner mood would have steered him clear.

"The Spanish Main is not Virginia!" he cried. "One does not live the life of a gentleman on it. Loot and murder are not the pastimes of a gentleman. The Spanish Main is not safe. But is Virginia safe? Is any spot safe? Eh, Abner? Show it to me if you know it!" And he plunged off into the deep broom sedge.

So it came about that an evil Frenchman with a cutlass in his teeth, and a vile old rum-soaked creature with a broken nose and a brace of pistols, got entangled in the common fancy with Dabney's legend.

Everybody in the Hills thought something was going to happen; but the wild thing that did happen came sooner than anybody thought.

One morning at sunrise a Negro house boy ran in, out of breath, to say that old Clayborne had gone by at a gallop on his way to Randolph, the justice of the peace, and shouted for my uncle to come to Highfield.

Randolph had the nearer road; but Abner met him at the Madison door and the two men went into the house together.

Old Charlie was sober; but he was drinking raw liquor and doing his best to get drunk. His face was ghastly, and his hands shook so that he could keep only a few spoonfuls of the white brandy in his big tumbler. My uncle said that if ever the terror of the damned was on a human creature in this world it was on old Charlie.

It was some time before they could get at what had happened. It was of no use to bother with Charlie until the liquor should begin to steady him. His loose underlip jerked and every faculty he could muster was massed on the one labor of getting the brandy to his mouth.

Old Mariah sat in the kitchen, with her apron over her head, rocking on the four legs of a split-bottomed chair. She was worse than useless.

My uncle and Randolph had got some things out of Clayborne on the way. There had been nothing to indicate the thing that night. Dabney had gone into old Thorndike's room, as usual, with the dog. Old Clayborne had put Charlie to bed drunk, snuffed out the candles and departed to his cabin, half a mile away. That was all old Clayborne could tell of the night before. Perhaps the sailor seemed a little more in fear than usual, and perhaps Charlie was a little more in liquor; but he could not be sure on those questions of degree. The sailor lately seemed to be in constant fear and Charlie had got back at his liquor with an increased and abandoned indulgence.

What happened after that my uncle and Randolph could see for themselves better than Clayborne could tell it.

Old Thorndike's room, like the other rooms of the house, had a door that opened on a long covered porch facing the river. This door now stood open. The ancient rusted lock plate, with its screws, was hanging to the frame. There were no marks of violence on the door. The sailor was gone. His pillow and the bedclothes were soaked with blood. All his clothes, including the red headcloth, were lying neatly folded on the arm of a chair.

The sailor's chest stood open and empty. There was a little sprinkling of blood drops from the bed to the door and into the weeds outside, but no blood anywhere else in the room. And from there, directly in a line to the river, the weeds and grass had been trampled. The ground was hard and dry, and no one could say how many persons had gone that way from the house. The dog lay just inside the door of the room, with his throat cut. It was the slash of a knife with the edge of a razor, for the dog's head was nearly severed from the neck.

It was noiseless, swift work—incredibly noiseless and swift. Dabney had not wakened, for the fowling piece stood unmoved at the head of the bed. When the door swung open somebody had caught the dog's muzzle and slipped the knife across his throat . . . and then the rest.

"It must have happened that way," Randolph said.

At any rate, the unwelcome sailor was gone. He had arrived in an abundance of mystery and he had departed in it, though where he went was clear enough. The great river, swinging round the high point of land, swallowed what it got.

A lost swimmer in that deadly water was sometimes found miles below, months later—or, rather, a hideous, unrecognizable human flotsam that the Hills accepted for the dead man.

The means, too, were not without the indication Dabney had given in his wild talk to my uncle. Besides, the Negroes had seen a figure—or more than one—at dusk, about an abandoned tobacco house beyond the great meadow on the landward side of Highfield.

It was a tumble-down old structure in a strip of bush between the line of the meadow and the acres of morass beyond it—called swamps in the South. It was ghost land—haunted, the Negroes said; and so what moved there before the tragedy, behind the great elm at the edge of the meadow, old Clayborne had seen only at a distance, with no wish to spy on it.

Was it the inevitable irony of chance that Dabney scouted the river with his glass while the thing he feared came in through the swamps behind him?

By the time my uncle and Randolph had got these evidences assembled the liquor had steadied Charlie. At first he pretended to know nothing at all about the affair. He had not wakened, and had heard nothing until the cries of old Mariah filled the house with bedlam.

Randolph said he had never seen my uncle so profoundly puzzled; he sat down in old Charlie's room, silent, with his keen, strong-featured face as immovable as wood. But the justice saw light in a crevice of the mystery and he drove directly at it, with no pretension.

"Charlie," he said, "you were not pleased to see Dabney turn up!"

The drunken creature did not lie.

"No; I didn't want to see him."

"Why not?"

"Because I thought he was dead."

"Because you did not wish to divide your father's estate with him—wasn't that it?"

"Well, it was all mine—wasn't it—if Dabney was dead?"

The justice went on:

"You tried to shoot Dabney on the night he arrived!"

c*

"I don't know," said Charlie. "I was drunk. Ask Clabe."

The man was in terror; but he kept his head—that was clear as light.

"Dabney knew he was in danger here, didn't he?"

"Yes; he did," said Charlie.

"And he was in fear?"

"Yes," said Charlie—"damnably in fear!"

"Of you!" cried the justice with a sudden, aggressive menace.

"Me?" Old Charlie looked strangely at the man. "Why, no —not me!"

"Of what, then?" said Randolph.

Old Charlie wavered; he got another measure of the brandy in him.

"Well," he said, "it was enough to be afraid of. Look what it did to him!"

Randolph got up, then, and stood over against the man across the table.

"You Madisons are all big men. Now listen to me! It required force to break that door in, and yet there is no mark on the door; that means somebody broke it in with the pressure of his shoulder, softly. And there is another thing, Charlie, that you have got to face: Dabney was killed in his bed while asleep. The dog in the room did not make a sound. Why?"

The face of the drunken man took on a strange, perplexed expression.

"That's so, Randolph," he said; "and it's strange—it's damned strange!"

"Not so very strange," replied the justice.

"Why not?" said Charlie.

"Because the dog knew the man who did that work in your father's room!"

And again, with menace and vigor, Randolph drove at the shaken drunkard:

"Where's the knife Dabney was killed with?"

Then, against all belief, against all expectation in the men, old Charlie fumbled in a drawer beside him and laid a knife on the table.

Randolph gasped at the unbelievable success of his driven query, and my uncle rose and joined him.

They looked closely at the knife. It was the common butcher knife of the countryside, made by a smith from a worn-out file and to be found in any kitchen; but it was ground to the point, and whetted to the hair-shearing edge of a razor.

"Look on the handle!" said Charlie.

They looked. And there, burned in the wood crudely, like the imitative undertaking of a child, was a skull and cross-bones.

"Where did you get this knife?" said my uncle.

"It was sticking here in my table, in my room, beside my bed, when I woke up." He indicated with his finger nail the narrow hole in the mahogany board where the point of the knife had been forced down. "And this was under it."

He stooped again to the drawer and put a sheet of paper on the table before the astonished men. It was a page of foolscap, with words printed in blood by the point of the knife: "Chest empty! Put thousand in gold—elm—meadow. Or the same to you!"

And there was the puncture in the center of the sheet where the point of the knife had gone through. My uncle laid it on the table, over the narrow hole in the mahogany board, and pressed it down with the knife. The point fitted into the paper and the board.

There was blood on the knife; and the gruesome thing, thus reset, very nearly threw old Charlie back into the panic of terror out of which the brandy had helped him. His fingers twitched, and he kept puffing out his loose underlip like a child laboring to hold back his emotions.

He went at the brandy bottle. And the tale he finally got out was the wildest lie anybody ever put forward in his own defense—if it was a lie. That was the point to judge. And this was Randolph's estimate at the time.

Charlie said that, to cap all of Dabney's strange acts, about a week before this night he asked for a thousand dollars. Charlie told him to go to hell. He said Dabney did not resent either the refusal or the harsh words of it. He simply sat still and began to take on an appearance of fear that sent old Charlie, tumbler in hand, straight to his liquor bottle. Dabney kept coming in every day or two to beg for money; so Charlie got drunk to escape the thing.

"Where was I to get a thousand dollars?" he queried in the tale to my uncle and Randolph.

He said the day before the tragedy was the worst. Dabney got at him in terror for the money. He must have it to save his life, he went on desperately, Charlie said. And then he cried!

Charlie spat violently at the recollection. There was something gruesome, helpless and awful in the memory—in the way Dabney quaked; the tears, and the jingle of the earrings; all the appearance of the man so set to a part of brutal courage—and this shattering fear! The flapping of the big half-moon earrings against the man's white quivering jowls was the worst, Charlie said.

Randolph thought old Charlie colored the thing if he was lying about it. If it was the truth the delusions of liquor would account for these overdrawn impressions. At any rate, the justice promptly spoke out what he thought.

"Charlie," he said, "you're trying to stage a sea yarn by the penny writers. It won't do!"

The man reflected, looking Randolph in the face.

"Why, yes," he said; "you're right—that's what it sounds like. But it isn't that. It's the truth." And he turned to my uncle. "You know it's the truth, Abner."

Randolph said that just here, at this point in the affair, all the established landmarks of common sense and sane credibility were suddenly jumbled up.

What my uncle answered was:

"I think it's all true."

Charlie took a big linen handkerchief out of his pocket and wiped his face. Then he said simply, quite simply, like a child:

"I'm afraid!"

One could doubt everything else, Randolph said; but not this. The man was in fear, beyond question.

"I've got it all figured out," Charlie continued. "They were after Dabney for something they thought he had in the chest. They offered to take a thousand dollars for their share and let him off. That's why he was so crazy to raise the money. When they found the chest empty they thought I had the thing, or knew where Dabney had concealed it; and now they are after me!",

Old Charlie stopped again and wiped his face.

"I don't want to die, Abner," he added, "like Dabney—in the bed. What shall I do."

"There is only one thing to do," replied my uncle. "Put the money by the elm in the meadow."

"But, Abner," replied the man, "where would I get a thousand dollars, as I said to Dabney?"

"I will lend it to you," replied my uncle.

"But, Abner," said Charlie, "you haven't got a thousand dollars in gold in your pocket."

"No," replied my uncle; "but if you will give me a lien on the land I will undertake to pay the money. The estate is in ruin, but it's worth double that sum."

And Randolph said that, among the other strange, mad, ridiculous things of that memorable, extraordinary day, he wrote a deed of trust on the Madison lands to secure Charlie's note to my uncle for a thousand dollars.

So great virtue was there in my uncle's word, and such power had he to inspire the faith of men, that he rode away, leaving old Charlie at peace and confident that he had escaped from peril—whether, as Randolph wondered, it was the peril of the pirate assassins in the great swamp or the gibbet of Virginia.

Two hundred yards from the house, where the strip of bush, skirting the meadow, touched the road, my uncle got down from his horse and tied the bridle rein to a sapling.

"What now, Abner?" cried Randolph, like a man swept along in a current of crazy happenings.

"I am going in to arrange about the payment of the money," replied my uncle.

The justice swore a great oath. If my uncle was setting out to interview desperate assassins—as his acts indicated—alone and unarmed, it was the extreme of foolhardy peril. Did he think murderers would parley with him and let him come away to tell it and to lead in a posse? It was a thing beyond all sane belief!

And it is evidence of the blood in Randolph that in this conviction, with the inevitable end of the venture before his face, he got down and went in with my uncle.

The path lay along a sort of dike, thrown up in some ancient time against the swamp. Now along the sides it was grown with great reeds, water beech and the common bush of wet lands.

They came to the old tobacco house noiselessly on the damp path. The tumble-down door had been set in place.

My uncle did not pause for any consideration of finesse or safety. He went straight ahead to the door and flung it open. It was rotten and insecurely set, and it fell with a clatter into the abandoned house.

At the sound a big, gaunt figure, asleep on the floor, sprang up.

In the dim light Randolph looked about for a weapon—a piece of the broken door would do. But my uncle was undisturbed.

"Dabney," he said, "I came to arrange about the money. My agent, Mr. Gray, in Memphis, will hand it to you. There will be nothing to sign."

Randolph said he cried out, because he was astonished:

"Dabney Madison, by the living God! I thought you were dead!"

My uncle turned about.

"How could you think that, Randolph?" he said. "You yourself pointed out how the dog was killed by somebody who knew him; and you must have seen that there was no blood on the floor where the dog lay—and consequently that the dog was killed in the bed to furnish blood for the pretended murder."

"But the money, Abner!" cried Randolph. "Why do you pay Dabney Madison this money?"

"Because it is his share of his father's estate," replied my uncle.

"So you were after that!" cried Randolph; "the half of your

father's estate. Damme, man, you took a lot of hell-turns on the road to that! Why didn't you sue in the courts? Your right was legal."

"Because a suit at law would have brought out his past," replied my uncle.

The man roused thus abruptly out of sleep had got now some measure of control.

"Randolph," he said, "no law of God or man runs on the sea. The trade of the sea south of the Bermudas is no business for a gentleman or to be told in the land of his father's honor. Abner knew where I'd been!"

"Yes," replied my uncle. "When I saw your bleached face; when I saw your cropped head under the pirate cloth; when I saw you take three steps in your nervous walk, and turn—I knew."

"That I had been in the Spanish Main?" said Dabney.

"That you had been in the penitentiary!" said my uncle.

Chapter 6

The House of the Dead Man

WE WERE on our way to the Smallwood place—Abner and I.
It was early in the morning and I thought we were the first on
the road; but at the Three Forks, where the Lost Creek turn-
pike trails down from the mountains, a horse had turned in
before us.

It was a morning out of Paradise, crisp and bright. The
spider-webs glistened on the fence rails. The timber cracked.
The ragweed was dusted with silver. The sun was moving upward from behind the world. I could have whistled out of
sheer joy in being alive on this October morning and the
horse under me danced; but Abner rode looking down his
nose. He was always silent when he had this trip to make. And
he had a reason for it.

The pastureland that we were going on to did not belong to
us. It had been owned by the sheriff, Asbury Smallwood. In
those days the sheriff collected the county taxes. One night
the sheriff's house had been entered, burned over his head and
a large sum of the county revenues carried off. No one ever
found a trace of those who had done this deed. The sheriff was
ruined. He had given up his lands and moved to a neighboring
county. His bondsmen had been forced to meet the loss. My
father had been one of them; but it was not the loss to my
father that bothered Abner.

"The thing does not hurt you, Rufus," he said; "but it
cripples Elnathan Stone and it breaks Adam Greathouse."

Stone was a grazier with heavy debts and Greathouse was a
little farmer. I remember how my father chaffed Abner when
he paid his portion of this loss.

" 'The Lord gave,' " he said, " 'and the Lord hath taken
away'—eh, Abner?"

"But, Rufus," replied Abner, "did the Lord take? We must be sure of that. There are others who take."

It was clear what Abner meant. If the Lord took he would be resigned to it; but if another took he would follow with a weapon in his hand and recover what had been taken. Abner's God was an exacting Overlord and His requisitions were to be met with equanimity; but He did not go halves with thieves and He issued no letters of marque.

When the sheriff failed Abner had put cattle on the land in an effort to make what he could for the bondsmen. It was good grazing land, but it was watered by springs, and we had to watch them. A beef steer does not grow fat without plenty of water. We went every week to give the cattle salt and to watch the springs.

As we rode I presently noticed that Abner was looking down at the horsetrack. And then I saw what I had not noticed before, that there were three horsetracks in the road—two going our way and one returning—but only one of the tracks was fresh. Finally Abner pulled up his big chestnut. We were passing the old burned house. The crumbled foundations and the blasted trees stood at the end of a lane. There had once been a gate before the house at the end of this lane, but it was now nailed up. The horse going before us had entered this lane for a few steps, then turned back into the road.

Abner did not speak. He looked at the track for a moment and then rode on. Presently we came to the bars leading from the road into the pasture. The horse had stopped here and its rider had got out of the saddle and let down the bars. One could see where the horse had gone through and the footprints of the rider were visible in the soft clay. The old horsetrack also went in and came out at these bars.

Abner examined the man's footprints with what I thought was an excess of interest. Travelers were always going through one's land; and, provided they closed the bars behind them, what did it matter? Abner seemed concerned about this traveler however. When we had entered the field he sat for some time in the saddle; and then, instead of going to the hills where the springs were, he rode up the valley toward a piece of woods. There was a little rivulet threading this valley and he watched it as he rode.

Finally, just before the rivulet entered the woods, he stopped and got down out of his saddle. When I came up he was looking at a track on the edge of the little stream. It was the footprint of a man, still muddy where the water had run into it. Abner stood on the bank beside the rivulet, and for a good while I could not imagine what he was waiting for. Then, as he watched the track, I understood. He was waiting for the muddy water to clear so he could see the imprint of the man's foot.

"Uncle Abner," I said, "what do you care about who goes through the field?"

"Ordinarily I do not care," he said, "if the man lays up the fence behind him; but there is something out of the ordinary about this thing. The man who crossed there on foot is the same man who came in on the horse. The footprints here and at the bar show the same plate on the bootheel. He rode a horse that had been here before today, because it remembered the lane and tried to turn in there. Moreover, the man did not wish to be seen, because he came early, hid the horse and went on foot back toward the burned house."

"How do you know that he had hidden the horse, Uncle Abner?"

For answer he beckoned to me and we rode into the woods. The leaves were damp and the horses made no sound. In a few moments Abner stopped and pointed through the beech trees, and I saw a bay horse tied to a sapling. The horse stood with his legs wide apart and his head down.

"The horse is asleep," said Abner; "it has been ridden all night. We must find the rider."

I was now alive with interest. The old story of the robbery floated before me in romantic colors. What innocent person would come here by stealth, ride his horse all night and then hide it in the woods? Moreover, as Abner said, this horse had been to the sheriff's house before today; and it had been there before the house was burned—because it had started to enter the old lane and had been turned back by its rider. We were all familiar with such striking examples of memory in horses. A horse, having once gone over a road and entered at a certain gate, will follow that road on a second trip and again enter that gate.

Then I remembered the old horsetrack that had preceded this one, and the solution of this thing appeared before me. The story had gone about that two men had robbed the sheriff and these evidences tallied with that story. Two men had ridden into that pasture; that one track was older was because one of the men had gone to tell the other to meet him here—had ridden back—and the other had followed. The horse of the first robber was doubtless concealed deeper in the wood. And why had they returned? That was clear enough—they had concealed the booty until now and had just come back for it.

The thrill of adventure tingled in my blood. We were on the trail of the robbers and they could not easily escape us. The one who had ridden this horse could not be far away, since his track in the brook was muddy when we found it; but why had he crossed the brook in the direction of the burned house? The way over the hill toward the house was wholly in the open—clean sod, not even a tree. The man on foot could not have been out of sight of us when we rode across the brook and round the brow of the hill—but he was out of sight. We sat there in our saddles and searched the land, lying smooth and open before us. There was the burned house below, bare as my hand, and the meadows, all open to the eye. A rabbit could not have hidden—where was the rider of that worn-out, sleeping horse?

Abner sat there looking down at this clean, open land. A man could not vanish into the air; he could not hide in a wisp of blue grass; he could not cross three hundred acres of open country while his track in a running brook remained muddy. He could have reached the brow of the hill and perhaps gone down to the house, but he could not have passed the meadows and the pasture field beyond without wings on his shoulders.

The morning was on its way; the air was like lotus. The sun, still out of sight, was beginning to gild the hilltops. I looked up; away on the knob at the summit of the hill there was an old graveyard—that was a curious custom, to put our dead on the highest point of land. A patch of sunlight lay on this village of the dead—and as I looked a thing caught my eye.

I turned in the saddle.

"I saw something flash up there, Uncle Abner."

"Flash," he said—"like a weapon?"

"Glitter," I said. And I caught up the bridle-rein.

But Abner put his hand on the bit.

"Quietly, Martin," he said. "We will ride slowly round the hill, as though we were looking for the cattle, and go up behind that knob; there is a ridge there and we shall not be seen until we come out on the crest of the hill beside the graveyard."

We rode idly away, stopping now and then, like persons at their leisure. But I was afire with interest. All the way to the crest of the hill the blood skipped in my veins. The horses made no sound on the carpet of green sod. And when we came out suddenly beside the ancient graveyard I fully expected to see there a brace of robbers—like some picture in a story—with bloody cloths around their heads and pistols in their belts; or two bewhiskered pirates before a heap of pieces-of-eight.

On the tick of the clock I was disillusioned, however. A man who had been kneeling by a grave rose. I knew him in the twinkling of an eye. He was the sheriff and in the twinkling of an eye I knew why he was there; and I was covered with confusion. His father was buried in this old graveyard. It was a land where men concealed their feelings as one conceals the practice of a crime; and one would have stolen his neighbor's goods before he would have intruded upon the secrecy of his emotions.

I pulled up my horse and would have turned back, pretending that I had not seen him, for I was ashamed; but Abner rode on and presently I followed in amazement. If Abner had cursed his horse or warbled a ribald song I could not have been more astonished. I was ashamed for myself and I was ashamed for Abner. How could he ride in on a man who had just got up from beside his father's grave? My mind flashed back over Abner's life to find a precedent for this conspicuous inconsiderate act; but there was nothing like it in all the history of the man.

When the sheriff saw us he wiped his face with his sleeve and went white as a sheet. And under my own shirt I felt and suffered with the man. I should have gone white like that if one had caught me thus. And in my throat I choked with bitterness at Abner. Had his heart tilted and every generous instinct been emptied out of it? Then I thought he meant to turn the thing with some word that would cover the man's confusion and save his feelings inviolate; but he shocked me out of that.

"Smallwood," said Abner, "you have come back!"

The man blinked as though the sun were in his eyes. He had not yet regained the mastery of himself.

"Yes," he said.

"And why do you come?" said Abner.

A flush of scarlet spread over the man's white face.

"And do you ask me that?" he cried. "It is the tomb of my father!"

"Your father," said Abner, "was an upright man. He lived in the fear of God. I respect his tomb."

"I thank you, Abner," replied the man. "I honor my father's grave."

"You honor it late," said Abner.

"Late!" echoed Smallwood.

"Late," said Abner.

The man spread out his hands with a gesture of resignation. "You mean that my misfortune has dishonored my father?"

"No," said Abner, "that is not what I mean; by a misfortune no man can be dishonored—neither his father nor his father's father."

"What is it you mean, then?" said the man.

"Smallwood," said Abner, "is it not before you; where you in your ownership allowed the fence around this grave to rot I have rebuilt it, and where you allowed the weeds to grow up I have cut them down?"

It was the truth. Abner had put up a fence and had cleaned the graveyard. Only the myrtle and cinquefoil covered it. I thought the sheriff would be ashamed at that, but his face brightened.

"It is disaster, Abner, that brings a man back to his duties to the dead. In prosperity we forget, but in poverty we remember."

"The Master," replied Abner, "was not very much concerned about the dead; nor am I. The dead are in God's keeping! It is our duties to the living that should move us. Do you remember, Smallwood, the story of the young man who wished to go and bury his father?"

"I do," said Smallwood, "and I have always held him in honor for it."

"And so, too, the Master would have held him, but for one thing."

"What thing?" said Smallwood.

"That the story was an excuse," replied Abner.

I saw the light go out of the man's face and his lips tremble; and then he said what I was afraid he would say.

"Abner," he said, "if you are determined to gouge this thing out of me, why here it is: I cannot bear to live in this community any longer. I am ashamed to see those upon whom I have brought misfortune—Elnathan Stone, and your brother Rufus, and Adam Greathouse. I have made up my mind to leave the country forever, but I wanted to see the place where my father was buried before I went, because I shall never see it again. You don't understand how a man can feel like that; but I tell you, when a man is in trouble he will remember his father's roof if he is living, and his father's grave if he is dead."

I was so mortified before this confession that Abner's heartless manner had forced out of the man that I reached over and caught my uncle by the sleeve. My horse stood by Abner's chestnut, and I hoped that he would yield to my importunity and ride on; but he turned in his saddle and looked first at me and then down upon the sheriff.

"Martin," he said, "thinks we ought to leave you to your filial devotions."

"It is a credit to the child's heart," replied the man, "and a rebuke to you, Abner. It is a pity that age robs us of charity."

Abner put his hands on the pommel of his saddle and regarded the sheriff.

"I have read St. Paul's epistle on charity," he said, "and,

after long reflection, I am persuaded that there exists a greater thing than charity—a thing of more value to the human family. Like charity, it rejoiceth not in iniquity, but it does not bear all things or believe all things, or endure all things; and, unlike charity, it seeketh its own. . . . Do you know what thing I mean, Smallwood? I will tell you. It is Justice."

"Abner," replied the man, "I am in no humor to hear a sermon."

"Those who need a sermon," said Abner, "are rarely in the humor to hear it."

"Abner," cried the man, "you annoy me! Will you ride on?"

"Presently," replied Abner; "when we have talked together a little further. You are about to leave the country. I shall perhaps never see you again and I would have your opinion upon a certain matter."

"Well," said the man, "what is it?"

"It is this," said Abner. "You appear to entertain great filial respect, and I would ask you a question touching that regard: What ought to be done with a man who would use a weapon against his father?"

"He ought to be hanged," said Smallwood.

"And would it change the case," said Abner, "if the father held something which the son had intrusted to him and would not give it up because it belonged to another, and the son, to take it, should come against his father with an iron in his hand?"

The sheriff's face became a land of doubt, of suspicion, of uncertainty and, I thought, of fear.

"Abner," cried the man, "I do not understand; will you explain it?"

"I will explain this thing which you do not understand," replied Abner, "when you have explained a thing which I do not understand. Why was it that you came here last night and again this morning? That was two visits to your father's grave within six hours. I do not understand why you should make two trips—and one upon the heels of the other."

For a moment the man did not reply; then he spoke.

"How do you know that I was here last night? Did you see me come or did another see and tell you?"

"I did not see you," replied Abner, "nor did any one tell me that you came; but I know it in spite of that."

"And how do you know it?" said Smallwood.

"I will tell you," said Abner. "On the road this morning I observed two horse-tracks leading this way; they both turned in at the same crossroads and they both came to this place. One was fresh, the other was some hours old—it is easy to tell that on a clay road. I compared those two tracks and the third returning track, and presently I saw that they had been made by the same horse."

Abner stopped and pointed down toward the beech woods.

"Moreover," he continued, "your horse, hidden among those trees, is worn out and asleep. Now you live only some twenty miles away—that journey this morning would not have so fatigued your horse that he would sleep on his feet; but to make two trips—to go all night—to travel sixty miles—would do it."

The sheriff's head did not move, but I saw his eyes glance down. The glance did not escape Abner and he went on.

"I saw the crowbar in the grass there some time ago," he said; "but what has the crowbar to do with your two trips?"

I, too, saw now the iron bar. It was the thing that had glittered in the sun.

The man threw back his shoulders; he lifted his face and stood up. There came upon him the pose and expression of one who steps out at last desperately into the open.

"Yes," he said, "I was here last night. It was my horse that made those tracks in the road and it is my horse that is hidden in the woods now. And that is my crowbar in the grass. . . . And do you want to know why I made those two trips, and why I brought that crowbar, and why I hid my horse? . . . Well, I'll tell you, since there is no shame in you and no decent feeling, and you are determined to have it. . . . You can't understand, Abner, because you have a heart of stone; but I tell you I wanted to see my father's grave before I left the country forever. I was ashamed to meet the people over here and so I came in the night. When I got here I saw that the heavy slab over my father's grave had settled down and was wedged in against the coping. I tried to straighten it up, but I could not. . . . Well, what would you have done, Abner—

gone away and left your father's tomb a ruin? . . . No matter
what you would have done! I went back twenty miles and got
that crowbar and came again to lift and straighten the stone
over my father's grave before I left it. . . . And now, will you
ride on and leave me to finish my work and go?"

"Smallwood," Abner said presently, "how do you know that
your house was robbed before it was burned? Might it not be
that the county revenues were burned with the house?"

"I will tell you how I know that, Abner," replied the man.
"The revenues of the county were all in my deerskin saddle-
pockets, under my pillow; when I awoke in the night the
house was dark and filled with smoke. I jumped up, seized my
clothes, which were on a chair by the bed, and ran downstairs;
but, first, I felt under the pillow for my saddle-pockets—and
they were gone."

"But, Smallwood," said Abner, "how can you be certain
that the money was stolen out of your saddle-pockets if you
did not find them?"

"I did find them," replied the sheriff; "I went back into the
house and got the saddle-pockets and brought them out—and
they were empty."

"That was a brave thing to do, Smallwood," said Abner—
"to go back into a burning house filled with smoke and dark.
You could have had only a moment."

"You speak the truth, Abner," replied the sheriff. "I had
only a moment—the house was a pot of smoke. But the
money was in my care, Abner. There was my duty—and what
is a man's life against that!"

I saw Abner's back straighten and I heard his feet grind on
the iron of his stirrups.

"And now, Smallwood," he said, and his voice was like the
menace of a weapon, "will you tell me how it was possible for
you to go into a house that was dark and filled with smoke,
and thus quickly—in a moment—find those empty saddle-
pockets, unless you knew exactly where they were?"

I saw that Abner's question had impaled the man, as one
pierces a fly through with a needle; and, like a fly, the man
in his confusion fluttered.

"Smallwood," said Abner, "you are a thief and a hypocrite

and a liar! And, like all liars, you have destroyed yourself! You not only stole this money but you tried to make your father an accomplice in that robbery. To conceal it, you hid it in this dead man's house. And, behold, the dead man has held his house against you! When you came here last night to carry away the money you found that the slab over your father's grave had fallen and wedged itself in against the limestone coping, and you could not lift it; and so you went back for that crowbar. . . . But who knows, you thief, what influence, though he be dead, a just man has with God! I came in time to help your father hold his house—and against his son, with a weapon in his hand!"

I saw the man cringe and writhe and shiver, as though he were unable to get out of his tracks; then the power came to him, and he vaulted over the fence and ran. He ran in fear down the hill and across the brook and into the wood; and a moment later he came out with his tired horse at a gallop.

Abner looked down from the hilltop on the flying thief, but he made no move to follow.

"Let him go," he said, "for his father's sake. We owe the dead man that much."

Then he got down from his horse, thrust the crowbar under the slab over the grave and lifted it up.

Beneath it were the sheriff's deerskin saddle-pockets and the stolen money!

Chapter 7

A Twilight Adventure

IT WAS A STRANGE scene that we approached. Before a cross-road leading into a grove of beech trees, a man sat on his horse with a rifle across his saddle. He did not speak until we were before him in the road, and then his words were sinister.

"Ride on!" he said.

But my Uncle Abner did not ride on. He pulled up his big chestnut and looked calmly at the man.

"You speak like one having authority," he said.

The man answered with an oath.

"Ride on, or you'll get into trouble!"

"I am accustomed to trouble," replied my uncle with great composure; "you must give me a better reason."

"I'll give you hell!" growled the man. "Ride on!"

Abner's eyes traveled over the speaker with a deliberate scrutiny.

"It is not yours to give," he said, "although possibly to receive. Are the roads of Virginia held by arms?"

"This one is," replied the man.

"I think not," replied my Uncle Abner, and, touching his horse with his heel, he turned into the crossroad.

The man seized his weapon, and I heard the hammer click under his thumb. Abner must have heard it, too, but he did not turn his broad back. He only called to me in his usual matter-of-fact voice:

"Go on, Martin; I will overtake you."

The man brought his gun up to his middle, but he did not shoot. He was like all those who undertake to command obedience without having first determined precisely what they will do if their orders are disregarded. He was prepared to threaten with desperate words, but not to support that threat with a

95

desperate act, and he hung there uncertain, cursing under his breath.

I would have gone on as my uncle had told me to do, but now the man came to a decision.

"No, by God!" he said; "if he goes in, you go in, too!"

And he seized my bridle and turned my horse into the crossroad; then he followed.

There is a long twilight in these hills. The sun departs, but the day remains. A sort of weird, dim, elfin day, that dawns at sunset, and envelops and possesses the world. The land is full of light, but it is the light of no heavenly sun. It is a light equal everywhere, as though the earth strove to illumine itself, and succeeded with that labor.

The stars are not yet out. Now and then a pale moon rides in the sky, but it has no power, and the light is not from it. The wind is usually gone; the air is soft, and the fragrance of the fields fills it like a perfume. The noises of the day and of the creatures that go about by day cease, and the noises of the night and of the creatures that haunt the night begin. The bat swoops and circles in the maddest action, but without a sound. The eye sees him, but the ear hears nothing. The whippoorwill begins his plaintive cry, and one hears, but does not see.

It is a world that we do not understand, for we are creatures of the sun, and we are fearful lest we come upon things at work here, of which we have no experience, and that may be able to justify themselves against our reason. And so a man falls into silence when he travels in this twilight, and he looks and listens with his senses out on guard.

It was an old wagon-road that we entered, with the grass growing between the ruts. The horses traveled without a sound until we began to enter a grove of ancient beech trees; then the dead leaves cracked and rustled. Abner did not look behind him, and so he did not know that I came. He knew that someone followed, but he doubtless took it for the sentinel in the road. And I did not speak.

The man with the cocked gun rode grimly behind me. I did not know whither we went or to what end. We might be shot down from behind a tree or murdered in our saddles. It was not a land where men took desperate measures upon a triviality. And I knew that Abner rode into something that little men, lacking courage, would gladly have stayed out of.

Presently my ear caught a sound, or, rather, a confused mingling of sounds, as of men digging in the earth. It was faint, and some distance beyond us in the heart of the beech woods, but as we traveled the sound increased and I could distinguish the strokes of the mattock, and the thrust of the shovel and the clatter of the earth on the dry leaves.

These sounds seemed at first to be before us, and then, a little later, off on our right-hand. And finally, through the gray boles of the beech trees in the lowland, I saw two men at work digging a pit. They had just begun their work, for there was little earth thrown out. But there was a great heap of leaves that they had cleared away, and heavy cakes of the baked crust that the mattocks had pried up. The length of the pit lay at right angles to the road, and the men were working with their backs toward us. They were in their shirts and trousers, and the heavy mottled shadows thrown by the beech limbs hovered on their backs and shoulders like a flock of night birds. The earth was baked and hard; the mattock rang on it, and among the noises of their work they did not hear us.

I saw Abner look off at this strange labor, his head half turned, but he did not stop and we went on. The old wagon-road made a turn into the low ground. I heard the sound of horses, and a moment later we came upon a dozen men.

I shall not easily forget that scene. The beech trees had been deadened by some settler who had chopped a ring around them, and they stood gaunt with a few tattered leaves, letting the weird twilight in. Some of the men stood about, others sat on the fallen trees, and others in their saddles. But upon every man of that grim company there was the air and aspect of one who waits for something to be finished.

An old man with a heavy iron-gray beard smoked a pipe, puffing out great mouthfuls of smoke with a sort of deliberate energy; another whittled a stick, cutting a bull with horns, and shaping his work with the nicest care; and still another traced letters on the pommel of his saddle with his thumbnail.

A little to one side a great pronged beech thrust out a gray arm, and under it two men sat on their horses, their elbows strapped to their bodies and their mouths gagged with a saddle-cloth. And behind them a man in his saddle was working with a colt halter, unraveling the twine that bound the head-piece and seeking thereby to get a greater length of rope.

This was the scene when I caught it first. But a moment later, when my uncle rode into it, the thing burst into furious life. Men sprang up, caught his horse by the bit and covered him with weapons. Some one called for the sentinel who rode behind me, and he galloped up. For a moment there was confusion. Then the big man who had smoked with such deliberation called out my uncle's name, others repeated it, and the panic was gone. But a ring of stern, determined faces were around him and before his horse, and with the passing of the flash of action there passed no whit of the grim purpose upon which these men were set.

My uncle looked about him.

"Lemuel Arnold," he said; "Nicholas Vance, Hiram Ward, you here!"

As my uncle named these men I knew them. They were cattle grazers. Ward was the big man with the pipe. The men with them were their renters and drovers.

Their lands lay nearest to the mountains. The geographical position made for feudal customs and a certain independence of action. They were on the border, they were accustomed to say, and had to take care of themselves. And it ought to be written that they did take care of themselves with courage and decision, and on occasion they also took care of Virginia.

Their fathers had pushed the frontier of the dominion northward and westward and had held the land. They had fought the savage single-handed and desperately, by his own methods and with his own weapons. Ruthless and merciless, eye for eye and tooth for tooth, they returned what they were given.

They did not send to Virginia for militia when the savage came; they fought him at their doors, and followed him through the forest, and took their toll of death. They were hardier than he was, and their hands were heavier and bloodier, until the old men in the tribes of the Ohio Valley forbade these raids because they cost too much, and turned the war parties south into Kentucky.

Certain historians have written severely of these men and their ruthless methods, and prattled of humane warfare; but they wrote nursing their soft spines in the security of a civilization which these men's hands had builded, and their words are hollow.

"Abner," said Ward, "let me speak plainly. We have got an account to settle with a couple of cattle thieves and we are not going to be interfered with. Cattle stealing and murder have got to stop in these hills. We've had enough of it."

"Well," replied my uncle, "I am the last man in Virginia to interfere with that. We have all had enough of it, and we are all determined that it must cease. But how do you propose to end it?"

"With a rope," said Ward.

"It is a good way," replied Abner, "when it is done the right way."

"What do you mean by the right way?" said Ward.

"I mean," answered my uncle, "that we have all agreed to a way and we ought to stick to our agreement. Now, I want to help you to put down cattle stealing and murder, but I want also to keep my word."

"And how have you given your word?"

"In the same way that you have given yours," said Abner, "and as every man here has given his. Our fathers found out that they could not manage the assassin and the thief when every man undertook to act for himself, so they got together and agreed upon a certain way to do these things. Now, we have indorsed what they agreed to, and promised to obey it, and I for one would like to keep my promise."

The big man's face was puzzled. Now it cleared.

"Hell!" he said. "You mean the law?"

"Call it what you like," replied Abner; "it is merely the agreement of everybody to do certain things in a certain way."

The man made a decisive gesture with a jerk of his head.

"Well," he said, "we're going to do this thing our own way."

My uncle's face became thoughtful.

D

"Then," he said, "you will injure some innocent people."

"You mean these two blacklegs?"

And Ward indicated the prisoners with a gesture of his thumb.

My uncle lifted his face and looked at the two men some distance away beneath the great beech, as though he had but now observed them.

"I was not thinking of them," he answered. "I was thinking that if men like you and Lemuel Arnold and Nicholas Vance violate the law, lesser men will follow your example, and as you justify your act for security, they will justify theirs for revenge and plunder. And so the law will go to pieces and a lot of weak and innocent people who depend upon it for security will be left unprotected."

These were words that I have remembered, because they put the danger of lynch law in a light I had not thought of. But I saw that they would not move these determined men. Their blood was up and they received them coldly.

"Abner," said Ward, "we are not going to argue this thing with you. There are times when men have to take the law into their own hands. We live here at the foot of the mountains. Our cattle are stolen and run across the border into Maryland. We are tired of it and we intend to stop it.

"Our lives and our property are menaced by a set of reckless desperate devils that we have determined to hunt down and hang to the first tree in sight. We did not send for you. You pushed your way in here; and now, if you are afraid of breaking the law, you can ride one, because we are going to break it—if to hang a pair of murderous devils is to break it."

I was astonished at my uncle's decision.

"Well," he said, "if the law must be broken, I will stay and help you break it!"

"Very well," replied Ward; "but don't get a wrong notion in your head, Abner. If you choose to stay, you put yourself on a footing with everybody else."

"And that is precisely what I want to do," replied Abner, "but as matters stand now, every man here has an advantage over me."

"What advantage, Abner?" said Ward.

"The advantage," answered my uncle, "that he has heard all the evidence against your prisoners and is convinced that they are guilty."

"If that is all the advantage, Abner," replied Ward, "you shall not be denied it. There has been so much cattle stealing here of late that our people living on the border finally got together and determined to stop every drove going up into the mountains that wasn't accompanied by somebody that we knew was all right. This afternoon one of my men reported a little bunch of about a hundred steers on the road, and I stopped it. These two men were driving the cattle. I inquired if the cattle belonged to them and they replied that they were not the owners, but that they had been hired to take the drove over into Maryland. I did not know the men, and as they met my inquiries with oaths and imprecations, I was suspicious of them. I demanded the name of the owner who had hired them to drive the cattle. They said it was none of my damned business and went on. I raised the county. We overtook them, turned their cattle into a field, and brought them back until we could find out who the drove belonged to. On the road we met Bowers."

He turned and indicated the man who was working with the rope halter.

I knew the man. He was a cattle shipper, somewhat involved in debt, but who managed to buy and sell and somehow keep his head above water.

"He told us the truth. Yesterday evening he had gone over on the Stone-Coal to look at Daniel Coopman's cattle. He had heard that some grazer from your county, Abner, was on the way up to buy the cattle for stockers. He wanted to get in ahead of your man, so he left home that evening and got to Coopman's place about sundown. He took a short cut on foot over the hill, and when he came out he saw a man on the opposite ridge where the road runs, ride away. The man seemed to have been sitting on his horse looking down into the little valley where Coopman's house stands. Bowers went down to the house, but Coopman was not there. The door was open, and Bowers says the house looked as though Coopman had just gone out of it and might come back any moment. There was no one about, because Coopman's wife had gone on a visit to her daughter, over the mountains, and the old man was alone.

"Bowers thought Coopman was out showing the cattle to the man whom he had just seen ride off, so he went out to the pasture field to look for him. He could not find him and he could not find the cattle. He came back to the house to wait until Coopman should come in. He sat down on the porch. As he sat there he noticed that the porch had been scrubbed and was still wet. He looked at it and saw that it had been scrubbed only at one place before the door. This seemed to him a little peculiar, and he wondered why Coopman had scrubbed his porch only in one place. He got up and as he went toward the door he saw that the jamb of the door was splintered at a point about halfway up. He examined this splintered place and presently discovered that it was a bullet hole.

"This alarmed him, and he went out into the yard. There he saw a wagon track leading away from the house toward the road. In the weeds he found Coopman's watch. He picked it up and put it into his pocket. It was a big silver watch, with Coopman's name on it, and attached to it was a buckskin string. He followed the track to the gate, where it entered the road. He discovered then that the cattle had also passed through this gate. It was now night. Bowers went back, got Coopman's saddle horse out of the stable, rode him home, and followed the track of the cattle this morning, but he saw no trace of the drove until we met him."

"What did Shifflet and Twiggs say to this story?" inquired Abner.

"They did not hear it," answered Ward; "Bowers did not talk before them. He rode aside with us when we met him."

"Did Shifflet and Twiggs know Bowers?" said Abner.

"I don't know," replied Ward; "their talk was so foul when we stopped the drove that we had to tie their mouths up."

"Is that all?" said Abner.

Ward swore a great oath.

"No!" he said. "Do you think we would hang men on that? From what Bowers told us, we thought Shifflet and

Twiggs had killed Daniel Coopman and driven off his cattle; but we wanted to be certain of it, so we set out to discover what they had done with Coopman's body after they had killed him and what they had done with the wagon. We followed the trail of the drove down to the Valley River. No wagon had crossed, but on the other side we found that a wagon and a drove of cattle had turned out of the road and gone along the basin of the river for about a mile through the woods. And there in a bend of the river we found where these devils had camped.

"There had been a great fire of logs very near to the river, but none of the ashes of this fire remained. From a circular space some twelve feet in diameter the ashes had all been shoveled off, the marks of the shovel being distinct. In the center of the place where this fire had burned the ground had been scraped clean, but near the edges there were some traces of cinders and the ground was blackened. In the river at this point, just opposite the remains of the fire, was a natural washout or hole. We made a raft of logs, cut a pole with a fork on the end and dragged the river. We found most of the wagon iron, all showing the effect of fire. Then we fastened a tin bucket to a pole and fished the washout. We brought up cinders, buttons, buckles and pieces of bone."

Ward paused.

"That settled it, and we came back here to swing the devils up."

My uncle had listened very carefully, and now he spoke.

"What did the man pay Twiggs and Shifflet?" said my uncle. "Did they tell you that when you stopped the drove?"

"Now that," answered Ward, "was another piece of damning evidence. When we searched the men we found a pocketbook on Shifflet with a hundred and fifteen dollars and some odd cents. It was Daniel Coopman's pocketbook, because there was an old tax receipt in it that had slipped down between the leather and the lining.

"We asked Shifflet where he got it, and he said that the fifteen dollars and the change was his own money and that the hundred had been paid to him by the man who had hired them to drive the cattle. He explained his possession of the pocketbook by saying that this man had the money in it, and when he went to pay them he said that they might just as well take it, too."

"Who was this man?" said Abner.

"They will not tell who he was."

"Why not?"

"Now, Abner," cried Ward, "why not, indeed! Because there never was any such man. The story is a lie out of the whole cloth. Those two devils are guilty as hell. The proof is all dead against them."

"Well," replied my uncle, "what circumstantial evidence proves, depends a good deal on how you get started. It is a somewhat dangerous road to the truth, because all the signboards have a curious trick of pointing in the direction that you are going. Now, a man will never realize this unless he turns around and starts back, then he will see, to his amazement that the signboards have also turned. But as long as his face is set one certain way, it is of no use to talk to him, he won't listen to you; and if he sees you going the other way, he will call you a fool."

"There is only one way in this case," said Ward.

"There are always two ways in every case," replied Abner, "that the suspected person is either guilty or innocent. You have started upon the theory that Shifflet and Twiggs are guilty. Now, suppose you had started the other way, what then?"

"Well," said Ward, "what then?"

"This, then," continued Abner. "You stop Shifflet and Twiggs on the road with Daniel Coopman's cattle, and they tell you that a man has hired them to drive this drove into Maryland. You believe that and start out to find the man. You find Bowers!"

Bowers went deadly white.

"For God's sake, Abner!" he said.

But my uncle was merciless and he drove in the conclusion. "What then?"

There was no answer, but the faces of the men about my uncle turned toward the man whose trembling hands fingered the rope that he was preparing for another.

"But the things we found, Abner?" said Ward.

"What do they prove," continued my uncle, "now that the signboards are turned? That somebody killed Daniel Coopman and drove off his cattle, and afterward destroyed the body and the wagon in which it was hauled away. . . . But who did that? . . . The men who were driving Daniel Coopman's cattle, or the man who was riding Daniel Coopman's horse, and carrying Daniel Coopman's watch in his pocket?"

Ward's face was a study in expression.

"Ah!" cried Abner. "Remember that the signboards have turned about. And what do they point to if we read them on the way we are going now? The man who killed Coopman was afraid to be found with the cattle, so he hired Twiggs and Shifflet to drive them into Maryland for him and follows on another road."

"But his story, Abner?" said Ward.

"And what of it?" replied my uncle. "He is taken and he must explain how he comes by the horse that he rides, and the watch that he carries, and he must find the criminal. Well, he tells you a tale to fit the facts that you will find when you go back to look, and he gives you Shifflet and Twiggs to hang."

I never saw a man in more mortal terror than Jacob Bowers. He sat in his saddle like a man bewildered.

"My God!" he said, and again he repeated it, and again.

And he had cause for that terror on him. My uncle was stern and ruthless. The pendulum had swung the other way, and the lawless monster that Bowers had allied was now turning on himself. He saw it and his joints were unhinged with fear.

A voice crashed out of the ring of desperate men, uttering the changed opinion.

"By God!" it cried, "we've got the right man now."

And one caught the rope out of Bowers' hand.

But my Uncle Abner rode in on them.

"Are you sure about that?" he said.

"Sure!" they echoed. "You have shown it yourself, Abner."

"No," replied my uncle, "I have not shown it. I have shown merely whither circumstantial evidence leads us when we go hotfoot after a theory. Bowers says that there was a man on the hill above Daniel Coopman's house, and this man will know that he did not kill Daniel Coopman and that his story is the truth."

They laughed in my uncle's face.

"Do you believe that there was any such person?"

My uncle seemed to increase in stature, and his voice became big and dominant.

"I do," he said, "because I am the man!"

They had got their lesson, and we rode out with Shifflet and Twiggs to a legal trial.

Chapter 8

The Age of Miracles

THE GIRL was standing apart from the crowd in the great avenue of poplars that led up to the house. She seemed embarrassed and uncertain what to do, a thing of April emerging into Summer.

Abner and Randolph marked her as they entered along the gravel road.

They had left their horses at the gate, but she had brought hers inside, as though after some habit unconsciously upon her.

But half-way to the house she had remembered and got down. And she stood now against the horse's shoulder. It was a black hunter, big and old, but age marred no beauty of his lines. He was like a horse of ebony, enchanted out of the earth by some Arabian magic, but not yet by that magic awakened into life.

The girl wore a long, dark riding-skirt, after the fashion of the time, and a coat of hunter's pink. Her dark hair was in a great wrist-thick plait. Her eyes, too, were big and dark, and her body firm and lithe from the out-of-doors.

"Ah!" cried Randolph, making his characteristic gesture, "Prospero has been piping in this grove. Here is a daughter of the immortal morning! We grow old, Abner, and it is youth that the gods love."

My uncle, his hands behind him, his eyes on the gravel road, looked up at the bewitching picture.

"Poor child," he said; "the gods that love her must be gods of the valleys and not gods of the hills."

"Ruth amid the alien corn! Is it a better figure, Abner? Well, she has a finer inheritance than these lands; she has youth!"

107

D*

"She ought to have both," replied my uncle. "It was sheer robbery to take her inheritance."

"It was a proceeding at law," replied the Justice. "It was the law that did the thing, and we can not hold the law in disrespect."

"But the man who uses the law to accomplish a wrong, we can so hold," said Abner. "He is an outlaw, as the highwayman and the pirate are."

He extended his arm toward the great house sitting at the end of the avenue.

"In spite of the sanction of the law, I hold this dead man for a robber. And I would have wrested these lands from him, if I could. But your law, Randolph, stood before him."

"Well," replied the Justice, "he takes no gain from it; he lies yonder waiting for the grave."

"But his brother takes," said Abner, "and this child loses."

The Justice, elegant in the costume of the time, turned his ebony stick in his fingers.

"One should forgive the dead," he commented in a facetious note; "it is a mandate of the Scripture."

"I am not concerned about the dead," replied Abner. "The dead are in God's hands. It is the living who concern me."

"Then," cried the Justice, "you should forgive the brother who takes."

"And I shall forgive him," replied Abner, "when he returns what he has taken."

"Returns what he has taken!" Randolph laughed. "Why, Abner, the devil could not filch a coin out of the clutches of old Benton Wolf."

"The devil," said my uncle, "is not an authority that I depend on."

"A miracle of Heaven, then," said the Justice. "But, alas, it is not the age of miracles."

"Perhaps," replied Abner, his voice descending into a deeper tone, "but I am not so certain."

They had come now to where the girl stood, her back against the black shoulder of the horse. The morning air moved the yellow leaves about her feet. She darted out to meet them, her face aglow.

"Damme!" cried Randolph. "William of Avon knew only witches of the second order! How do you do, Julia? I have hardly seen you since you were no taller than my stick, and told me that your name was 'Pete-George,' and that you were a circus-horse, and offered to do tricks for me."

A shadow crossed the girl's face.

"I remember," she said, "it was up there on the porch!"

"Egad!" cried Randolph, embarrassed. "And so it was!"

He kissed the tips of the girl's fingers and the shadow in her face fled.

For the man's heart was good, and he had the manner of a gentleman. But it was Abner that she turned to in her dilemma.

"I forgot," she said, "and almost rode into the house. Do you think I could leave the horse here? He will stand if I drop the rein."

Then she went on to make her explanation. She wanted to see the old house that had been so long her home. This was the only opportunity, to-day, when all the countryside came to the dead man's burial. She thought she might come, too, although her motive was no tribute of respect.

She put her hand through Abner's arm and he looked down upon her, grave and troubled.

"My child," he said, "leave the horse where he stands and come with me, for my motive, also, is no tribute of respect; and you go with a better right than I do."

"I suppose," the girl hesitated, "that one ought to respect the dead, but this man—these men—I can not."

"Nor can I," replied my uncle. "If I do not respect a man when he is living, I shall not pretend to when he is dead. One does not make a claim upon my honor by going out of life."

They went up the avenue among the yellow poplar leaves and the ragweed and fennel springing up along the unkept gravel.

It was a crisp and glorious morning. The frost lay on the rail fence. The spider-webs stretched here and there across the high grasses of the meadows in intricate and bewildering lace-work. The sun was clear and bright, but it carried no oppressive heat as it drew on in its course toward noon.

The countryside had gathered to see Adam Wolf buried. It was a company of tenants, the idle and worthless mostly, drawn by curiosity. For in life the two old men who had seized upon this property by virtue of a defective acknowledgment to a deed, permitted no invasion of their boundary.

Everywhere the lands were posted; no urchin fished and no schoolboy hunted. The green perch, fattened in the deep creek that threaded the rich bottom lands, no man disturbed. But the quail, the pheasant, the robin and the meadow-lark, old Adam pursued with his fowling-piece. He tramped about with it at all seasons. One would have believed that all the birds of heaven had done the creature some unending harm and in revenge he had declared a war. And so the accident by which he met his death was a jeopardy of the old man's habits, and to be looked for when one lived with a fowling-piece in one's hands and grew careless in its use.

The two men lived alone and thus all sorts of mystery sprang up around them, elaborated by the Negro fancy and gaining in grim detail at every story-teller's hand. It had the charm and thrilling interest of an adventure, then, for the countryside to get this entry.

The brothers lived in striking contrast. Adam was violent, and his cries and curses, his hard and brutal manner were the terror of the Negro who passed at night that way, or the urchin overtaken by darkness on his road home. But Benton got about his affairs in silence, with a certain humility of manner, and a mild concern for the opinion of his fellows. Still, somehow, the Negro and the urchin held him in a greater terror. Perhaps because he had got his coffin made and kept it in his house, together with his clothes for burial. It seemed uncanny thus to prepare against his dissolution and to bargain for the outfit, with anxiety to have his shilling's worth.

And yet, with this gruesome furniture at hand, the old man, it would seem, was in no contemplation of his death. He spoke sometimes with a marked savor and an unctuous kneading of the hands of that time when he should own the land, for he was the younger and by rule should have the expectancy of life.

There was a crowd about the door and filling the hall inside, a crowd that elbowed and jostled, taken with a quivering interest, and there to feed its maw of curiosity with every item.

The girl wished to remain on the portico, where she could see the ancient garden and the orchard and all the paths and byways that had been her wonderland of youth, but Abner asked her to go in.

Randolph turned away, but my uncle and the girl remained some time by the coffin. The rim of the dead man's forehead and his jaw were riddled with bird-shot, but his eyes and an area of his face below them, where the thin nose came down and with its lines and furrows made up the main identity of features, were not disfigured. And these preserved the hard stamp of his violent nature, untouched by the accident that had dispossessed him of his life.

He lay in the burial clothes and the coffin that Benton Wolf had provided for himself, all except the gloves upon his hands. These the old man had forgot. And now when he came to prepare his brother for a public burial, for no other had touched the man, he must needs take what he could find about the house, a pair of old, knit gloves with every rent and moth-hole carefully darned, as though the man had sat down there with pains to give his brother the best appearance that he could.

This little touch affected the girl to tears, so strange is a woman's heart. "Poor thing!" she said. And for this triviality she would forget the injury that the dead man and his brother had done to her, the loss they had inflicted, and her long distress.

She took a closer hold upon Abner's arm, and dabbed her eyes with a tiny kerchief.

"I am sorry for him," she said, "for the living brother. It is so pathetic."

And she indicated the old, coarse gloves so crudely darned and patched together.

But my uncle looked down at her, strangely, and with a cold, inexorable face.

"My child," he said, "there is a curious virtue in this thing that moves you. Perhaps it will also move the man whose handiwork it is. Let us go up and see him."

Then he called the Justice.

"Randolph," he said, "come with us."

The Justice turned about. "Where do you go?" he asked.

"Why, sir," Abner answered, "this child is weeping at the sight of the dead man's gloves, and I thought, perhaps, that old Benton might weep at them too, and in the softened mood return what he has stolen."

The Justice looked upon Abner as upon one gone mad.

"And be sorry for his sins! And pluck out his eye and give it to you for a bauble! Why, Abner, where is your common sense. This thing would take a miracle of God."

My uncle was undisturbed.

"Well," he said, "come with me, Randolph, and help me to perform that miracle."

He went out into the hall, and up the wide old stairway, with the girl, in tears, upon his arm. And the Justice followed, like one who goes upon a patent and ridiculous fool's errand.

They came into an upper chamber, where a great bulk of a man sat in a padded chair looking down upon his avenue of trees. He looked with satisfaction. He turned his head about when the three came in and then his eyes widened in among the folds of fat.

"Abner and Mr. Randolph and Miss Julia Clayborne!" he gurgled. "You come to do honor to the dead!"

"No, Wolf," replied my uncle, "we come to do justice to the living."

The room was big, and empty but for chairs and an open secretary of some English make. The pictures on the wall had been turned about as though from a lack of interest in the tenant. But there hung in a frame above the secretary—with its sheets of foolscap, its iron ink-pot and quill pens—a map in detail, and the written deed for the estate that these men had taken in their lawsuit. It was not the skill of any painter that gave pleasure to this mountain of a man; not fields or groves imagined or copied for their charm, but the fields and groves that he possessed and mastered. And he would be reminded at his ease of them and of no other.

The old man's eyelids fluttered an instant as with some indecision, then he replied, "It was kind to have this thought of me. I have been long neglected. A little justice of recognition, even now, does much to soften the sorrow at my brother's death." Randolph caught at his jaw to keep in the laughter. And the huge old man, his head crouched into his billowy shoulders, his little reptilian eye shining like a crum of glass, went on with his speech.

"I am the greater moved," he said, "because you have been aloof and distant with me. You, Abner, have not visited my house, nor you, Randolph, although you live at no great distance. It is not thus that one gentleman should treat another. And especially when I and my dead brother, Adam, were from distant parts and came among you without a friend to take us by the hand and bring us to your door."

He sighed and put the fingers of his hands together.

"Ah, Abner," he went on, "it was a cruel negligence, and one from which I and my brother Adam suffered. You, who have a hand and a word at every turning, can feel no longing for this human comfort. But to the stranger, alone, and without the land of his nativity, it is a bitter lack."

He indicated the chairs about him.

"I beg you to be seated, gentlemen and Miss Clayborne. And overlook that I do not rise. I am shaken at Adam's death."

Randolph remained planted on his feet, his face now under control. But Abner put the child into a chair and stood behind it, as though he were some close and masterful familiar.

"Wolf," he said, "I am glad that your heart is softened."

"My heart—softened!" cried the man. "Why, Abner, I have the tenderest heart of any of God's creatures. I can not endure to kill a sparrow. My brother Adam was not like that. He would be for hunting the wild creatures to their death with firearms. But I took no pleasure in it."

"Well," said Randolph, "the creatures of the air got their revenge of him. It was a foolish accident to die by."

"Randolph," replied the man, "it was the very end and extreme of carelessness. To look into a fowling-piece, a finger on the hammer, a left hand holding the barrel half-way up, to see if it was empty. It was a foolish and simple habit of my brother, and one that I abhorred and begged him to forego, again and again, when I have seen him do it.

"But he had no fear of any firearms, as though by use and habit he had got their spirit tamed—as trainers, I am told, grow careless of wild beasts, and jugglers of the fangs and poison of their reptiles. He was growing old and would forget if they were loaded."

He spoke to Randolph, but he looked at Julia Clayborne and Abner behind her chair.

The girl sat straight and composed, in silence. The body of my uncle was to her a great protecting presence. He stood with his broad shoulders above her, his hands on the back of the chair, his face lifted. And he was big and dominant, as painters are accustomed to draw Michael in Satan's wars.

The pose held the old man's eye, and he moved in his chair; then he went on, speaking to the girl.

"It was kind of you, Abner, and you, Randolph, to come in to see me in my distress, but it was fine and noble in Miss Julia Clayborne. Men will understand the justice of the law and by what right it gives and takes. But a child will hardly understand that. It would be in nature for Miss Clayborne in her youth, to hold the issue of this lawsuit against me and my brother Adam, to feel that we had wronged her; had by some unfairness taken what her father bequeathed to her at his death, and always regarded as his own. A child would not see how the title had never vested, as our judges do. How possession is one thing, and the title in fee simple another and distinct. And so I am touched by this consideration."

Abner spoke then.

"Wolf," he said, "I am glad to find you in this mood, for now Randolph can write his deed, with consideration of love and affection instead of the real one I came with."

The old man's beady eye glimmered and slipped about.

"I do not understand, Abner. What deed?"

"The one Randolph came to write," replied my uncle.

"But, Abner," interrupted the Justice, "I did not come to write a deed." And he looked at my uncle in amazement.

"Oh, yes," returned Abner, "that is precisely what you came to do."

He indicated the open secretary with his hand.

"And the grantor, as it happens, has got everything ready for you. Here are foolscap and quill pens and ink. And here, exhibited for your convenience, is a map of the lands with all the metes and bounds. And here," he pointed to the wall, "in a frame, as though it were a work of art with charm, is the court's deed. Sit down, Randolph, and write." And such virtue is there in a dominant command, that the Justice sat down before the secretary and began to select a goose quill.

Then he realized the absurdity of the direction and turned about.

"What do you mean, Abner?" he cried.

"I mean precisely what I say," replied my uncle. "I want you to write a deed."

"But what sort of deed," cried the astonished Justice, "and by what grantor, and to whom, and for what lands?"

"You will draw a conveyance," replied Abner, "in form, with covenants of general warranty for the manor and lands set out in the deed before you and given in the plat. The grantor will be Benton Wolf, esquire, and the grantee Julia Clayborne, infant, and mark you, Randolph, the consideration will be love and affection, with a dollar added for the form."

The old man was amazed. His head, bedded into his huge shoulders, swung about; his pudgy features worked; his expression and his manner changed; his reptilian eyes hardened; he puffed with his breath in gusts.

"Not so fast, my fine gentleman!" he gurgled. "There will be no such deed."

"Go on, Randolph," said my uncle, as though there had been no interruption, "let us get this business over."

"But, Abner," returned the Justice, "it is fool work, the grantor will not sign."

"He will sign," said my uncle, "when you have finished, and seal and acknowledge—go on!"

"But, Abner, Abner!" the amazed Justice protested.

"Randolph," cried my uncle, "will you write, and leave this thing to me?"

And such authority was in the man to impose his will that the bewildered Justice spread out his sheet of foolscap, dipped his quill into the ink and began to draw the instrument, in form and of the parties, as my uncle said. And while he wrote, Abner turned back to the gross old man.

"Wolf," he said, "must I persuade you to sign the deed?"

"Abner," cried the man, "do you take me for a fool?"

He had got his unwieldy body up and defiant in the chair.

"I do not," replied my uncle, "and therefore I think that you will sign."

The obese old man spat violently on the floor, his face a horror of great folds.

"Sign!" he sputtered. "Fool, idiot, madman! Why should I sign away my lands?"

"There are many reasons," replied Abner calmly. "The property is not yours. You got it by a legal trick, the judge who heard you was bound by the technicalities of language. But you are old, Wolf, and the next Judge will go behind the record. He will be hard to face. He has expressed Himself on these affairs. 'If the widow and the orphan cry to me, I will surely hear their cry.' Sinister words, Wolf, for one who comes with a case like yours into the court of Final Equity."

"Abner," cried the old man, "begone with your little sermons!"

My uncle's big fingers tightened on the back of the chair.

"Then, Wolf," he said, "if this thing does not move you, let me urge the esteem of men and this child's sorrow, and our high regard."

The old man's jaw chattered and he snapped his fingers.

"I would not give that for the things you name," he cried, and he set off a tiny measure on his index-finger with the thumb.

"Why, sir, my whim, idle and ridiculous, is a greater power to move me than this drivel."

Abner did not move, but his voice took on depth and volume.

"Wolf," he said, "a whim is sometimes a great lever to move a man. Now, I am taken with a whim myself. I have a fancy, Wolf, that your brother Adam ought to go out of the world barehanded as he came into it."

The old man twisted his great head, as though he would get Abner wholly within the sweep of his reptilian eye.

"What?" he gurgled. "What is that?"

"Why, this," replied my uncle. "I have a whim—'idle and ridiculous,' did you say, Wolf? Well, then, idle and ridiculous, if you like, that your brother ought not to be buried in his gloves."

Abner looked hard at the man and, although he did not move, the threat and menace of his presence seemed somehow to advance him. And the effect upon the huge old man was like some work of sorcery. The whole mountain of him began to quiver and the folds of his face seemed spread over with thin oil. He sat piled up in the chair and the oily sweat gathered and thickened on him. His jaw jerked and fell into a baggy gaping and the great expanse of him worked as with an ague.

Finally, out of the pudgy, undulating mass, a voice issued, thin and shaken.

"Abner," it said, "has any other man this fancy?"

"No," replied my uncle, "but I hold it, Wolf, at your decision."

"And, Abner," his thin voice trebled, "you will let my brother be buried as he is?"

"If you sign!" said my uncle.

The man reeked and grew wet in the terror on him, and one thought that his billowy body would never be again at peace. "Randolph," he quavered, "bring me the deed."

Outside, the girl sobbed in Abner's arms. She asked for no explanation. She wished to believe her fortune a miracle of God, forever—to the end of all things. But Randolph turned on my uncle when she was gone.

"Abner! Abner!" he cried. "Why in the name of the Eternal was the old creature so shaken at the gloves?"

"Because he saw the hangman behind them," replied my

uncle. "Did you notice how the rim of the dead man's face was riddled by the bird-shot and the center of it clean? How could that happen, Randolph?"

"It was a curious accident of gun-fire," replied the Justice.

"It was no accident at all," said Abner. "That area of the man's face is clean because it was protected. Because the dead man put up his hands to cover his face when he saw that his brother was about to shoot him.

"The backs of old Adam's hands, hidden by the gloves, will be riddled with bird-shot like the rim of his face."

Chapter 9

The Tenth Commandment

THE AFTERNOON sun was hot, and when the drove began to descend the long wooded hill we could hardly keep them out of the timber. We were bringing in our stock cattle. We had been on the road since daybreak and the cattle were tired. Abner was behind the drove and I was riding the line of the wood. The mare under me knew as much about driving cattle as I did, and between us we managed to keep the steers in the road; but finally a bullock broke away and plunged down into the deep wood. Abner called to me to turn all the cattle into the grove on the upper side of the road and let them rest in the shade while we got the runaway steer out of the underbrush. I turned the drove in among the open oak trees, left my mare to watch them and went on foot down through the underbrush. The long hill descending to the river was unfenced wood grown up with thickets. I was perhaps three hundred yards below the road when I lost sight of the steer, and got up on a stump to look.

I did not see the steer, but in a thicket beyond me I saw a thing that caught my eye. The bushes had been cut out, the leaves trampled, and there was a dogwood fork driven into the ground. About fifty feet away there was a steep bank and below it a horse path ran through the wood.

The thing savored of mystery. All round was a dense tangle of thicket, and here, hidden at a point commanding the horse path, was this cleared spot with the leaves trampled and the forked limb of a dogwood driven into the ground. I was so absorbed that I did not know that Abner had ridden down the hill behind me until I turned and saw him sitting there on his great chestnut gelding looking over the dense bushes into the thicket.

He got down out of his saddle, parted the bushes carefully

and entered the thicket. There was a hollow log lying beyond the dogwood fork. Abner put his hand into the log and drew out a gun. It was a bright, new, one-barreled fowling-piece— a muzzle-loader, for there were no breech-loaders in that country then. Abner turned the gun about and looked it over carefully. The gun was evidently loaded, because I could see the cap shining under the hammer. Abner opened the brass plate on the stock, but it contained only a bit of new tow and the implement, like a corkscrew, which fitted to the ramrod and held the tow when one wished to clean the gun. It was at this moment that I caught sight of the steer moving in the bushes and I leaped down and ran to head him off, leaving Abner standing with the gun in his hands.

When I got the steer out and across the road into the drove Abner had come up out of the wood. He was in the saddle, his clenched hand lay on the pommel.

I was afraid to ask Abner questions when he looked like that, but my curiosity overcame me.

"What did you do with the gun, Uncle Abner?"

"I put it back where it was," he said.

"Do you know who the owner is?"

"I do not know who he is," replied Abner without looking in my direction, "but I know what he is—he is a coward!"

The afternoon drew on. The sun moved towards the far-off chain of mountains. Silence lay on the world. Only the tiny creatures of the air moved with the hum of a distant spinner, and the companies of yellow butterflies swarmed on the road. The cattle rested in the shade of the oak trees and we waited. Abner's chestnut stood like a horse of bronze and I dozed in the saddle.

Shadows were entering the world through the gaps and passes of the mountains when I heard a horse. I stood up in my stirrups and looked.

The horse was traveling the path running through the wood below us. I could see the rider through the trees. He was a grazer whose lands lay westward beyond the wood. In the deep, utter silence I could hear the creak of his saddle-leather. Then suddenly as he rode there was the roar of a gun, and a cloud of powder smoke blotted him out of sight.

In that portentous instant of time I realized the meaning of the things that I had seen there in the thicket. It was an ambush to kill this man! The fork in the ground was to hold the gun-barrel so the assassin could not miss his mark.

And with this understanding came an appalling sense of my Uncle Abner's negligence. He must have known all this when he stood there in the thicket, and when he knew it, why had he left that gun there? Why had he put it back into its hiding-place? Why had he gone his way thus unconcernedly and left this assassin to accomplish his murder? Moreover, this man riding there through the wood was a man whom Abner knew. His house was the very house at which Abner expected to stop this night. We were on our way there!

It was in one of those vast spaces of time that a second sometimes stretches over that I put these things together and jerked my head toward Abner, but he sat there without the tremor of a muscle.

The next second I saw the frightened horse plunging in the path and I looked to see its saddle empty, or the rider reeling with the blood creeping through his coat, or some ghastly thing that clutched and swayed. But I did not see it. The rider sat firmly in his saddle, pulled up the horse, and, looking idly about him, rode on. He believed the gun had been fired by some hunter shooting squirrels.

"Oh," I cried, "he missed!"

But Abner did not reply. He was standing in his stirrups searching the wood.

"How could he miss, Uncle Abner," I said, "when he was so near to the path and had that fork to rest his gun-barrel in? Did you see him?"

It was some time before Abner answered, and then his reply was to my final query.

"I did not see him," he said deliberately. "He must have slipped away somehow through the thicket."

That was all he said, and for a good while he was silent, drumming with his fingers on the pommel of his saddle and looking out over the distant treetops.

The sun was touching the mountains before Abner began to move the drove. We got the cattle out of the wood and started the line down the long hill. The road forked at the bottom of the hill—one branch of it, the main road, went on to the house of the grazer with whom we had expected to spend the night and the other turned off through the wood.

I was astonished when Abner turned the drove into this other road, but I said nothing, for I presently understood the reason for this change of plans. One could hardly accept the hospitality of a man when he had negligently stood by to see him murdered.

In half a mile the road came out into the open. There was a big new house on a bit of rising land and, below, fields and meadows. I did not know the crossroad, but I knew this place. The man, Dillworth, who lived here had been sometime the clerk of the county court. He had got this land, it was said, by taking advantage of a defective record, and he had now a suit in chancery against the neighboring grazers for the land about him. He had built this great new house, in pride boasting that it would sit in the center of the estate that he would gain. I had heard this talked about—this boasting, and how one of the grazers had sworn before the courthouse that he would kill Dillworth on the day that the decree was entered. I knew in what esteem Abner held this man and I wondered that he should choose him to stay the night with.

When we first entered the house and while we ate our supper Abner had very little to say, but after that, when we had gone with the man out on to the great porch that overlooked the country, Abner changed—I think it was when he picked up the county newspaper from the table. Something in this paper seized on his attention and he examined it with care. It was a court notice of the sale of lands for delinquent taxes, but the paper had been torn and only half of the article was there. Abner called our host's attention to it.

"Dillworth," he said, "what lands are included in this notice?"

"Are they not there?" replied the man.

"No," said Abner, "a portion of the newspaper is gone. It is torn off at a description of the Jenkins' tract"—and he put his finger on the line and showed the paper to the man—"what lands follow after that?"

"I do not remember the several tracts," Dillworth answered, "but you can easily get another copy of the newspaper. Are you interested in these lands?"

"No," said Abner, "but I am interested in this notice."

Then he laid the newspaper on the table and sat down in a chair. And then it was that his silence left him and he began to talk.

Abner looked out over the country.

"This is fine pasture land," he said.

Dillworth moved forward in his chair. He was a big man with a bushy chestnut beard, little glimmering eyes and a huge body.

"Why, Abner," he said, "it is the very best land that a beef steer ever cropped the grass on."

"It is a corner of the lands that Daniel Davisson got in a grant from George the Third," Abner continued. "I don't know what service he rendered the crown, but the pay was princely—a man would do king's work for an estate like this."

"King's work he would do," said Dillworth, "or hell's work. Why, Abner, the earth is rich for a yard down. I saw old Hezekiah Davisson buried in it, and the shovels full of earth that the Negroes threw on him were as black as their faces, and the sod over that land is as clean as a woman's hair. I was a lad then, but I promised myself that I would one day possess these lands."

"It is a dangerous thing to covet the possession of another," said Abner. "King David tried it and he had to do—what did you call it, Dillworth?—'hell's work.'"

"And why not," replied Dillworth, "if you get the things you want by it?"

"There are several reasons," said Abner, "and one is that it requires a certain courage. Hell's work is heavy work, Dillworth, and the weakling who goes about it is apt to fail."

Dillworth laughed. "King David didn't fail, did he?"

"He did not," replied Abner; "but David, the son of Jesse, was not a coward."

"Well," said Dillworth, "I shall not fail either. My hands are not trained to war like this, but they are trained to lawsuits."

"You got this wedge of land on which your house is built by a lawsuit, did you not?" said Abner.

"I did," replied Dillworth; "but if men do not exercise ordinary care they must suffer for that negligence."

"Well," said Abner, "the little farmer who lived here on this wedge suffered enough for his. When you dispossessed him he hanged himself in his stable with a halter."

"Abner," cried Dillworth, "I have heard enough about that. I did not take the man's life. I took what the law gave me. If a man will buy land and not look up the title it is his own fault."

"He bought at a judicial sale," said Abner, "and he believed the court would not sell him a defective title. He was an honest man, and he thought the world was honest."

"He thought wrong," said Dillworth.

"He did," said Abner.

"Well," cried Dillworth, "am I to blame because there is a fool the less? Will the people never learn that the court does not warrant the title to the lands that it sells in a suit in chancery? The man who buys before the courthouse door buys a pig in a poke, and it is not the court's fault if the poke is empty. The judge could not look up the title to every tract of land that comes into his court, nor could the title to every tract be judicially determined in every suit that involves it. To do that, every suit over land would have to be a suit to determine title and every claimant would have to be a party."

"What you say may be the truth," said Abner, "but the people do not always know it."

"They could know it if they would inquire," answered Dillworth; "why did not this man go before the judge?"

"Well," replied Abner, "he has gone before a greater Judge." Abner leaned back in his chair and his fingers rapped on the table.

"The law is not always justice," he said. "Is it not the law that a man may buy a tract of land and pay down the price in gold and enter into the possession of it, and yet, if by inadvertence, the justice of the peace omits to write certain words into the acknowledgment of the deed, the purchaser takes no title and may be dispossessed of his lands?"

"That is the law," said Dillworth emphatically; "it is the very point in my suit against these grazers. Squire Randolph could not find his copy of Mayo's Guide on the day that the deeds were drawn and so he wrote from memory."

Abner was silent for a moment.

"It is the law," he said, "but is it justice, Dillworth?"

"Abner," replied Dillworth, "how shall we know what justice is unless the law defines it?"

"I think every man knows what it is," said Abner.

"And shall every man set up a standard of his own," said Dillworth, "and disregard the standard that the law sets up? That would be the end of justice."

"It would be the beginning of justice," said Abner, "if every man followed the standard that God gives him."

"But, Abner," replied Dillworth, "is there a court that could administer justice if there were no arbitrary standard and every man followed his own?"

"I think there is such a court," said Abner.

Dillworth laughed.

"If there is such a court it does not sit in Virginia."

Then he settled his huge body in his chair and spoke like a lawyer who sums up his case.

"I know what you have in mind, Abner, but it is a fantastic notion. You would saddle every man with the thing you call a conscience, and let that ride him. Well, I would unsaddle him from that. What is right? What is wrong? These are vexed questions. I would leave them to the law. Look what a burden is on every man if he must decide the justice of every act as it comes up. Now the law would lift that burden from his shoulders, and I would let the law bear it."

"But under the law," replied Abner, "the weak and the ignorant suffer for their weakness and for this ignorance, and the shrewd and the cunning profit by their shrewdness and by their cunning. How would you help that?"

"Now, Abner," said Dillworth, "to help that you would have to make the world over."

Again Abner was silent for a while.

"Well," he said, "perhaps it could be done if every man put his shoulder to the wheel."

"But why should it be done?" replied Dillworth. "Does Nature do it? Look with what indifference she kills off the weakling. Is there any pity in her or any of your little soft concerns? I tell you these things are not to be found anywhere in Nature—they are man-made."

"Or God-made," said Abner.

"Call it what you like," replied Dillworth, "it will be equally fantastic, and the law would be fantastic to follow after it. As for myself, Abner, I would avoid these troublesome refinements. Since the law will undertake to say what is right and what is wrong I shall leave her to say it and let myself go free. What she requires me to give I shall give, and what she permits me to take I shall take, and there shall be an end of it."

"It is an easy standard," replied Abner, "and it simplifies a thing that I have come to see you about."

"And what have you come to see me about?" said Dillworth; "I knew that it was for something you came."

And he laughed a little, dry, nervous laugh.

I had observed this laugh breaking now and then into his talk and I had observed his uneasy manner ever since we came. There was something below the surface in this man that made him nervous and it was from that under thing that this laugh broke out.

"It is about your lawsuit," said Abner.

"And what about it?"

"This," said Abner: "That your suit has reached the point where you are not the man to have charge of it."

"Abner," cried Dillworth, "what do you mean?"

"I will tell you," said Abner. "I have followed the progress of this suit, and you have won it. On any day that you call it up the judge will enter a decree, and yet for a year it has stood there on the docket and you have not called it up. Why?"

Dillworth did not reply, but again that dry, nervous laugh broke out.

"I will answer for you, Dillworth," said Abner—"you are afraid!"

Abner extended his arm and pointed out over the pasture

lands, growing dimmer in the gathering twilight, across the river, across the wood to where lights moved and twinkled.

"Yonder," said Abner, "lives Lemuel Arnold; he is the only man who is a defendant in your suit, the others are women and children. I know Lemuel Arnold. I intended to stop this night with him until I thought of you. I know the stock he comes from. When Hamilton was buying scalps on the Ohio, and haggling with the Indians over the price to be paid for those of the women and the children, old Hiram Arnold walked into the conference: 'Scalp-buyer,' he said, 'buy my scalps; there are no little ones among them,' and he emptied out on to the table a bagful of scalps of the king's soldiers. That man was Lemuel Arnold's grandfather and that is the blood he has. You would call him violent and dangerous, Dillworth, and you would be right. He is violent and he is dangerous. I know what he told you before the courthouse door. And, Dillworth, you are afraid of that. And so you sit here looking out over these rich lands and coveting them in your heart—and are afraid to take them."

The night was descending, and I sat on a step of the great porch, in the shadow, forgotten by these two men. Dillworth did not move, and Abner went on.

"That is bad for you, Dillworth, to sit here and brood over a thing like this. Plans will come to you that include 'hell's work'; this is no thing for you to handle. Put it into my hands."

The man cleared his throat with that bit of nervous laugh.

"How do you mean—into your hands?" he said.

"Sell me the lawsuit," replied Abner.

Dillworth sat back in his chair at that and covered his jaw with his hand, and for a good while he was silent.

"But it is these lands I want, Abner, not the money for them."

"I know what you want," said Abner, "and I will agree to give you a proportion of all the lands that I recover in the suit."

"It ought to be a large proportion, then, for the suit is won."

"As large as you like," said Abner.

Dillworth got up at that and walked about the porch. One could tell the two things that were moving in his mind: That Abner was, in truth, the man to carry the thing through—he stood well before the courts and he was not afraid; and the other thing—How great a proportion of the lands could he demand? Finally he came back and stood before the table.

"Seven-eighths then. Is it a bargain?"

"It is," said Abner. "Write out the contract."

A Negro brought foolscap paper, ink, pens, and a candle and set them on the table. Dillworth wrote, and when he had finished he signed the paper and made his seal with a flourish of the pen after his signature. Then he handed the contract to Abner across the table.

Abner read it aloud, weighing each legal term and every lawyer's phrase in it. Dillworth had knowledge of such things and he wrote with skill. Abner folded the contract carefully and put it into his pocket, then he got a silver dollar out of his leather wallet and flung it on to the table, for the paper read: "In consideration of one dollar cash in hand paid, the receipt of which is hereby acknowledged." The coin struck hard and spun on the oak board. "There," he said, "is your silver. It is the money that Judas was paid in and, like that first payment to Judas, it is all you'll get."

Dillworth got on his feet. "Abner," he said, "what do you drive at now?"

"This," replied Abner: "I have bought your lawsuit; I have paid you for it, and it belongs to me. The terms of that sale are written down and signed. You are to receive a portion of what I recover; but if I recover nothing you can receive nothing."

"Nothing?" Dillworth echoed.

"Nothing!" replied Abner.

Dillworth put his big hands on the table and rested his body on them; his head drooped below his shoulders, and he looked at Abner across the table.

"You mean—you mean——"

"Yes," said Abner, "that is what I mean. I shall dismiss this suit."

"Abner," the other wailed, "this is ruin—these lands—these rich lands!" And he put out his arms, as toward something that one loves. "I have been a fool. Give me back my paper." Abner arose.

"Dillworth," he said, "you have a short memory. You said that a man ought to suffer for his lack of care, and you shall suffer for yours. You said that pity was fantastic, and I find it fantastic now. You said that you would take what the law gives you; well, so shall I."

The sniveling creature rocked his big body grotesquely in his chair.

"Abner," he whined, "why did you come here to ruin me?"

"I did not come to ruin you," said Abner. "I came to save you. But for me you would have done a murder."

"Abner," the man cried, "you are mad. Why should I do a murder?"

"Dillworth," replied Abner, "there is a certain commandment prohibited, not because of the evil in it, but because of the thing it leads to—because there follows it—I use your own name, Dillworth, 'hell's work.' This afternoon you tried to kill Lemuel Arnold from an ambush."

Terror was on the man. He ceased to rock his body. He leaned forward, staring at Abner, the muscles of his face flabby.

"Did you see me?"

"No," replied Abner, "I did not."

The man's body seemed, at that, to escape from some hideous pressure. He cried out in relief, and his voice was like air wheezing from the bellows.

"It's a lie! a lie! a lie!"

I saw Abner look hard at the man, but he could not strike a thing like that.

"It's the truth," he said, "you are the man; but when I stood in the thicket with your weapon in my hand I did not know it, and when I came here I did not know it. But I knew that this ambush was the work of a coward, and you were the only coward that I could think of. No," he said, "do not delude yourself—that was no proof. But it was enough to bring me here. And the proof? I found it in this house. I will show it to you. But before I do that, Dillworth, I will return to you something that is yours."

He put his hand into his pocket, took out a score of buckshot and dropped them on the table. They clattered off and rolled away on the floor.

"And that is how I saved you from murder, Dillworth. Before I put your gun back into the hollow log I drew all the charge in it except the powder."

He advanced a step nearer to the table.

"Dillworth," he said, "a little while ago I asked you a question that you could not answer. I asked you what lands were included in the notice of sale for delinquent taxes printed in that county newspaper. Half of the newspaper had been torn off, and with it the other half of that notice. And you could not answer. Do you remember that question, Dillworth? Well, when I asked it of you I had the answer in my pocket. The missing part of that notice was the wadding over the buckshot!"

He took a crumpled piece of newspaper out of his pocket and joined it to the other half lying before Dillworth on the table.

"Look," he said, "how the edges fit!"

Chapter 10

The Devil's Tools

I was about to follow my Uncle Abner into the garden when at a turn of the hedge, I stopped. A step or two beyond me in the sun, screened by a lattice of vines, was a scene that filled me full of wonder. Abner was standing quite still in the path, and a girl was clinging to his arm, with her face buried against his coat. There was no sound, but the girl's hands trembled and her shoulders were convulsed with sobs.

Whenever I think of pretty women, even now, I somehow always begin with Betty Randolph, and yet, I cannot put her before the eye, for all the memories. She remains in the fairy-land of youth, and her description is with the poets; their extravagances intrude and possess me, and I give it up.

I cannot say that a woman is an armful of apple blossoms, as they do, or as white as milk, and as playful as a kitten. These are happy collocations of words and quite descriptive of her, but they are not mine. Nor can I draw her in the language of a civilization to which she does not belong— one of wheels and spindles with its own type; superior, no doubt, but less desirable, I fancy. The age that grew its women in romance and dowered them with poetic fancies was not so impracticable as you think. It is a queer world; those who put their faith in the plow are rewarded by the plow, and those who put their faith in miracles are rewarded by miracles.

I remained in the shelter of the hedge in some considerable wonder. We had come to pay our respects to this young woman on her approaching marriage, and to be received like this was somewhat beyond our expectations. There could be nothing in this marriage on which to found a tragedy of tears. It was a love match if ever there was one.

Edward Duncan was a fine figure of a man; his lands

adjoined, and he had ancestors enough for Randolph. He stood high in the hills, but I did not like him. You will smile at that, seeing what I have written of Betty Randolph, and remembering how, at ten, the human heart is desperately jealous.

The two had been mated by the county gossips from the cradle, and had lived the prophecy. The romance, too, had got its tang of denial to make it sharper. The young man had bought his lands and builded his house, but he must pay for them before he took his bride in, Randolph said, and he had stood by that condition.

There had been some years of waiting, and Randolph had been stormed. The debt had been reduced, but a mortgage remained, until now, by chance, it had been removed, and the gates of Paradise were opened. Edward Duncan had a tract of wild land in the edge of Maryland which his father had got for a song at a judicial sale. He had sold this land, he said, to a foreign purchaser, and so got the money to clear off his debt. He had written to Betty, who was in Baltimore at the time, and she had hurried back with frocks and furbelows. The day was set, we had come to see how happy she would be, and here she was clinging to my Uncle Abner's arm and crying like her heart would break.

It was some time before the girl spoke, and Abner stood caressing her hair, as though she were a little child. When the paroxysms of tears was over she told him what distressed her, and I heard the story, for the turn of the hedge was beside them, and I could have touched the girl with my hand. She took a worn ribbon from around her neck and held it out to Abner. There was a heavy gold cross slung to it on a tiny ring. I knew this cross, as every one did; it had been her mother's, and the three big emeralds set in it were of the few fine gems in the county. They were worth five thousand dollars, and had been passed down from the divided heirlooms of an English grandmother. I knew what the matter was before Betty Randolph said it. The emeralds were gone. The cross lying in her hand was bare.

She told the story in a dozen words. The jewels had been gone for some time, but her father had not known it until to-day. She had hoped he would never know, but by accident he had found it out. Then he had called an inquisition, and sat down to discover who had done the robbery. And here it was that Betty Randolph's greatest grief came in. The loss of the emeralds was enough; but to have her old Mammy Liza, who had been the only mother that she could remember, singled out and interrogated for the criminal, was too much to be borne. Her father was now in his office proceeding with the outrage. Would my Uncle Abner go and see him before he broke her heart?

Abner took the cross and held it in his hand. He asked a question or two, but, on the whole, he said very little, which seemed strange to me, with the matter to clear up. How long had the emeralds been missing? And she replied that they had been in the cross before her trip to Baltimore, and missing at her return. She had not taken the cross on the journey. It had remained among her possessions in her room. She did not know when she had seen it on her return.

And she began once more to cry, and her dainty mouth to tremble, and the big tears to gather in her brown eyes.

Abner promised to go in and brave Randolph at his inquisition, and bring Mammy Liza out. He bade Betty walk in the garden until he returned, and she went away comforted.

But Abner did not at once go in. He remained for some moments standing there with the cross in his hand; then, to my surprise, he turned about and went back the way that he had come. I had barely time to get out of his way, for he walked swiftly along the path to the gate, and down to the stable. I followed, for I wondered why he went here instead of to the house, as he had promised. He crossed before the stables and entered a big shed where the plows and farm tools were kept, the scythes hung up, and the corn hoes. The shed was of huge logs, roofed with clapboards, and open at each end.

I lost a little time in making a detour around the stable, but when I looked into the shed between a crack of the logs, my Uncle Abner was sitting before the big grindstone, turning it with his foot, and very delicately holding the cross on the edge of the stone. He paused and examined his work, and then continued. I could not understand what he was at. Why had he come here, and why did he grind the cross on the stone? At any rate, he presently stopped, looked about until he found a piece of old leather, and again sat down to rub the cross, as though to polish what he had ground.

He examined his work from time to time, until at last it pleased him, and he got up. He went out of the shed and up the path toward the garden. I knew where he was going now and I took some short cuts.

Randolph's office was a wing built on to the main residence, after the fashion of the old Virginia mansion house. It was a single story with a separate entrance, so arranged that the master of the house could receive his official visitors and transact his business without disturbing his domestic household.

I was a very good Indian at that period of my life, and skilled in the acts of taking cover. I was ten years old and had lived the life of the Mohawk, with much care for accuracy of detail. True, it was a life I had now given up for larger affairs, but I retained its advantages. One does not spend whole afternoons at the blood-thirsty age of five, in stalking the turkeycock in the wooded pasture, noiselessly on his belly, with his wooden knife in his hand, and not come to the maturity of ten with the accomplishments of Uncas.

I was presently in a snowball bush, with a very good view of Randolph's inquisition, and I think that if Betty had waited to see it, she need not have gone away in so great a grief. Randolph was sitting behind his table in his pompous manner and with the dignity of kings. But for all his attitudes, he took no advantage over Mammy Liza.

The old woman sat beyond him, straight as a rod in her chair, her black silk dress smoothed into straight folds, her white cap prim and immaculate, her square-rimmed spectacles on her nose, and her hands in her lap. If there was royal blood on the Congo, she carried it in her veins, for her dignity was real. And there I think she held Randolph back from any definite accusation. He advanced with specious and sententious innuendoes and arguments, *a priori* and conclusion *post hoc ergo propter hoc* to inclose her as the guilty agent. But

from the commanding position of a blameless life, she did not
see it, and he could not make her see it. She regarded this
conference as that of two important persons in convention
assembled,—a meeting together of the heads of the House of
Randolph to consider a certain matter touching its goods and
its honor. And, for all his efforts, he could not dislodge her
from the serenity of that position.

"Your room adjoins Betty's?" he said.

"Yes, Mars Ran," she answered. "I's always slep' next to
my chile, ever since her ma handed her to me outen the bed
she was borned in."

"And no one goes into her room but you?"

"No, sah, 'ceptin' when I's there to see what they's doin'."

"Then no other servant in this house could have taken
anything out of Betty's room without your knowing it?"

"That's right, Mars Ran. I'd 'a' knowed it."

"Then," said Randolph, tightening the lines of his premises, "if you alone have access to the room, and no one goes
in without your consent or knowledge, how could any other
servant in this house have taken these jewels?"

"They didn't!" said the old woman. "I's done had all the
niggers up before me, an' I's ravaged 'em an' searchified 'em."

Her mouth tightened with the savage memory.

"I knows 'em! I knows 'em all—mopin' niggers, an' mealy
mouthed niggers, an' shoutin' niggers, an' cussin' niggers, an'
I knows all their carryin's-on, an' all their underhan' oneryness,
an' all their low-down contraptions. An' they knows I knows
it." She paused and lifted a long, black finger.

"They fools Miss Betty, an' they fools you, Mars Ran, but
they don't fool Mammy Liza."

She replaced her hands together primly in the lap of her
silk dress and continued in a confidential tone.

" 'Course we knows niggers steals, but they steals eatables,
an' nobody pays any 'tention to that. Your Grandpap never
did, nor your pap, nor us. You can't be too hard on niggers,
jist as you can't be too easy on 'em. If you's too hard, they
gits down in the mouth, an' if you's too easy they takes the
place. A down in the mouth nigger is always a wuthless nigger,
an' a biggity nigger is a 'bomination!"

She paused a moment, but she had entered upon her discourse, and she continued.

"I ain't specifyin' but what there's some on this place that would b'ar watchin', an' I's had my eye on 'em; but they's like the unthinking horse, they'd slip a fril-fral outen the kitchen, or a side of bacon outen the smoke-house, but they wouldn't do none of your gran' stealin'.

"No, sah! No, sah! Mars Ran, them jules wasn't took by nobody in this house."

She paused and reflected, and her face filled with the energy of battle.

"I'd jist like to see a nigger tech a whip-stitch that belongs to my chile. I'd shore peel the hide offen 'em. Tech it! No, sah, they ain't no nigger on this place that's a-goin' to rile me."

And in her energy she told Randolph some homely truths.

"They ain't afeared of you, Mars Ran, 'cause they knows they can make up some cock an' bull story to fool you; an' they ain't afeared of Miss Betty 'cause they knows they can whip it 'roun' her with a pitiful face; but I's different. I rules 'em with the weepen of iron! They ain't none of 'em that can stand up before me with a lie, for I knows the innermost and hidden searchings of a nigger."

She extended her clenched hand with a savage gesture.

"An' I tells 'em, Mars Ran'll welt you with a withe, but I'll scarify you with a scorpeen!"

It was at this moment that my Uncle Abner entered.

Mammy Liza immediately assumed her company manners. She rose and made a little courtesy.

" 'Eben', Mars Abner," she said; "is you all well?"

Abner replied, and Randolph came forward to receive him. He got my uncle a chair, and began to explain the matter with which he was engaged. Abner said that he had already got the story from Betty.

Randolph went back to his place behind the table, and to his judicial attitudes.

"There is no direct evidence bearing upon this robbery," he said, "consequently, in pursuing an investigation of it, we must follow the established and orderly formula laid down by the law writers. We must carefully scrutinize all the circumstances of time, place, motive, means, opportunity, and conduct. And, while upon a trial, a judge must assume the innocence of everybody indicated, upon an investigation, the inquisitor must assume their guilt."

He compressed his lips and continued with exalted dignity.

"No one is to be exempt from consideration, not even the oldest and most trusted servants. The wisdom of this course was strikingly shown in Lord William Russell's case, where the facts indicated suicide, but a rigid application of this rule demonstrated that my Lord Russell had been, in fact, murdered by his valet."

My uncle did not interrupt. But Mammy Liza could not restrain her enthusiasm. She was very proud of Randolph, and, like all Negroes, associated ability with high sounding words. His grandiloquence and his pomposity were her delight. Her eyes beamed with admiration.

"Go on, Mars Ran," she said; "you certainly is a gran' talker."

Randolph banged the table.

"Shut up!" he roared. "A man can't open his mouth in this house without being interrupted."

But Mammy Liza only beamed serenely. She was accustomed to these outbursts of her lord, and unembarrassed by them. She sat primly in her chair with the radiance of the beloved disciple.

It is one of the excellences of vanity that it cannot be overthrown by a chance blow. However desperately rammed, it always topples back upon its pedestal. Another would have gone hopelessly to wreckage under that, but not Randolph. He continued in his finest manner.

"Bearing this in mind," he said, "let us analyze the indicatory circumstances. It is possible, of course, that a criminal agent may plan his crime with skill, execute it without accident, and maintain the secret with equanimity, and that all interrogation following upon his act, will be wholly futile; but this is not usually true, as was conspicuously evidenced in Sir Ashby Cooper's case."

He paused and put the tips of his extended fingers together.

"What have we here to indicate the criminal agent? No human eye has seen the robber at his work, and there are no witnesses to speak; but we are not to abandon our investigation for that. The writers on the law tell us that circumstantial evidence in the case of crimes committed in secret is the most satisfactory from which to draw conclusions of guilt, for men may be seduced to perjury from base motives, but facts, as Mr. Baron Legg so aptly puts it, 'cannot lie.' "

He made a large indicatory gesture toward his bookshelf.

"True," he said, "I would not go so far as Mr. Justice Butler in Donellan's case. I would not hold circumstantial evidence to be superior to direct evidence, nor would I take the position that it is wholly beyond the reach and compass of human abilities to invent a train of circumstances that might deceive the ordinary inexperienced magistrate. I would recall the Vroom case, and the lamentable error of Sir Matthew Hale, in hanging some sailors for the murder of a shipmate who was, in fact, not dead. But even that error, sir," and he addressed my uncle directly in the heat and eloquence of his oration, "if in the law one may ever take an illustration from the poets, bore a jewel in its head. It gave us Hale's Rule."

He paused for emphasis, and my uncle spoke.

"And what was that rule?" he said.

"That rule, sir," replied Randolph, "ought not to be stated from memory. It is a nefarious practice of our judges, whereby errors creep into the sound text. It should be read as it stands, sir, in the elegant language of Sir Matthew."

"Leaving out the elegant language of Sir Matthew," replied Abner, "what does the rule mean?"

"In substance and effect," continued Randolph, "but by no means in these words, the rule directs the magistrate to be first certain that a crime has been committed before he undertakes to punish anybody for it."

"Precisely!" said my uncle; "and it is the very best sense that I ever heard of in the law."

He held the gold cross out in his big palm.

"Take this case," he said. "What is the use to speculate

about who stole the emeralds, when it is certain that they have not been stolen!"

"Not stolen!" cried Randolph. "They are gone!"

"Yes," replied Abner, "they are gone, but they are not stolen. . . . I would ask you to consider this fact: If these emeralds had been stolen out of the cross, the tines of the metal which held the stones in place, would have been either broken off or pried up, and we would find either the new break in the metal, or the twisted projecting tines. . . . But, instead," he continued, "the points of the setting are all quite smooth. What does that indicate?"

Randolph took the cross and examined it with care.

"You are right, Abner," he said; "the settings are all worn away. I am not surprised; the cross is very old."

"And if the settings are worn away," continued my uncle, "what has become of the stones?"

Randolph banged the table with his clenched hand.

"They have fallen out. Lost! By gad, sir!"

My uncle leaned back in his chair, like one to whom a comment is superfluous. But Randolph delivered an oration. It was directed to Mammy Liza, and the tenor of it was felicitations upon the happy incident that turned aside suspicion from any member of his household. He grew eloquent, pictured his distress, and how his stern, impartial sense of justice had restrained it, and finally, with what seigniorial joy he now received the truth.

And the old woman sat under it in ecstatic rapture. She made little audible sighs and chirrups. Her elbows were lifted and she moved her body rhythmically to the swing of Randolph's periods. She was entranced at the eloquence, but the intent of Randolph's speech never reached her. She was beyond the acquittal, as she had been beyond the accusation.

She continued to bow radiantly after Randolph had made an end.

"Yes, sah," she said; "yes, sah, Mars Ran, I done tole you that them jules wan't took by none of *our* niggers."

But, as for me, I was overcome with wonder. Here was my uncle convincing Randolph by a piece of evidence which he,

E*

himself, had deliberately manufactured on the face of the grindstone.

So that was what he had been at in the shed—grinding off the tines and polishing the settings with a piece of leather, so they would give the appearance of being worn. From my point of vantage in the snowball bush, I looked upon him with a growing interest. He sat, oblivious to Randolph's vaporings, looking beyond him, through the open window at the far-off green fields. He had taken these pains to acquit Mammy Liza. But some one was guilty then! And who? I got a hint of that within the next five minutes, and I was appalled.

"Liza," said Randolph, descending to the practical, "who sweeps Miss Betty's room?"

"Laws, Mars Ran," replied the old negro, " 'course I does everything fo' my chile. The house niggers don't do nothin'— that is, they don't do nothin' 'thouten I sets an' watches 'em. I sets when they washes the winders, and I sets when they sweeps, an' I sets when they makes the bed up. I's been a-settin' there all the time Miss Betty's been gone, 'ceptin', of course, when Mars Cedward was there."

She paused and tittered.

"Bless my life, how young folks does carry on! Every day heah comes Mars Cedward a-ridin' up, an' he says, 'Howdy, Mammy, I reckon if I can't see Miss Betty, I'll have to run upstairs an' look at her Ma.' An' he lights offen his horse, 'Get your key, Mammy,' he says, 'an' open the sacred po'tals.' And I gets the key outen my pocket an' unlocks the do' an' he whippits in there to that little picture of Miss Betty's Ma, that hangs over her bureau."

The old woman paused and wiped a mist from her spectacles with an immaculate and carefully folded handkerchief.

"Yes, yes, sah, 'co'se Miss Betty does look like her Ma— she's the very spit-an'-image of her. . . . Well, I goes along back an' sets down on the stair-steps, an' waits till Mars Cedward gets done with his worshipin's, an' he comes along an' says, 'Thankee, Mammy, I reckon that'll have to last me until to-morrow,' an' then I goes back an' locks the do'. I's mighty keerful to lock do's. I ain't minded to have no 'quisitive nigger ramshakin' 'roun'."

But my uncle stopped her and sent her to Betty as evidence in the flesh that she had come acquit of Randolph's inquisition. And the two men fell into a talk upon other matters.

But I no longer listened. I sat within my bush and studied the impassive face of my Uncle Abner, and tried to join these contradictory incidents into something that I could understand. Slowly the thing came to me! But I did not push on into the inevitable conclusion. Its consequences were too appalling. I saw it and let it lie.

Somebody had pried the emeralds out of that cross,— somebody having access to the room. And that person was not Mammy Liza! Abner knew that. . . . And he deliberately falsified the evidence. To acquit Mammy Liza? Something more than that, I thought. She was in no danger; even Randolph behind his judicial attitudes, had never entertained the idea for a moment. Then, this thing meant that my uncle had deliberately screened the real criminal. But why? Abner was no respecter of men. He stood for justice—clean and ruthless justice, tempered by no distinctions. Why, then, indeed?

And then I had an inspiration. Abner was thinking of some one beyond the criminal, and of the consequences to that one if the truth were known; and this thing he had done, he had done for her! And now I thought about her, too.

Her faith, her trust, the dearest illusion of her life had been imperiled, had been destroyed, but for my uncle's firm, deliberate act.

And then, another thing rose up desperately before me. How could he let this girl go on in ignorance of the truth? Must he not, after all, tell her what he knew? And my tongue grew dry in contemplation of that ordeal. And yet again, why? Love of her had been ultimately the motive. She need never know, and the secret might live out everybody's life. Moreover, for all his iron ways, Abner was a man who saw justice in its large and human aspect, and he stood for the spirit, above the letter, of the truth.

And yet, even there under the limited horizon of a child, I seemed to feel that he must tell her. And so when he finally got away from Randolph, and turned into the garden, I stalked him with desperate cunning. I was on fire to know what he would do. Would he speak? Or would he keep the thing for-ever silent? I had sat before two acts of this drama, and I would see what the curtains went down on. And I did see it from the shelter of the tall timothy-grass.

He found Betty at the foot of the garden. She ran to him in joy at Mammy Liza's vindication, and with pretty evidences of her affection. But he took her by the hand without a word and led her to a bench.

And when she was seated he sat down beside her. I could not see her face, but I could hear his voice and it was won-derfully kind.

"My child," he said, "there is always one reason, if no other, why good people must not undertake to work with a tool of the devil, and that reason is because they handle it so badly."

He paused and took the gold cross out of his pocket.

"Now here," he continued, "I have had to help somebody out who was the very poorest bungler with a devil's tool. I am not very skilled myself with that sort of an implement, but, dear me, I am not so bad a workman as this person! . . . Let me show you. . . . The one who got the emeralds out of this cross left the twisted and broken tines to indicate a deliberate criminal act, so I had to grind them off in order that the thing might look like an accident. . . . That cleared everybody —Mammy Liza, who had no motive for this act, and Edward Duncan, who had."

The girl stood straight up.

"Oh," she said, and her voice was a long shuddering whis-per, "no one could think he did it!"

"And why not?" continued my uncle. "He had the oppor-tunity and the motive. He was in the room during your absence, and he needed the money which those emeralds would bring in order to clear his lands of debt."

The girl clenched her hands and drew them in against her heart.

"But you don't think he stole them?" And again her voice was in that shuddering whisper.

I lay trembling.

"No," replied Abner, "I do not think that Edward Duncan stole these emeralds, because I know that they were never stolen at all."

He put out his hand and drew the girl down beside him.

"My child," he continued, "we must always credit the poorest thief with some glimmering of intelligence. When I first saw this cross in your hand, I knew that this was not the work of a thief, because no thief would have painfully pried the emeralds out, in order to leave the cross behind as an evidence of his guilt. Now, there is a reason why this cross was left behind, but it is not the reason of a thief—two reasons, in fact: because some one wished to keep it, and because they were not afraid to do so.

"Now, my child," and Abner put his arm tenderly around the girl's shoulders, "who could that person be who treasured this cross and was not afraid to keep it?"

She clung to my uncle then, and I heard the confession among her sobbings. Edward Duncan was making every sacrifice for her, and she had made one for him. She had sold the emeralds in Baltimore, and through an agent, bought his mountain land. But he must never know, never in this world, and my Uncle Abner must promise her that upon his honor.

And lying in the deep timothy-grass, I heard him promise.

Chapter 11

The Hidden Law

WE HAD COME out to Dudley Betts' house and were standing in a bit of meadow. It was an afternoon of April; there had been a shower of rain, and now the sun was on the velvet grass and the white-headed clover blossoms. The sky was blue above and the earth green below, and swimming between them was an air like lotus. Facing the south upon this sunny field was a stand of bees, thatched with rye-straw and covered over with a clapboard roof, the house of each tribe a section of a hollow gum-tree, with a cap on the top for the tribute of honey to the human tyrant. The bees had come out after the shower was gone, and they hummed at their work with the sound of a spinner.

Randolph stopped and looked down upon the humming hive. He lifted his finger with a little circling gesture.

" 'Singing masons building roofs of gold,' " he said. "Ah, Abner, William of Avon was a great poet."

My uncle turned about at that and looked at Randolph and then at the hive of bees. A girl was coming up from the brook below with a pail of water. She wore a simple butternut frock, and she was clean-limbed and straight like those first daughters of the world who wove and spun. She paused before the hive and the bees swarmed about her as about a great clover blossom, and she was at home and unafraid like a child in a company of yellow butterflies. She went on to the spring house with her dripping wooden pail, kissing the tips of her fingers to the bees. We followed, but before the hive my uncle stopped and repeated the line that Randolph had quoted:

" 'Singing masons building roofs of gold,' . . . and over a floor of gold and pillars of gold." He added, "He was a good riddle maker, your English poet, but not so good as Samson, unless I help him out."

145

I received the fairy fancy with all children's joy. Those little men singing as they laid their yellow floor, and raised their yellow walls, and arched their yellow roof! Singing! The word seemed to open up some sunlit fairy world.

It pleased Randolph to have thus touched my uncle.

"A great poet, Abner," he repeated, "and more than that; he drew lessons from nature valuable for doctrine. Men should hymn as they labor and fill the fields with song and so suck out the virus from the curse. He was a great philosopher, Abner—William of Avon."

"But not so great a philosopher as Saint Paul," replied Abner, and he turned from the bees toward old Dudley Betts, digging in the fields before his door. He put his hands behind him and lifted his stern bronze face.

"Those who coveted after money," he said, "have 'pierced themselves through with many sorrows.' And is it not the truth? Yonder is old Dudley Betts. He is doubled up with aches; he has lost his son; he is losing his life, and he will lose his soul—all for money—'Pierced themselves through with many sorrows,' as Saint Paul said it, and now, at the end he has lost the hoard that he slaved for."

The man was a by-word in the hills; mean and narrow, with an economy past belief. He used everything about him to one end and with no thought but gain. He cultivated his fields to the very door, and set his fences out into the road, and he extracted from those about him every tithe of service. He had worked his son until the boy had finally run away across the mountains. He had driven his daughter to the makeshifts of the first patriarchal people—soap from ashes, linen from hemp, and the wheel and the loom for the frock upon her limbs.

And like every man under a single dominating passion, he grew in suspicion and in fear. He was afraid to lend out his money lest he lose it. He had given so much for this treasure that he would take no chance with it, and so kept it by him in gold.

But caution and fear are not harpies to be halted; they wing on. Betts was dragged far in their claw-feet. There is a land of dim things that these convoys can enter. Betts arrived there. We must not press the earth too hard, old, forgotten

peoples believed, lest evil things are squeezed out that strip us
and avenge it. And ancient crones, feeble, wrapped up by the
fire, warned him: The earth suffered us to reap, but not to
glean her. We must not gather up every head of wheat. The
earth or dim creatures behind the earth would be offended. It
was the oldest belief. The first men poured a little wine out
when they drank and brought an offering of their herds and
the first fruits of the fields. It was written in the Book. He
could get it down and read it.

What did they know that they did this? Life was hard then;
men saved all they could. There was some terrible experience
behind this custom, some experience that appalled and stamped
the race with a lesson!

At first Betts laughed at their warnings; then he cursed at
them, and his changed manner marked how far he had got.
The laugh meant disbelief, but the curse meant fear.

And now, the very strangest thing had happened: The
treasure that the old man had so painfully laid up had mys-
teriously vanished clear away. No one knew it. Men like
Betts, cautious and secretive, are dumb before disaster. They
conceal the deep mortal hurt as though to hide it from
themselves.

He had gone in the night and told Randolph and Abner,
and now they had come to see his house.

He put down his hoe when we came up and led us in. It
was a house like those of the first men, with everything in it
home-made—hand-woven rag-carpets on the floor, and hand-
woven coverlets on the beds; tables and shelves and benches of
rude carpentry. These things spoke of the man's economy. But
there were also things that spoke of his fear: The house was a
primitive stockade. The door was barred with a beam, and
there were heavy shutters at the window; an ax stood by the
old man's bed and an ancient dueling pistol hung by its trig-
ger-guard to a nail.

I did not go in, for youth is cunning. I sat down on the
doorstep and fell into so close a study of a certain wasp at
work under a sill that I was overlooked as a creature without
ears; but I had ears of the finest and I lost no word.

The old man got two splint-bottom chairs and put them

by the table for his guests, and then he brought a blue earthen jar and set it before them. It was one of the old-fashioned glazed jars peddled by the hucksters, smaller but deeper than a crock, with a thick rim and two great ears. In this he kept his gold pieces until on a certain night they had vanished.

The old man's voice ran in and out of a whisper as he told the story. He knew the very night, because he looked into his jar before he slept and every morning when he got out of his bed. It had been a devil's night—streaming clouds drove across an iron sky, a thin crook of a moon sailed, and a high bitter wind scythed the earth.

Everybody remembered the night when he got out his almanac and named it. There had been noises, old Betts said, but he could not define them. Such a night is full of voices; the wind whispers in the chimney and the house frame creaks. The wind had come on in gusts at sunset, full of dust and whirling leaves, but later it had got up into a gale. The fire had gone out and the house inside was black as a pit. He did not know what went on inside or out, but he knew that the gold was gone at daylight, and he knew that no living human creature had got into his house. The bar on his door held and the shutters were bolted. Whatever entered, entered through the keyhole or through the throat of the chimney that a cat would stick in.

Abner said nothing, but Randolph sat down to an official inquiry:

"You have been robbed, Betts," he said. "Somebody entered your house that night."

"Nobody entered it," replied the old man in his hoarse, half-whispered voice, "either on that night or any other night. The door wast fast, Squire."

"But the thief may have closed it behind him."

Betts shook his head. "He could not put up the bar behind him, and besides, I set it in a certain way. It was not moved. And the windows—I bolt them and turn the bolt at a certain angle. No human touched them."

It was not possible to believe that this man could be mistaken. One could see with what care he had set his little traps —the bar across the door precisely at a certain hidden line;

the bolts of the window shutters turned precisely to an angle that he alone knew. It was not likely that Randolph would suggest anything that this cautious old man had not already thought of.

"Then," continued Randolph, "the thief concealed himself in your house the day before the robbery and got out of it on the day after."

But again Betts shook his head, and his eyes ran over the house and to a candle on the mantelpiece.

"I look," he said, "every night before I go to bed."

And one could see the picture of this old, fearful man, looking through his house with the smoking tallow candle, peering into every nook and corner. Could a thief hide from him in this house that he knew inch by inch? One could not believe it. The creature took no chance; he had thought of every danger, this one among them, and every night he looked! He would know, then, the very cracks in the wall. He would have found a rat.

Then, it seemed to me, Randolph entered the only road there was out of this mystery.

"Your son knew about this money?"

"Yes," replied Betts, " 'Lander knew about it. He used to say that a part of it was his because he had worked for it as much as I had. But I told him," and the old man's voice cheeped in a sort of laugh, "that he was mine."

"Where was your son Philander when the money disappeared?" said Randolph.

"Over the mountains," said Betts; "he had been gone a month." Then he paused and looked at Randolph. "It was not 'Lander. On that day he was in the school that Mr. Jefferson set up. I had a letter from the master asking for money. . . . I have the letter," and he got up to get it.

But Randolph waved his hand and sat back in his chair with the aspect of a brooding oracle.

It was then that my uncle spoke.

"Betts," he said, "how do you think the money went?"

The old man's voice got again into that big crude whisper. "I don't know, Abner."

But my uncle pressed him.

"What do you think?"

Betts drew a little nearer to the table.

"Abner," he said, "there are a good many things going on around a man that he don't understand. We turn out a horse to pasture, and he comes in with hand-holts in his mane. . . . You have seen it?"

"Yes," replied my uncle.

And I had seen it, too, many a time, when the horses were brought up in the spring from pasture, their manes twisted and knotted into loops, as though to furnish a hand-holt to a rider.

"Well, Abner," continued the old man in his rustling whisper, "who rides the horse? You cannot untie or untwist those hand-holts—you must cut them out with shears—with iron. Is it true?"

"It is true," replied my uncle.

"And why, eh, Abner? Because those hand-holts were never knotted in by any human fingers! You know what the old folk say?"

"I know," answered my uncle. "Do you believe it, Betts?"

"Eh, Abner!" he croaked in the guttural whisper. "If there were no witches, why did our fathers hang up iron to keep them off? My grandmother saw one burned in the old country. She had ridden the king's horse, and greased her hands with shoemakers' wax so her fingers would not slip in the mane. . . . Shoemakers' wax! Mark you that, Abner!"

"Betts," cried Randolph, "you are a fool; there are no witches!"

"There was the Witch of Endor," replied my uncle. "Go on, Betts."

"By gad, sir!" roared Randolph, "if we are to try witches, I shall have to read up James the First. That Scotch king wrote a learned work on demonology. He advised the magistrates to search on the body of the witch for the seal of the devil; that would be a spot insensible to pain, and, James said, 'Prod for it with a needle.'"

But my uncle was serious.

"Go on, Betts," he said. "I do not believe that any man

entered your house and robbed you. But why do you think that a witch did?"

"Well, Abner," answered the old man, "who could have got in but such a creature? A thief cannot crawl through a keyhole, but there are things that can. My grandmother said that once in the old country a man awoke one night to see a gray wolf sitting by his fireside. He had an ax, as I have, and he fought the wolf with that and cut off its paw, whereupon it fled screaming through the keyhole. And the paw lying on the floor was a woman's hand!"

"Then, Betts," cried Randolph, "it's damned lucky that you didn't use your ax, if that is what one finds on the floor."

Randolph had spoken with pompous sarcasm, but at the words there came upon Abner's face a look of horror.

"It is," he said, "in God's name!"

Betts leaned forward in his chair.

"And what would have happened to me, Abner, do you think, if I had used my ax? Would I have died there with the ax in my hand?"

The look of horror remained upon my uncle's face.

"You would have wished for that when the light came; to die is sometimes to escape the pit."

"I would have fallen into hell, then?"

"Aye, Betts," replied my uncle, "straightway into hell!"

The old man rested his hands on the posts of the chair.

"The creatures behind the world are baleful creatures," he muttered in his big whisper.

Randolph got up at that.

"Damme!" he said. "Are we in the time of Roger Williams, and is this Massachusetts, that witches ride and men are filched of their gold by magic and threatened with hell fire? What is this cursed foolery, Abner?"

"It is no foolery, Randolph," replied my uncle, "but the living truth."

"The truth!" cried Randolph. "Do you call it the truth that creatures, not human, able to enter through the keyhole and fly away, have Betts' gold, and if he had fought against this robbery with his ax he would have put himself in torment?

Damme, man! In the name of common sense, do you call this the truth?"

"Randolph," replied Abner, and his voice was slow and deep, "it is every word the truth."

Randolph moved back the chair before him and sat down. He looked at my uncle curiously.

"Abner," he said, "you used to be a crag of common sense. The legends and theories of fools broke on you and went to pieces. Would you now testify to witches?"

"And if I did," replied my uncle, "I should have Saint Paul behind me."

"The fathers of the church fell into some errors," replied Randolph.

"The fathers of the law, then?" said Abner.

Randolph took his chin in his hand at that. "It is true," he said, "that Sir Matthew Hale held nothing to be so well established as the fact of witchcraft for three great reasons, which he gave in their order, as became the greatest judge in England: First, because it was asserted in the Scriptures; second, because all nations had made laws against it; and, third, because the human testimony in support of it was overwhelming. I believe that Sir Matthew had knowledge of some six thousand cases. . . . But Mr. Jefferson has lived since then, Abner, and this is Virginia."

"Nevertheless," replied my uncle, "after Mr. Jefferson, and in Virginia, this thing has happened."

Randolph swore a great oath.

"Then, by gad, sir, let us burn the old women in the villages until the creatures who carried Betts' treasure through the keyhole bring it back!"

Betts spoke then.

"They have brought some of it back!"

My uncle turned sharply in his chair.

"What do you mean, Betts?" he said.

"Why this, Abner," replied the old man, his voice descending into the cavernous whisper; "on three mornings I have found some of my gold pieces in the jar. And they came as they went, Abner, with every window fastened down and the bar across the door. And there is another thing about these pieces that have come back—they are mine, for I know every piece—but they have been in the hands of the creatures that ride the horses in the pasture—they have been handled by witches!" He whispered the word with a fearful glance about him. "How do I know that? Wait, I will show you!"

He went over to his bed and got out a little box from beneath his cornhusk mattress—a worn, smoke-stained box with a sliding lid. He drew the lid off with his thumb and turned the contents out on the table.

"Now look," he said; "look, there is wax on every piece! Shoemakers' wax, mark you. . . . Eh, Abner! My mother said that—the creatures grease their hands with that so their fingers will not slip when they ride the barebacked horses in the night. They have carried this gold clutched in their hands, see, and the wax has come off!"

My uncle and Randolph leaned over the table. They examined the coins.

"By the Eternal!" cried Randolph. "It *is* wax! But were they clean before?"

"They were clean," the old man answered. "The wax is from the creatures' fingers. Did not my mother say it?"

My uncle sat back in his chair, but Betts strained forward and put his fearful query:

"What do you think, Abner; will all the gold come back?"

My uncle did not at once reply. He sat for some time silent, looking through the open door at the sunny meadowland and the far off hills. But finally he spoke like one who has worked out a problem and got the answer.

"It will not all come back," he said.

"How much, then?" whispered Betts.

"What is left," replied Abner, "when the toll is taken out."

"You know where the gold is?"

"Yes."

"And the creatures that have it, Abner," Betts whispered, "they are not human?"

"They are not human!" replied my uncle.

Then he got up and began to walk about the house, but not to search for clews to this mysterious thing. He walked like one who examines something within himself—or something beyond the eye—and old Betts followed him with his straining face. And Randolph sat in his chair with his arms folded and his chin against his stock, as a skeptic overwhelmed by proof might sit in a house of haunted voices. He was puzzled upon every hand. The thing was out of reason at every point, both in the loss and in the return of these coins upon the table, and my uncle's comments were below the soundings of all sense. The creatures who now had Betts' gold could enter through the keyhole! Betts would have gone into the pit if he had struck out with his ax! A moiety of this treasure would be taken out and the rest returned! And the coins testified to no human handling! The thing had no face nor aspect of events in nature. Mortal thieves enjoyed no such supernal powers. These were the attributes of the familiar spirit. Nor did the human robber return a per cent upon his gains!

I have said that my uncle walked about the floor. But he stopped now and looked down at the hard, miserly old man.

"Betts," he said, "this is a mysterious world. It is hedged about and steeped in mystery. Listen to me! The Patriarchs were directed to make an offering to the Lord of a portion of the increase in their herds. Why? Because the Lord had need of sheep and heifers? Surely not, for the whole earth and its increase were His. There was some other reason, Betts. I do not understand what it was, but I do understand that no man can use the earth and keep every tithe of the increase for himself. They did not try it, but you did!"

He paused and filled his big lungs.

"It was a disastrous experiment. . . . What will you do?"

"What must I do, Abner?" the old man whispered. "Make a sacrifice like the Patriarchs?"

"A sacrifice you must make, Betts," replied my uncle, "but not like the Patriarchs. What you received from the earth you must divide into three equal parts and keep one part for yourself."

"And to whom shall I give the other two parts, Abner?"

"To whom would you wish to give them, Betts, if you had the choice?"

The old man fingered about his mouth.

"Well," he said, "a man would give to those of his own household first—if he had to give."

"Then," said Abner, "from this day keep a third of your increase for yourself and give the other two-thirds to your son and your daughter."

"And the gold, Abner? Will it come back?"

"A third part will come back. Be content with that."

"And the creatures that have my gold? Will they harm me?"

"Betts," replied my uncle, "the creatures that have your gold on this day hidden in their house will labor for you as no slaves have ever labored—without word or whip. Do you promise?"

The fearful old man promised, and we went out into the sun.

The tall straight young girl was standing before the spring-house, kneading a dish of yellow butter and singing like a blackbird. My uncle strode down to her. We could not hear the thing he said, but the singing ceased when he began to talk and burst out in a fuller note when he had finished—a big, happy, joyous note that seemed to fill the meadow.

We waited for him before the stand of bees, and Randolph turned on him when he came.

"Abner," he said, "what is the answer to this damned riddle?"

"You gave it, Randolph," he replied—" 'Singing masons building roofs of gold.' " And he pointed to the bees. "When I saw that the cap on one of the gums had been moved I thought Betts' gold was there, and when I saw the wax on the coins I was certain."

"But," cried Randolph, "you spoke of creatures not human —creatures that could enter through the keyhole—creatures——"

"I spoke of the bees," replied my uncle.

"But you said Betts would have fallen into hell if he had struck out with his ax!"

"He would have killed his daughter," replied Abner. "Can you think of a more fearful hell? She took the gold and hid it in the bee cap. But she was honest with her father; whenever she sent a sum of money to her brother she returned an equal number of gold pieces to old Betts' jar."

"Then," said Randolph, with a great oath, "there is no witch here with her familiar spirits?"

"Now that," replied my uncle, "will depend upon the imagery of language. There is here a subtle maiden and a stand of bees!"

Chapter 12

The Riddle

I HAVE NEVER seen the snow fall as it fell on the night of the seventeenth of February. It had been a mild day with a soft, stagnant air. The sky seemed about to descend and enclose the earth, as though it were a thing which it had long pursued and had now got into a corner. All day it seemed thus to hover motionless above its quarry, and the earth to be apprehensive like a thing in fear. Animals were restless, and men, as they stood about and talked together, looked up at the sky.

We were in the county seat on that day. The grand jury was sitting, and Abner had been summoned to appear before it. It was the killing of old Christian Lance that the grand jury was inquiring into. He had been found one morning in his house, bound into a chair. The body sat straining forward, death on it, and terror in its face. There was no one in the house but old Christian, and it was noon before the neighbors found him. The tragedy had brought the grand jury together, and had filled the hills with talk, for it left a mystery unsolved.

This mystery that Christian sealed up in his death was one that no man could get a hint at while he was living—what had the old man done with his money? He grazed a few cattle and got a handsome profit. He spent next to nothing; he gave nothing to any one, and he did not put his money out to interest. It was known that he would take only gold in payment for his cattle. He made no secret of that. The natural inference was that he buried his coin in some spot about his garden, but idle persons had watched his house for whole nights after he had sold his cattle, and had never seen him come out with a spade. And young bloods, more curious, I think, than criminal, had gone into his house when he was absent, and searched it more than once. There was no corner that they had not

looked into, and no floor board that they had not lifted, nor
any loose stone about the hearth that they had not felt under.

Once, in conference on this mystery, somebody had sug-
gested that the knobs on the andirons and the handles on the
old high-boy were gold, having gotten the idea from some tale.
And a little later, when the old man returned one evening
from the grist-mill, he found that one of these knobs on the
andirons had been broken off. But, as the thief never came
back for the other, it was pretty certain that this fantastic notion was not the key to Christian's secret.

It was after one of these mischievous searchings that he
put up his Delphic notice when he went away—a leaf from a
day-book, scrawled in pencil, and pinned to the mantelpiece:
"Why don't you look in the cow?"

The idle gossips puzzled over that. What did it mean? Was
the thing a sort of taunt? And did the old man mean that
since these persons had looked into every nook and corner of
his house, they ought also to have looked into the red mouth
of the cow? Or did he mean that his money was invested in
cattle and there was the place to look? Or was the thing a
cryptic sentence—like that of some ancient oracle—in which
the secret to his hoarded gold was hidden?

At any rate it was certain that old Christian was not afraid
to go away and leave his door open, and the secret to guard
itself. And he was justified in that confidence. The mischievous
gave over their inquisitions, and the mystery became a sort of
legend.

With the eyes of the curious thus on him, and that mystery
for background, it was little wonder that his tragic death fired
the country.

I have said there was a horror about the dead man's face as
he sat straining in the chair. And the thing was in truth a horror! But that word does not tell the story. The eyes, the
muscles of his jaw, the very flesh upon his bones seemed to
strain with some deadly resolution, as though the indomitable
spirit of the man, by sheer determination, would force the
body to do its will, even after death was on it. And here there
was a curious thing. It was not about the house, where his
treasure might have been concealed, that the dead man

strained, but toward the door, as though he would follow after some one who had gone out there.

The neighbors cut him from the chair, straightened out his limbs, and got him buried. But his features, set in that deadly resolution, they could not straighten out. Neither the placidity of death, nor the fingers of those who prepared the man for burial, could relax the muscles or get down his eyelids. He lay in the coffin with that hideous resolution on his face, and he went into the earth with it.

When the man was found, Randolph sent for Abner, and the two of them looked through the house. Nothing had been disturbed. There was a kettle on the crane, and a crock beside the hearth. The ears of seed corn hung from the rafters, trussed up by their shucks; the bean pods together in a cluster; the cakes of tallow sat on a shelf above the mantel; the festoons of dried apples and the bunches of seasoned herbs hung against the chimney. The bed and all the furniture about the house was in its order.

When they had finished with that work they did not know who it was that had killed old Christian. Abner did not talk, but he said that much, and the Justice of the Peace told all he knew to every casual visitor. True, it was nothing more than the county knew already, but his talk annoyed Abner.

"Randolph's a leaky pitcher," he said. And I think it was this comment that inspired the notion that Abner knew something that he had not told the Justice.

At any rate he was a long time before the grand jury on this February day. The grand jury sat behind closed doors. They were stern, silent men, and nothing crept out through the keyhole. But after the witnesses were heard, the impression got about that the grand jury did not know who had killed old Christian, and this conclusion was presently verified when they came in before the judge. They had no indictment to find. And when the judge inquired if they knew of anything that would justify the prosecuting attorney in taking any further action on behalf of the state, the foreman shook his head.

Night was descending when we left the county-seat. Abner sat in his saddle like a man of bronze, his face stern, as it always was when he was silent, and I rode beside him. I wish I could get my Uncle Abner before your eye. He was one of those austere, deeply religious men who might have followed Cromwell, with a big iron frame, a grizzled beard and features forged out by a smith. His god was the god of the Tishbite, who numbered his followers by the companies who drew the sword. The land had need of men like Abner. The government of Virginia was over the Alleghenies, and this great, fertile cattle country, hemmed in by the far-off mountains like a wall of the world, had its own peace to keep. And it was these iron men who kept it. The fathers had got this land in grants from the King of England; they had held it against the savage and finally against the King himself . . . And the sons were like them.

The horses were nervous; they flung their heads about, and rattled the bit rings and traveled together like men apprehensive of some danger to be overtaken. That deadly stillness of the day remained, but the snow was now beginning to appear. It fell like no other snow that I have ever seen—not a gust of specks or a shower of tiny flakes, but now and then, out of the dirty putty-colored sky, a flake as big as a man's thumb-nail winged down and lighted on the earth like some living creature. And it clung to the thing that it lighted on as though out of the heavens it had selected that thing to destroy. And, while it clung, there came another of these soft white creatures to its aid, and settled beside it, and another and another, until the bare stem of the ragweed, or the brown leaf of the beech tree snapped under the weight of these clinging bodies.

It is a marvel how quickly this snow covered up the world, and how swiftly and silently it descended. The trees and fences were grotesque and misshapen with it. The landscape changed and was blotted out. Night was on us, and always the invading swarm of flakes increased until they seemed to crowd one another in the stagnant air.

Presently Abner stopped and looked up at the sky, but he did not speak and we went on. But now the very road began to be clogged with this wet snow; great limbs broke at the tree trunks under the weight of it; the horses began to flounder, and at last Abner stopped. It seemed to be at a sort of cross-road in a forest, but I was lost. The snow had covered every landmark that I knew. We had been traveling for an hour in a country as unfamiliar as the Tartar Steppes.

Abner turned out of the road into the forest. My horse followed. We came presently into the open, and stopped under the loom of a house. It was a great barn of hewn logs, but unused and empty. The door stood open on its broken hinges. We got down, took the horses in, removed the saddles, and filled the mangers with some old hay from the loft. I had no idea where we were. We could not go on, and I thought we would be forced to pass the night here. But this was not Abner's plan.

"Let us try to find the house, Martin," he said, "and build a fire."

We set out from the stable. Abner broke a trail through the deep snow, and I followed at his heels. He must have had some sense of direction, for we could not see. We seemed an hour laboring in that snow, but it could only have been a few minutes at the furthest. Presently we came upon broad steps, and under the big columns of a portico. And I knew the place for an old abandoned manor house, set in a corner of worn-out fields, in the edge of the forest, where the river bowed in under sheer banks a dozen fathoms down. The estate was grown up with weeds, and the house falling to decay. But now, when we came into the portico, a haze of light was shining through the fan-shaped glass over the door. It was this light that disturbed Abner. He stopped and stood there in the shelter of the columns, like a man in some perplexity.

"Now, who could that be?" he said, not to me, but to himself.

And he remained for some time, watching the blur of light, and listening for a sound. But there was no sound. The house had been abandoned. The windows were nailed up. Finally he went over to the ancient door and knocked. For answer there was the heavy report of a weapon, and a white splinter leaped out of a panel above his head. He sprang aside, and the weapon bellowed again, and I saw another splinter. And then I saw a thing that I had not noticed, that the door and the boards over the windows were riddled with these bullet holes. Abner shouted out his name and called on the man within to stop shooting and open the door.

For some time there was silence; then, finally the door did open, and a man stood there with a candle in his hand. He was a little old man with a stub of wiry beard, red grizzled hair, keen eyes like a crumb of glass, and a body knotted and tawny like a stunted oak tree. He wore a sort of cap with a broad fur collar fastened with big brass wolf-head clasps. And I knew him. He was the old country doctor, Storm, who had come into the hills, from God knows where. He lived not far away, and as a child, I feared him. I feared the flappings of his cape on some windy ridge, for he walked the country in his practice, and only rode when the distances were great. No one knew his history, and about him the Negroes had conjured up every sort of fancy. These notions took a sort of form. Storm was a rival of the Devil and jousted with him for the lives of men and beasts. He would work on a horse, snapping his jaws and muttering his strange oaths, as long and as patiently as upon the body of a man. And surely, if one stood and watched him, one would presently believe that Storm contended with something for its prey. I can see him now, standing in the door with the candle held high up so he could peer into the darkness.

He cried out when he saw Abner.

"Come in," he said, "by the Eternal, you are welcome!"

"Storm!" said Abner, "you in this house!"

"And why not?" replied the man. "I walk and am overtaken by a snow; and you ride and do not escape it."

He laughed, showing his twisted, yellow teeth, and turned about in the doorway, and we followed him into the house. There was a fire burning on the hearth and another candle guttering on the table. It was a hall that the door led into—the conventional hall of the great old Southern manor house, wide mahogany doors on either side stood closed in their white frames, a white stairway going up to a broad landing, and a huge fireplace with brass andirons. The place was warm, but musty. It had long been stripped and gutted. It was hung with cobwebs and powdered down with dust. There was a small portmanteau on the table, such as one's father used to carry, of black leather with little flaps and buckles. And beside it a blue iron stone jug and a dirty tumbler.

The man set down the candle and indicated the jug and the fireplace with a queer, ironical gesture.

"I offer you the hospitality of the cup and the hearth, Abner,'" he said.

"We will take the hearth, Storm," replied Abner, "if you please."

And we went over to the fireplace, took off our great coats, beat out the wet snow, and sat down on the old mahogany settle by the andirons.

"Every man to the desire of his heart and the custom of his life," said Storm.

He took up the jug, turned it on end, and drained its contents into the glass. There was only a little of the liquor left. It was brewed from apples, raw and fiery, and the odor of it filled the place. Then he held up the glass, watching the firelight play in the white-blue liquor.

"You fill the mind with phantoms," he said, turning the glass about as though it held some curious drug. "We swallow you and see things that are not, and dead men from their graves."

He toyed with the glass, put it on the table, and sat down.

"Abner," he said, "I know the body of a man down to the fiber of his bones; but the mind—it is a land of mystery. We dare not trust it." He paused and rapped the table with his callous fingers.

"Against another we may be secure, but against himself what one of us is safe? A man may have no fear of your Hebrew God, Abner, or your Assyrian Devil, and yet, his own mind may turn against him and fill him full of terror. . . . A man may kill his enemy in secret and hide him, and return to his house secure—and find the dead man sitting in his chair with the wet blood on him. And with all his philosophies he cannot eject that phantom from its seat. He will say this thing does not exist. But what avails the word when the thing is there!"

He got on his feet and leaned over the table with his crooked fingers out before him.

F

I was afraid and I drew closer to my uncle. This strange old man, straining over the table, peering into the shadows, held me with a gripping fascination. His wiry, faded red hair seemed to rise on his scalp, and I looked to see some horror in its grave clothes appear before him.

Abner turned his stern face upon him. It was some time before he spoke.

"Storm," he said, "what do you fear?"

"Fear!" cried the old man, his voice rising in a sharp staccato; and he made a gesture outward with his hand.

"You fear your God, Abner, and I fear myself!"

But there was something in Abner's voice and in this query launched at him that changed the man as by some sorcery. He sat down, fingered the glass of liquor, and looked at Abner closely. He did not speak for some time. He appeared to be turning some problem slowly in his mind. There was a lot of mystery here to clear up. We had discovered him by chance, and surely he had received us in the strangest manner. His explanation could not be true that he had come into the house before us on this night, for the house was warm, and it could not have been heated in that time. What was the creature's secret? Why was he here, and who besieged him. These were things which he must fear to have known, and yet, he was glad to see us, glad to find us there in the snow, instead of another whom he feared to find there. And yet, we disturbed him, and he was uncertain what to do. He sat beyond the table, and I could see his eyes run over us, and wander off about the hall and return and glance at the black portmanteau.

And while he hung there between his plans, Abner spoke.

"Storm," he said, "what does all this mean?"

The old man looked about him swiftly, furtively, I thought; then he spoke in a voice so low that we could hardly hear him.

"Let me put it this way, Abner," he said: "One comes here, as you come; he is met as you are met; well, what happens from all this? . . . A suspicion enters the visitor's mind. There is peril to the host in that, and he is put to an alternative. He must explain or he must shoot the guest. . . . Well, he chooses to make his explanation first, and if that fail, there is the other!

" 'And,' he says, 'you have done me a service to come in; I am glad to see you.' And you say, 'What do you fear?' He answers, 'Robbers.' You say, 'What have you in this house to lose?' And he tells you this:

"Michael Dale owned this house. He was rich. When he was dying he sat here by this hearth, tapping the bricks with his cane, and peering at his worthless son. You remember that son, Abner; he looked like the Jupiter of Elis before the Devil got him. 'Wellington,' he said, 'I am leaving you a treasure here.' He had been speaking of this estate, and one thought he meant the lands, and so gave the thing no notice. But later one remembered that expression and began to think it over. One recalled where it was that Michael Dale sat and the tapping of his stick. Well, when one is going down, any straw is worth the clutching. One slips into this house and looks."

He indicated the brick hearth with a gesture.

"No, it is not there now. The gold is in that portmanteau."

He arose, opened the bag, and fumbled in it. Then he came to us with some pieces in his hand.

Abner took the gold and examined it carefully by the fire-light. They were old pieces, and he rubbed them between his fingers and scraped something from their faces with his thumb-nail. Then he handed them back, and Storm cast them into the portmanteau and buckled it together. Then he sat down and drew the stone jug over beside him.

"Now, Abner," he said, "there is this evil about a treasure. It fills one full of fear. You must stand guard over it, and the thing gets on your nerves. The wind in the chimney is a voice, and every noise a footstep. At first one goes about with the weapon in his hand, and then, when he can bear it no more, he shoots at every sound."

Abner did not move, and I listened to the man as to a tale of Bagdad. Every mystery was now cleared up—his presence in this house, his fear, the bullet holes, and why he was glad to see us, and yet disturbed that we had come. And I saw what he had been turning in his mind—whether he should trust us with the truth or leave us to our own conclusions. I understood and verified in myself every detail of this story. I should have acted as he did at every step, and I could realize this fear, and how, as the thing possessed him, one might come at last to shoot up the shadows. I looked at the man with a sort of wonder.

Abner had been stroking his bronze face with his great sinewy hand, and now he spoke.

"Storm," he said, "Michael Dale's riddle is not the only one that has been read." And he told of Christian Lance's death, and the Delphic sentence that had doubtless caused it. "You knew old Christian, Storm, and his curious life?"

"I did," replied Storm, "and I knew the man who carried off the knob of the andiron. But how do you say that any man read his riddle, Abner, and how do you know that there was any riddle in it? I took the thing to be an idle taunt."

"And so did Randolph," said Abner, "but you were both wrong. The secret was in that scrawled sentence, and some one guessed it."

"How do you know that, Abner?" said Storm.

Abner did not reply directly to the point.

"Old Christian loved money," he went on. "He would have died before he told where it was hidden. And his straining toward the door, as though in death he would follow one who had gone out there, meant that his secret had been divined, and that his gold had gone that way."

"You ride to a conclusion on straws, Abner," said Storm, "if that is all the proof you have."

"Well," replied Abner, "I have also a theory."

"And what is your theory?" said Storm.

"It is this," continued Abner; "when old Christian wrote, 'Why don't you look in the cow,' he meant a certain thing. There was a row of tallow cakes on a shelf. My theory is that each year when he got the gold from his cattle, he molded it into one of these tallow cakes, turned it out of the crock, and put it on the shelf. And there, in the heart of these tallow cakes, was the old man's treasure!"

"But you tell me that the cakes were there on this shelf when you found old Christian," said Storm.

"They were," replied Abner.

"Every one of them," said Storm.

"Every one of them," answered Abner.

"Had any one of them been cut or broken?"

"Not one of them; they were smooth and perfect."

"Then your first conclusion goes to pieces, Abner. No man carried Christian's money through the door; it is there on the shelf."

"No," said Abner, "it is not there. The man who killed old Christian Lance got the gold out of those cakes of tallow."

"And, now, Abner," cried the man, "the bottom of your theory falls. How could one get the gold out of these cakes, and leave them perfect?"

"I will tell you that," replied Abner. "There was a kettle on the crane and a crock beside the hearth, and every cake of tallow on the shelf was white . . . They had been remolded! Randolph did not see that, but I did."

Storm got on his feet.

"Then you do not believe this explanation, Abner—that the gold comes from the hearth?"

"I do not," replied Abner, and his voice was deep and level. "There is tallow on these coins!"

I saw Abner glance at the iron poker and watch Storm's hand.

But the old man did not draw his weapon. He laughed noiselessly, twisting his crooked mouth.

"You are right, Abner," he said, "it is Christian's gold, and this tale a lie. But you are wrong in your conclusion. Lance was not killed by a little man like I am; he was killed by a big man like you!"

He paused and leaned over, resting his hands on the table.

"The man who killed him did not guess that riddle, Abner. . . . Put the evidences together. . . . Lance was tied into his chair before the assassin killed him. Why? That was to threaten him with death unless he told where his gold was hidden. . . . Well, Lance would not tell that, but the assassin found it out by chance. He stooped to put the poker into the fire to heat it, and torture Christian. The cakes of tallow were on a hanging shelf against the white-washed chimney; as the assassin arose, he struck this shelf with his shoulder, and one of the tallow cakes fell and burst on the hearth. Then he killed Christian with a blow of the heated poker. I know that because the hair about the wound was scorched!

"You saw a good deal in that house, Abner, but did you see a crease in the chimney where the shelf smote it, and the mark of a man's shoulder on the whitewash? And that shoulder, Abner," he raised his hand above his head, "it was as high as yours!"

There was silence.

And as the two men looked thus at each other, there was a sound as of something padding about the house outside. For a moment I did not understand these sounds, then I realized that the wind was rising, and clumps of snow falling from the trees. But to another in that house these sounds had no such explanation.

Then a thing happened. One of the mahogany doors entering the hall leaped back, and a man stood there with a pistol in his hand. And in all my life I have never seen a creature like him! There was everything fine and distinguished in his face, but the face was a ruin. It was a loathsome and hideous ruin. Made for the occupancy of a god, the man's body was the dwelling of a devil. I do not mean a clean and vicious devil, but one low and bestial, that wallowed and gorged itself with sins. And there was another thing in that face that to understand, one must have seen it. There was terror, but no fear! It was as though the man advanced against a thing that filled him full of horror, but he advanced with courage. He had a spirit in him that saw and knew the aspect and elements of danger, but it could not be stampeded into flight.

I heard Abner say, "Dale!" like one who pronounces the name of some extraordinary thing. And I heard Storm say, "Mon dieu! With a teaspoonful of laudanum in him, he walks!"

The creature did not see us; he was listening to the sounds outside, and he started for the door.

"You there," he bellowed, "again! . . . Damn you! . . . Well, I'll get you this time. . . . I'll hunt you to hell!" . . . And his drunken voice rumbled off into obscenities and oaths.

He flung the door open and went out. His weapon thundered, and by it and the drunken shouting, we could track him. He seemed to move north, as though lured that way. We stood and listened.

"He goes toward the river," said Abner. "It is God's will."

Then far off there was a last report of the weapon and a great bellowing cry that shuddered through the forest.

That night over the fire, Storm told us how he had come in from the snow and found Dale drunk and fighting the ghost of Christian Lance; how he listened to his story, and slipped the drug into his glass, and how he got him hidden, when we came, on the promise to keep his secret; and how he had fenced with Abner, seeing that Abner suspected him.

But it was the failure of his drug that vexed him.

"It would put a brigadier and his horse to sleep—that much, if it were pure. I shall take ten drops to-morrow night and see."

Chapter 13

The Straw Man

IT WAS A DAY of early June in Virginia. The afternoon sun lay warm on the courthouse with its great plaster pillars; on the tavern with its two-story porch; on the stretches of green fields beyond and the low wooded hill, rimmed by the far-off mountains like a wall of the world.

It was the first day of the circuit court, which all the country attended. And on this afternoon, two men crossed the one thoroughfare that lay through the county seat, and went up the wide stone steps into the courthouse.

The two men were in striking contrast. One, short of stature and beginning to take on the rotundity of age, was dressed with elaborate care, his great black stock propping up his chin, his linen and the cloth of his coat immaculate. He wore a huge carved ring and a bunch of seals attached to his watch-fob. The other was a big, broad-shouldered, deep-chested Saxon, with all those marked characteristics of a race living out of doors and hardened by wind and sun. His powerful frame carried no ounce of surplus weight. It was the frame of the empire builder on the frontier of the empire. The face reminded one of Cromwell, the craggy features in repose seemed molded over iron, but the fine gray eyes had a calm serenity, like remote spaces in the summer sky. The man's clothes were plain and somber. And he gave one the impression of things big and vast.

As the two entered between the plaster pillars, a tall old man came out from the county clerk's office. But for his face, he might have been one of a thousand Englishmen in Virginia. There was nothing in the big, spare figure or the cranial lines of the man to mark.

But the face seized you. In it was an unfathomable disgust with life, joined, one would say, with a cruel courage. The

171

hard, bony jaw protruded; bitter lines descended along the planes of the face, and the eyes circled by red rims were expressionless and staring, as though, by some abominable negligence of nature, they were lidless.

The two approached, and the one so elaborately dressed spoke to the old man.

"How do you do, Northcote Moore?" he said. "You know Abner?"

The old man stopped instantly and stood very still. He moved the stick in his hand a trifle before him. Then he spoke in a high-pitched, irascible voice.

"Abner, eh! Well, what the devil is Abner here for?"

The little pompous man clenched his fingers in his yellow gloves, but his voice showed no annoyance.

"I asked him to have a look at Eastwood Court."

"Damn the justice of the peace of every county," cried the old man, "and you included, Randolph! You never make an end of anything."

He gave no attention to Abner, who remained unembarrassed, regarding the impolite old man as one regards some strange, new, and particularly offensive beast.

"Chuck the whole business, Randolph, that's what I say," the irascible old man continued, "and forget about it. Who the devil cares? A drooling old paralytic is snuffed out. Well, he ought to have gone five and twenty years ago! He couldn't manage his estate and he kept me out. I was like to hang about until I rotted, while the creature played at Patience, propped up against the table and the wall. A nigger, on a search for shillings, knocks him on the head. Shall I hunt the nigger down and hang him? Damme! I would rather get him a patent of state lands!"

The face of Randolph was a study in expression.

"But, sir," he said, "there are some things about this affair that are peculiar—I may say extraordinarily peculiar."

Again the old man stood still. When he spoke his voice was in a lower note.

"And so," he said, "you have nosed out a new clew and got Abner over, and we are to have another inquisition."

He reflected, moving his stick idly before him. Then he went on in a petulant, persuasive tone.

"Why can't you let sleeping dogs lie? The country is beginning to forget this affair, and you set about to stir it up. Shall I always have the thing clanking at my heels like a ball and chain?"

Then he rang the paved court with the ferrule of his stick.

"Damme, man!" he cried. "Has Virginia no mysteries, that you yap forever on old scents at Eastwood? What does it matter who did this thing? It was a public service. Virginia needs a few men on her lands with a bit of courage. This state is rotten with old timber. In youth, Duncan Moore was a fool. In age, he was better dead. Let there be an end to this, Randolph."

And he turned about and went back into the county clerk's office.

Randolph was a justice of the peace in Virginia. He looked a moment after the departing figure; then he spoke to his companion.

"He is here to have the lands of Duncan Moore transferred on the assessor's book to his own name. He takes the estate under the Life and Lives statute of Virginia, that the legislature got up to soften the rigor of Mr. Jefferson's Statute of Descents. Under it, this estate with its great English manor house was devised by the original ancestor to Duncan Moore for his life, and after him to Northcote Moore for his life, and at his death to Esdale Moore. It could have run twenty-one years farther if the scrivener had known the statute. Mr. Jefferson did not entirely decapitate the law of entail."

He paused and lifted his finger with a curious gesture.

"It is a queer family—I think the very queerest in Virginia. There is something defective about every one of them. Duncan Moore, the decedent, had no children. His two brothers died epileptics. This man, the son of the elder brother, is blind. And the son of the junior, Mr. Esdale Moore, the attorney-at-law——"

The Justice of the Peace was interrupted. A little dapper man, sunburned and bareheaded, dressed like a tailor's print, but with the smart, aggressive air of a well-bred colonial Englishman, pushed through the crowd and clapped the Justice on the shoulder.

"What luck, Randolph?" he cried. "I am sure Abner has run the assassin to cover." And he bobbed his head to Abner like one whose profession permits a certain familiarity. "Come along to the tavern; 'I would listen to your wondrous tales,' as Homer says it."

He led the way, calling out to a member of the bar, hailing an acquaintance, and hurling banter about him in the bluff, hearty fashion which he imagined to be the correct manner of a man of the people who is getting on. He was in the strength and vigor of his race at forty.

"Beastly dull, Randolph," he rattled; "nothing exciting since the dawn expect old Baron-Vitch's endless suit in chancery. But one must sit tight, rain or shine. The people must know where to find a lawyer when they want him."

He swung along with a big military stride.

"The life of a lawyer is far from jolly. I should like to cut it, Randolph, if I had a good shooting and a bit of trout water. Alas, I am poor!" And he made a dramatic gesture.

One felt that under this froth the man was calling out the truth. For all his hearty interest in affairs, the law was merely a sort of game. It was nothing real. He played to win, and he had chosen his profession with care and after long reflection, as a breeder chooses a colt for the Derby, or as an English family of influence selects a crack regiment for the heir at Oxford. He cared not one penny what the laws were or the great policies of Virginia. But he did care, with an inbred and abiding interest, about the value of a partridge shooting, or the damming of a trout stream by the grist mills. These things were the realities of life, and not the actions at law or the suits in chancery.

"How does one get a fortune nowadays, Abner?" he called back across his shoulder, "for I need one like the devil. Marriage or crime, eh? Crime requires a certain courage, and they say out in the open that lawyers are decadent. With you and Randolph on the lookout, I should be afraid to go in for crime!"

He clapped a passing giant on the back, called him Harrison, accused him of having an eye on Congress, and went on across his shoulder to Abner:

"Marriage, then? Do you know a convenient orphan with a golden goose? Pleasure and a certain gain would be idyllic! The simplest men understand that. Do not the writers in Paris tell us that the French peasant on his marriage night, while embracing his bride with one arm, extends the other in order to feel the sack that contains her dowry?"

They were now on the upper floor of the tavern porch. Mr. Esdale Moore sent a Negro for a dish of tea, after the English fashion.

Then he got a table at the end of the porch, somewhat apart, and the three men sat down.

"And now, Randolph," he said, "what did you find in Eastwood?"

"I am afraid," replied the Justice of the Peace, "that we found little new there. The evidence remains, with trifling additions, what it was; but Abner has arrived at some interesting opinions upon this evidence."

"I am sure Abner can clap his hand on the assassin," said the attorney. "Come, sir, let me fill your cup, and while I stand on one foot, as St. Augustine used to say, tell me who ejected my uncle, the venerable Duncan Moore, out of life."

The Negro servant had returned with a great silver pot, and a tray of cups with queer kneeling purple cows on them.

Abner held out his cup.

"Sir," he said, "one must be very certain, to answer that question." His voice was deep and level, like some balanced element in nature.

He waited while the man filled the cup; then he replaced it on the table.

"And, sir," he continued slowly, "I am not yet precisely certain."

He slipped a lump of sugar slowly into the cup.

"It is the Ruler of Events who knows, sir; we can only conjecture. We cannot see the truth naked before us as He does; we must grope for it from one indication to another until we find it."

"But, reason, Abner," interrupted the lawyer, bustling in his chair; "we have that, and God has nothing better!"

"Sir," replied Abner, "I cannot think of God depending on a thing so crude as reason. If one reflects upon it, I think one will immediately see that reason is a quality exclusively peculiar to the human mind. It is a thing that God could never, by any chance, require. Reason is the method by which those who do not know the truth, step by step, finally discover it."

He paused and looked out across the table at the far-off mountains.

"And so, sir, God knows who in Virginia has a red hand from this work at Eastwood Court, without assembling the evidence and laboring to determine whither these signboards point. But Randolph and I are like children with a puzzle. We must get all the pieces first, and then sit down and laboriously fit them up."

He looked down into his cup, his face in repose and reflective.

"Ah, sir," he went on, "if one could be certain that one had always every piece, there would no longer remain such a thing as a human mystery. Every event dovetails into every other event that precedes and follows. With the pieces complete, the truth could never elude us. But, alas, sir, human intelligence is feeble and easily deludes itself, and the relations and ramifications of events are vast and intricate."

"Then, sir," said Mr. Esdale Moore, "you do not believe that the criminal can create a series of false evidences that will be at all points consistent with the truth."

"No man can do it," replied Abner. "For to do that, one must know everything that goes before and everything that follows the event which one is attempting to falsify. And this omniscience only the intelligence of God can compass. It is impossible for the human mind to manufacture a false consistency of events except to a very limited extent."

"Then, gentlemen," cried the lawyer, "you can make me no excuse for leaving this affair a mystery."

"Yes," replied my uncle, "we could make you an excuse—a valid and sound excuse: the excuse of incompetency."

Mr. Esdale Moore laughed in his big, hearty voice.

"With your reputation, Abner, and that of Squire Randolph in Virginia, I should refuse to receive it."

"Alas," continued Abner, "we are no better than other men. A certain experience, some knowledge of the habits of criminals, and a little skill in observation are the only advantages we have. If one were born among us with, let us say, a double equipment of skull space, no criminal would ever escape him."

"He would laugh at us, Abner," said the Justice.

"He would never cease to laugh," returned my uncle, "but he would laugh the loudest at the bungling criminal. To him, the most cunning crime would be a botch; fabricated events would be conspicuous patch-work, and he would see the identity of the criminal agent in a thousand evidences."

He hesitated a moment; then he added:

"Fortunately for human society, the inconsistency of false evidence is usually so glaring that any one of us is able to see it."

"As in Lord William Russell's case," said the Justice, "where the valet, having killed his master in such a manner as to create the aspect of suicide, inadvertently carried away the knife with which his victim was supposed to have cut his own throat."

"Precisely," said Abner. "And there is, I think, in every case something equally inconsistent, if we only look close enough to find it."

He turned to Mr. Esdale Moore.

"With a little observation, sir, to ascertain the evidence, and a little common sense to interpret its intent, Randolph and I manage to get on."

The lawyer put a leading question.

"What glaring inconsistency did you find at Eastwood?" he said.

Abner looked at Randolph, as though for permission to go on. The Justice nodded.

"Why, this thing, sir," he answered, "that a secretary that was not locked should be broken open."

"But, Abner," said the lawyer, "who, but myself, knew that this secretary was not locked? It was the custom to lock it, although it contained nothing but my uncle's playing cards. As I told Randolph, on the day of my uncle's death I put the key down among the litter of papers inside the secretary, after I had opened it, and could not find it again, so I merely closed the lid. But I alone knew this. Everybody else would imagine the secretary to be locked as usual."

"Not everybody," continued my uncle. "Reflect a n ment: To believe the secretary locked on this night, one must have known that it was locked on every preceding night. To believe that it was locked on this night because the lid was closed, one must have known that it was always locked on every preceding night when the lid was closed. And further, sir, one must have known this custom so well—one must have been so certain of it—that one knew it was not worth while to attempt to open the secretary by pulling down the lid on the chance that it might not be locked, and so, broke it open at once.

"Now, sir," he went on, "does this not exclude the theory that Duncan Moore was killed by a common burglar who entered the house for the purpose of committing a robbery? Such a criminal agent could not have known this custom. He might have believed the secretary to be locked, or imagined it to be, but he could not have known it conclusively. He could not have been so certain that he would fail to lay hold of the lid to make sure. One must assume the lowest criminal will act with some degree of intelligence."

"By Jove!" cried the attorney, striking the table, "I had a feeling that my uncle was not killed by a common thief! I thought the authorities were not at the bottom of this thing, and that is why I kept at Randolph, why I urged him to get you out to Eastwood Court."

"Sir," replied Abner, "I am obliged to you for the compliment. But your feeling was justified, and your persistence in this case will, I think, be rewarded.

"Nevertheless, sir, if you will pardon the digression, permit me to say that your remark interests me profoundly. Whence, I wonder, came this feeling that caused you to reject the obvious explanation and to urge a further and more elaborate inquiry?"

"Now, Abner," returned Mr. Esdale Moore, "I cannot answer that question. The thing was a kind of presentiment. I had a sort of feeling, as we express it. I cannot say more than that."

"I have had occasion," continued Abner, "to examine the theory of presentiments, and I find that we are forced to one of two conclusions: Either they are of an origin exterior to the individual, of which we have no reliable proof, or they are founded upon some knowledge of which the correlation in the mind is, for the moment, obscure. That is to say, a feeling, presentiment, or premonition, may be a sort of shadow thrown by an unformed conclusion.

"An unconscious or subconscious mental process produces an impression. We take this impression to be from behind the stars, when, in fact, it merely indicates the rational conclusion at which we would have arrived if we had made a strong, conscious effort to understand the enigma before us."

He drank a little tea and put the cup back gently on the table.

"Perhaps, sir, if you had gone forward with the mental processes that produced your premonition, you would have worked out the solution of this mystery. Why, I wonder, did your deductions remain subconscious?"

"That is a question in mental science," replied the lawyer.

"Is not all science mental?" continued my uncle. "Do not men take their facts in a bag to the philosopher that he may put them together? Let us reflect a moment, sir: Are not the primitive emotions—as, for example, fear—in their initial stages always subconscious, or, as we say, instinctive? Thus, a thousand times in the day do not our bodies draw back from danger of which we are wholly unconscious? We do not go forward into these perils, and we pass on with no realization of their existence. Can we doubt, sir, that the mind also instinctively perceives danger at the end of certain mental processes and does not go forward upon them?"

The lawyer regarded my uncle in a sort of wonder.

"Abner," he said, "you forget my activities in this affair. It is I who have kept at Randolph. What instinctive fear, then, could have mentally restrained me?"

"Why, sir," replied Abner, "the same fear that instinctively restrained Randolph and myself."

Mr. Esdale Moore looked my uncle in the face.

"What fear?" he said.

"The fear," continued Abner, "of what these deductions lead to."

Abner moved his chair a little nearer to the table and went on in a lower voice.

"Now, sir, if we exclude the untenable hypothesis that this crime was committed by an unknown thief, from the motive of robbery, what explanation remains? Let us see: This secretary could have been broken open only by some one who knew that it was the custom to keep it locked. Who was certain of that custom? Obviously, sir, only those in the household of the aged Duncan Moore."

The face of the lawyer showed a profound interest. He leaned over, put his right elbow on the table, rested his chin in the trough of the thumb and finger, and with his other hand, took a box of tobacco cigarettes from his pocket and began to break it open. It was one of the elegancies of that day.

Abner went on, "Was it a servant at Eastwood Court?"

He paused, and Randolph interrupted.

"On the night of this tragedy," said the Justice of the Peace, "all the Negroes in the household attended a servants' ball on a neighboring estate. They went in a body and returned in a body. The aged Duncan Moore was alive when they left the house, and dead when they returned."

"But, Randolph," Abner went on, "independent of this chance event, conclusive in itself—which I feel is an accident to which we are hardly entitled—do not our inferences legitimately indicate a criminal agent other than a servant at Eastwood Court?

"Sane men do not commit violent crimes without a motive. There was no motive to move any servant except that of gain, and there was no gain to be derived from the death of the aged Duncan Moore, except that to be got from rifling his secretary. But the one who knew so much about this secretary that he was certain it was locked, would also have known enough about it to know that it contained nothing of value."

He hesitated and moved the handle of his cup.

"Now, sir," he added, "two persons remain."

The lawyer, fingering the box of cigarettes, broke it open and presented them to my uncle and Randolph. He lighted one, and over the table looked Abner in the face.

"You mean Northcote Moore and myself," he said in a firm, even voice. "Well, sir, which one was it?"

My uncle remained undisturbed.

"Sir," he said, "there was at least a pretense of consistency in the work of the one who manufactured the evidences of a burglar. There was a window open in the north wing at the end of the long, many-cornered passage that leads through Eastwood Court to the room in the south wing where the aged Duncan Moore was killed. Now some one had gone along that passage, as you pointed out to Randolph when Eastwood Court was first inspected, because there were finger-prints on the walls at the turns and angles. These finger-prints were marked in the dust on the walls of the passage on the east side, but on the west side, beginning heaviest near Duncan Moore's room, the prints were in blood.

"These marks on the wall show that the assassin did, in fact, enter by this passage and return along it. But he did not enter by the open window. The frame of this window was cemented into the casement with dust. This dust was removed only on the inside. Moreover, violence had been used to force it open, and the marks of this violence were all plainly visible on the inside of the frame."

He stopped, remained a moment silent, and then continued:

"This corridor is the usual and customary way—in fact, the only way leading from the north wing of Eastwood Court to the south wing. Duncan Moore alone occupied the south wing. And, sir, on this night, Northcote Moore and yourself alone occupied the north wing. You were both equally familiar with this passage, since you lived in the house, and used it constantly."

Abner paused and looked at Mr. Esdale Moore.

"Shall I go on, sir?" he said.

"Pray do," replied the lawyer.

Abner continued, in his deep, level voice.

"Now, sir, you will realize why Randolph and I felt an instinctive fear of the result of these deductions, and perhaps, sir, why your subconscious conclusions went no further than a premonition."

"But the law of Virginia," put in the Justice, "is no respecter of persons. If the Governor should do a murder, his office would not save him from the gallows."

"It would not," said the lawyer. "Go on, Abner."

My uncle moved slightly in his chair.

"If the aged Duncan Moore were removed," he continued, "Northcote Moore would take the manor-house and the lands. For Esdale Moore to take the estate, both the aged Duncan Moore and the present incumbent must be removed. Only the aged Duncan Moore was removed. Who was planning a gain, then, by this criminal act? Esdale Moore or Northcote Moore?

"Another significant thing: Mr. Esdale Moore knew this secretary was unlocked on this night; Northcote Moore did not. Who, then, was the more likely to break it open as evidence of a presumptive robbery?

"And, finally, sir, who would grope along this corridor feeling with his hands for the corners and angles of the wall, one who could see, or a blind man?"

My uncle stopped and sat back in his chair.

The lawyer leaned over and put both arms on the table.

"Gentlemen," he said, since he addressed both Randolph and Abner, "you amaze me! You accuse the most prominent man in Virginia."

"Before the law," said the Justice, "all men are equal."

The lawyer turned toward my uncle, as to one of more consideration.

"While you were making your deductions," he said, "I had to insist that you go on, for I was myself included. I was bound to hear you to the end, although you shocked me at every step. But now, I beg you to reflect. Northcote Moore belongs to an ancient and honorable family. He is old; he is blind. Surely something can be done to save him."

"Nothing," replied the Justice firmly.

Abner lifted his face, placid, unmoving, like a mask.

"Perhaps," he said.

The two men before him at the table moved with astonishment.

"Perhaps!" cried the Justice of the Peace. "This is Virginia!"

But it was the lawyer who was the more amazed. He had not moved; he did not move; but his face, as by some sorcery, became suddenly perplexed.

The tavern was now deserted; every one had gone back into the courthouse. The three men were alone. There was silence except for the noises of the village and the far-off hum of winged insects in the air. Mr. Esdale Moore sat facing north along the upper porch; Abner opposite; Randolph looking eastward toward the courthouse. My uncle did not go on at once. He reached across the table for one of the tobacco cigarettes. The lawyer mechanically took up the box with his hand nearest to the Justice of the Peace and opened the lid with his thumb and finger. Abner selected one but did not light it.

"Writers on the law," he began, "warn us against the obvious inference when dealing with the intelligent criminal agent, and for this reason: while the criminal of the lowest order seeks only to cover his identity, and the criminal of the second order to indicate another rather than himself, the criminal of the first order, sir, will sometimes undertake a subtle finesse—a double intention.

"The criminal of the lowest order gives the authorities no one to suspect. The criminal of the second order sets up a straw man before his own door, hoping to mislead the authorities. But the criminal of the first order sets it before the door of another, expecting the authorities of the state to knock it down and take the man behind it.

"Now, sir,"—my uncle paused—"looked at from this quarter, do not our obvious deductions lack a certain conclusiveness?

"If Northcote Moore were hanged for murder, Esdale Moore would take the manor-house and the landed estate.

Therefore, he might wish Northcote Moore hanged, just as Northcote Moore might wish Duncan Moore murdered.

"And, if one were deliberately placing a straw man, would there be any inconsistency in breaking open a secretary obviously unlocked? The straw, sir, would be only a trifle more conspicuous!

"And the third deduction"—his gray eyes narrowed, and he spoke slowly: "If one born blind, and another, were accustomed to go along a passage day after day; in the dark, who would grope, feeling his way in the night, step by step, along the angles of the wall—the one who could see, or the blind man?"

The amazed Justice struck the table with his clenched hand.

"By the gods," he cried, *"not the blind man!* For to the blind man, the passage was always dark!"

The lawyer had not moved, but his face, in its desperate perplexity, began to sweat. The Justice swung around upon him, but Abner put out his hand.

"A moment, Randolph," he said. "The human body is a curious structure. It has two sides, as though two similar mechanisms were joined with a central trunk—the dexter side, or that which is toward the south when the man is facing the rising sun, and the sinister side, or that which is toward the north. These sides are not coequal. One of them is controlling and dominates the man, and when the task before him is difficult, it is with this more efficient controlling side that he approaches it.

"Thus, one set on murder and desperately anxious to make no sound, to make no false step, to strike no turn or angle, would instinctively follow the side of the wall that he could feel along with his controlling hand. This passage runs north and south. The bloody finger-prints are all on the west side of the wall, the prints in the dust on the east side; therefore, the assassin followed the east side of the wall when he set out on his deadly errand, and the west side when he returned with the blood on him.

"That is to say," and his voice lifted into a stronger note, "he always followed the left side of the wall.

"Why, sir?" And he got on his feet, his voice ringing, his finger pointing at the sweating, cornered man. "Because his controlling side was on the left—because he was left handed!

"And you, sir—I have been watching you——"

The pent-up energies of Mr. Esdale Moore seemed to burst asunder.

"It's a lie!" he cried.

And he lunged at Abner across the table, with his clenched *left* hand.

Chapter 14

The Mystery of Chance

IT WAS a night like the pit. The rain fell steadily. Now and then a gust of wind rattled the shutters, and the tavern sign, painted with the features of George the Third, now damaged by musket-balls and with the eyes burned out, creaked.

The tavern sat on the bank of the Ohio. Below lay the river and the long, flat island, where the ill-starred Blennerhasset had set up his feudal tenure. Flood water covered the island and spread everywhere—a vast sea of yellow that enveloped the meadow-lands and plucked at the fringe of the forest.

The scenes in the tavern were in striking contrast. The place boomed with mirth, shouts of laughter, ribald tales and songs. The whole crew of the *Eldorado* of New Orleans banqueted in the guest-room of the tavern. This was the open room for the public. Beyond it and facing the river was the guest-room for the gentry, with its floor scrubbed with sand, its high-boy in veneered mahogany, its polished andirons and its various pretensions to a hostelry of substance.

At a table in this room, unmindful of the bedlam beyond him, a man sat reading a pamphlet. He leaned over on the table, between two tall brass candlesticks, his elbows on the board, his thumb marking the page. He had the dress and manner of a gentleman—excellent cloth in his coat, a rich stock and imported linen. On the table sat a top hat of the time, and in the corner by the driftwood fire was a portmanteau with silver buckles, strapped up as for a journey. The man was under forty, his features regular and clean-cut; his dark brows joined above eyes big and blue and wholly out of place in the olive skin.

Now and then he got up, went over to the window and looked out, but he was unable to see anything, for the rain continued and the puffs of wind. He seemed disturbed and uneasy. He drummed on the sill with his fingers, and then, with a glance at his portmanteau, returned to his chair between the two big tallow candles.

From time to time the tavern-keeper looked in at the door with some servile inquiry. This interruption annoyed the guest.

"Damme, man," he said, "are you forever at the door?"

"Shall I give the crew rum, sir?" the landlord asked.

"No," replied the man; "I will not pay your extortions for imported liquor."

"They wish it, sir."

The man looked up from his pamphlet.

"They wish it, eh," he said with nice enunciation. "Well, Mr. Castoe, I do not!"

The soft voice dwelt on the "Mr. Castoe" with ironical emphasis. The mobile upper lip, shadowed with a silken mustache, lifted along the teeth with a curious feline menace.

The man was hardly over his table before the door opened again. He turned abruptly, like a panther, but when he saw who stood in the door, he arose with a formal courtesy.

"You are a day early, Abner," he said. "Are the Virginia wagons in for their salt and iron?"

"They will arrive to-morrow," replied my uncle; "the roads are washed out with the rains."

The man looked at my uncle, his hat and his greatcoat splashed with mud.

"How did you come?" he asked.

"Along the river," replied my uncle, "I thought to find you on the *Eldorado*."

"On the *Eldorado!*" cried the man. "On such a night, when the Tavern of George the Third has a log fire and kegs in the cellar!"

My uncle entered, closed the door, took off his greatcoat and hat, and sat down by the hearth.

"The boat looked deserted," he said.

"To the last nigger," said the man. "I could not take the comforts of the tavern and deny them to the crew."

My uncle warmed his hands over the snapping fire.

"A considerate heart, Byrd," he said, with some deliberation, "is a fine quality in a man. But how about the owners of your cargo, and the company that insures your boat?"

"The cargo, Abner," replied the man, "is in Benton's warehouse, unloaded for your wagons. The boat is tied up in the back-water. No log can strike it."

He paused and stroked his clean-cut, aristocratic jaw.

"The journey down from Fort Pitt was damnable," he added, "—miles of flood water, yellow and running with an accursed current. It was no pleasure voyage, believe me, Abner. There was the current running logs, and when we got in near the shore, the settlers fired on us. A careless desperado, your settler, Abner!"

"More careless, Byrd, do you think," replied my uncle, "than the river captain who overturns the half-submerged cabins with the wash of his boat?"

"The river," said the man, "is the steamboat's highway."

"And the cabin," replied my uncle, "is the settler's home."

"One would think," said Byrd, "that this home was a palace and the swamp land a garden of the Hesperides, and your settler a King of the Golden Mountains. My stacks are full of bullet holes."

My uncle was thoughtful by the fire.

"This thing will run into a river war," he said. "There will be violence and murder done."

"A war, eh!" echoed the man. "I had not thought of that, and yet, I had but now an ultimatum. When we swung in tonight, a big backwoodsman came out in a canoe and delivered an oration. I have forgotten the periods, Abner, but he would burn me at the stake, I think, and send the boat to Satan, unless I dropped down the river and came in below the settlement."

He paused and stroked his jaw again with that curious gesture.

"But for the creature's command," he added, "I would have made the detour. But when he threatened, I ran in as I liked and the creature got a ducking for his pains. His canoe went bottom upward, and if he had not been a man of oak, he would have gone himself to Satan."

"And what damage did you do?" inquired my uncle.

"Why, no damage, as it happened," said the man. "Some cabins swayed, but not one of them went over. I looked, Abner, for a skirmish in your war. There was more than one rifle at a window. If I were going to follow the river," he continued, "I would mount a six-pounder."

"You will quit the river, then," remarked my uncle.

"It is a dog's life, Abner," said the man. "To make a gain in these days of Yankee trading, the owner must travel with his boat. Captains are a trifle too susceptible to bribe. I do not mean gold-pieces, slipped into the hand, but the hospitalities of the shopkeeper. Your Yankee, Abner, sees no difference in men, or he will waive it for a sixpence in his till. The captain is banqueted at his house, and the cargo is put on short. One cannot sit in comfort at New Orleans and trade along the Ohio."

"Is one, then, so happy in New Orleans?" asked my uncle.

"In New Orleans, no," replied the man, "but New Orleans is not the world. The world is in Piccadilly, where one can live among his fellows like a gentleman, and see something of life—a Venetian dancer, ladies of fashion, and men who dice for something more than a trader's greasy shillings."

Byrd again got up and went to the window. The rain and gusts of wind continued. His anxiety seemed visibly to increase.

My uncle arose and stood with his back to the driftwood fire, his hands spread out to the flame. He glanced at Byrd and at the pamphlet on the table, and the firm muscles of his mouth hardened into an ironical smile.

"Mr. Evlyn Byrd," he said, "what do you read?"

The man came back to the table. He sat down and crossed one elegant knee over the other.

"It is an essay by the Englishman, Mill," he said, "reprinted in the press that Benjamin Franklin set up at Philadelphia. I agree with Lord Fairfax where the estimable Benjamin is concerned: 'Damn his little maxims! They smack too much of New England!' But his press gives now and then an English thing worth while."

"And why is this English essay worth while?" asked my uncle.

"Because, Abner, in its ultimate conclusions, it is a justification of a gentleman's most interesting vice. 'Chance,' Mr. Mill demonstrates, 'is not only at the end of all our knowledge, but it is also at the beginning of all our postulates.' We begin with it, Abner, and we end with it. The structure of all our philosophy is laid down on the sills of chance and roofed over with the rafters of it."

"The Providence of God, then," said my uncle, "does not come into Mr. Mill's admirable essay."

Mr. Evlyn Byrd laughed.

"It does not, Abner," he said. "Things happen in this world by chance, and this chance is no aide-de-camp of your God. It happens unconcernedly to all men. It has no rogue to ruin and no good churchman, pattering his prayers, to save. A man lays his plans according to the scope and grasp of his intelligence, and this chance comes by to help him or to harm him, as it may happen, with no concern about his little morals, and with no divine intent."

"And so you leave God out," said my uncle, with no comment.

"And why not, Abner?" replied the man. "Is there any place in this scheme of nature for His intervention? Why, sir, the intelligence of man that your Scriptures so despise can easily put His little plan of rewards and punishments out of joint. Not the good, Abner, but the intelligent, possess the earth. The man who sees on all sides of his plan, and hedges it about with wise precaution, brings it to success. Every day the foresight of men outwits your God."

My uncle lifted his chin above his wet stock. He looked at the window with the night banked behind it, and then down at the refined and elegant gentleman in the chair beside the table, and then at the strapped-up portmanteau in the corner. His great jaw moved out under the massive chin. From his face, from his manner, he seemed about to approach some business of vital import. Then, suddenly, from the room beyond there came a great boom of curses, a cry that the dice had fallen against a platter, a blow and a gust of obscenities and oaths.

My uncle extended his arm toward the room.

"Your gentleman's vice," he said; "eh, Mr. Byrd!"

The man put out a jeweled hand and snuffed the candles.

"The vice, Abner, but not the gentlemen."

Mr. Byrd flicked a bit of soot from his immaculate sleeve. Then he made a careless gesture.

"These beasts," he said, "are the scum of New Orleans. They would bring any practice into disrepute. One cannot illustrate a theory by such creatures. Gaming, Abner, is the diversion of a gentleman; it depends on chance, even as all trading does. The Bishop of London has been unable to point out wherein it is immoral."

"Then," said Abner, "the Bishop does little credit to his intelligence."

"It has been discussed in the coffee-houses of New Orleans," replied Mr. Byrd, "and no worthy objection found."

"I think I can give you one," replied my uncle.

"And what is your objection, Abner?" asked the man.

"It has this objection, if no other," replied my uncle, "it encourages a hope of reward without labor, and it is this hope, Byrd, that fills the jail house with weak men, and sets strong ones to dangerous ventures."

He looked down at the man before him, and again his iron jaw moved.

"Byrd," he said, "under the wisdom of God, labor alone can save the world. It is everywhere before all benefits that we would enjoy. Every man must till the earth before he can eat of its fruits. He must fell the forest and let in the sun before his grain will ripen. He must spin and weave. And in his trading he must labor to carry his surplus stuff to foreign people, and to bring back what he needs from their abundance. Labor is the great condition of reward. And your gentleman's vice, Byrd, would annul it and overturn the world."

But the man was not listening to Abner's words. He was on his feet and again before the window. He had his jaw gathered into his hand. The man swore softly.

"What disturbs you, Byrd?" said my uncle.

He stood unmoving before the fire, his hands to the flame. The man turned quickly.

"It is the night, Abner—wind and driving rain. The devil has it!"

"The weather, Byrd," replied my uncle, "happens in your

philosophy by chance, so be content with what it brings you, for this chance regards, as you tell me, no man's plans; neither the wise man nor the fool hath any favor of it."

"Nor the just nor the unjust, Abner."

My uncle looked down at the floor. He locked his great bronze fingers behind his massive back.

"And so you believe, Byrd," he said. "Well, I take issue with you. I think this thing you call 'chance' is the Providence of God, and I think it favors the just."

"Abner," cried the man, now turning from the window, "if you believe that, you believe it without proof."

"Why, no," replied my uncle; "I have got the proof on this very night."

He paused a moment; then he went on.

"I was riding with the Virginia wagons," he said, "on the journey here. It was my plan to come on slowly with them, arriving on the morrow. But these rains fell; the road on this side of the Hills was heavy; and I determined to leave the wagons and ride in to-night.

"Now, call this what you like—this unforeseen condition of the road, this change of plan. Call it 'chance,' Byrd!"

Again he paused and his big jaw tightened.

"But it is no chance, sir, nor any accidental happening that Madison of Virginia, Simon Carroll of Maryland and my brother Rufus are upright men, honorable in their dealings and fair before the world.

"Now, sir, if this chance, this chance of my coming on to-night before the Virginia wagons, this accidental happening, favored Madison, Simon Carroll and my brother Rufus as though with a direct and obvious intent, as though with a clear and preconceived design, you will allow it to me as a proof, or, at least, Mr. Evlyn Byrd, as a bit of evidence, as a sort of indisputable sign, that honorable men, men who deal fairly with their fellows, have some favor of these inscrutable events."

The man was listening now with a careful attention. He came away from the window and stood beside the table, his clenched fingers resting on the board.

"What do you drive at, Abner?" he asked.

My uncle lifted his chin above the big wet stock.

"A proof of my contention, Byrd," he answered.

"But your story, Abner? What happened?"

My uncle looked down at the man.

"There is no hurry, Byrd," he said; "the night is but half advanced and you will not now go forward on your journey."

"My journey!" echoed the man. "What do you mean?"

"Why, this," replied my uncle: "that you would be setting out for Piccadilly, I imagine, and the dancing women, and the gentlemen who live by chance. But as you do not go now, we have ample leisure for our talk."

"Abner," cried Mr. Byrd, "what is this riddle?"

My uncle moved a little in his place before the fire.

"I left the Virginia wagons at midday," he went on; "night fell in the flatland; I could hardly get on; the mud was deep and the rains blew. The whole world was like the pit.

- "It is a common belief that a horse can see on any night, however dark, but this belief is error, like that which attributes supernatural perception to the beast. My horse went into the trees and the fence; now and then there was a candle in a window, but it did not lighten the world; it served only to accentuate the darkness. It seemed impossible to go forward on a strange road, now flooded. I thought more than once to stop in at some settler's cabin. But mark you, Byrd, I came on. Why? I cannot say. 'Chance,' Mr. Evlyn Byrd, if you like. I would call it otherwise. But no matter."

He paused a moment, and then continued:

"I came in by the river. It was all dark like the kingdom of Satan. Then, suddenly, I saw a light and your boat tied up. This light seemed somewhere inside, and its flame puzzled me. I got down from my horse and went onto the steamboat. I found no one, but I found the light. It was a fire just gathering under way. A carpenter had been at work; he had left some shavings and bits of candle, and in this line of rubbish the fire had started."

The man sat down in his chair beside the two tallow candles.

"Fire!" he said. "Yes, there was a carpenter at work in my

office cabin to-day. He left shavings, and perhaps bits of candle, it is likely. Was it in my office cabin?"

"Along the floor there," replied my uncle, "beginning to flame up."

"Along the floor!" repeated Mr. Byrd. "Then nothing in my cabin was burned? The wall desk, Abner, with the long mahogany drawer—it was not burned?"

He spoke with an eager interest.

"It was not burned," replied my uncle. "Did it contain things of value?"

"Of great value," returned the man.

"You leave, then, things of value strangely unprotected," replied my uncle. "The door was open."

"But not the desk, Abner. It was securely locked. I had that lock from Sheffield. No key would turn it but my own."

Byrd sat for some moments unmoving, his delicate hand fingering his chin, his lips parted. Then, as with an effort, he got back his genial manner.

"I thank you, Abner," he said. "You have saved my boat. And it was a strange coincidence that brought you there to do it."

Then he flung back in his big chair with a laugh.

"But your theory, Abner? This chance event does not support it. It is not the good or Christian that this coincidence has benefited. It is I, Abner, who am neither good nor Christian."

My uncle did not reply. His face remained set and reflective.

The rain beat on the window-pane, and the drunken feast went on in the room beyond him.

"Byrd," he said, "how do you think that fire was set? A half-burned cigar dropped by a careless hand, or an enemy?"

"An enemy, Abner," replied the man. "It will be the work of these damned settlers. Did not their envoy threaten if I should come in, to the peril of their cabins? I gave them no concern then, but I was wrong in that. I should have looked out for their venom. Still, they threaten with such ease and with no hand behind it that one comes, in time, to take no notice of their words."

He paused and looked up at the big man above him.

"What do you think, Abner? Was the fire set?"

"One cannot tell from the burning rubbish," replied my uncle.

"But your opinion, Abner?" said the man. "What is your opinion?"

"The fire was set," replied my uncle.

Byrd got up at that, and his clenched hand crashed on the table.

"Then, by the kingdom of Satan, I will overturn every settler's cabin when the boat goes out tomorrow."

My uncle gave no attention to the man's violence.

"You would do wanton injury to innocent men," he said. "The settlers did not fire your boat."

"How can you know that, Abner?"

My uncle changed. Vigor and energy and an iron will got into his body and his face.

"Byrd," he said, "we had an argument just now; let me recall it to your attention. You said 'chance' happened equally to all, and I that the Providence of God directs it. If I had failed to come on to-night, the boat would have burned. The settlers would have taken blame for it. And Madison of Virginia, Simon Carroll of Mayland and my brother Rufus, whose company at Baltimore insure your boat, would have met a loss they can ill afford."

His voice was hard and level like a sheet of light.

"Not you, Byrd, who, as you tell me, are neither good nor Christian, but these men, who are, would have settled for this loss. Is it the truth—eh, Mr. Evlyn Byrd?"

The man's big blue eyes widened in his olive skin.

"I should have claimed the insurance, of course, as I had the right to do," he said coldly, for he was not in fear. "But, Abner——"

"Precisely!" replied my uncle. "And now, Mr. Evlyn Byrd, let us go on. We had a further argument. You thought a man in his intelligence could outwit God. And, sir, you undertook to do it! With your crew drunken here, the boat deserted, the settlers to bear suspicion and your portmanteau packed up for your journey overland to Baltimore, you watched at that window to see the flames burst out."

The man's blue eyes—strange, incredible eyes in that olive skin—were now hard and expressionless as glass. His lips moved, and his hand crept up toward a bulging pocket of his satin waistcoat.

Grim, hard as iron, inevitable, my uncle went on:

"But you failed, Byrd! God outwitted you! When I put that fire out in the rubbish, the cabin was dark, and in the dark, Byrd, there, I saw a gleam of light shining through the keyhole of your wall desk—the desk that you alone can open, that you keep so securely locked. Three bits of candle were burning in that empty drawer."

The man's white hand approached the bulging pocket.

And my uncle's voice rang as over a plate of steel.

"Outwit God!" he cried. "Why, Byrd, you had forgotten a thing that any schoolboy could have told you. You had forgotten that a bit of candle in a drawer, for lack of air, burns more slowly than a bit outside. Your pieces set to fire the rubbish were consumed, but your pieces set in that locked drawer to make sure—to outwit God, if, by chance, the others failed—were burning when I burst the lid off."

The man's nimble hand, lithe like a snake, whipped a derringer out of his bulging pocket.

But, quicker than that motion, quicker than light, quicker than the eye, my uncle was upon him. The derringer fell harmless to the floor. The bones of the man's slender fingers snapped in an iron palm. And my uncle's voice, big, echoing like a trumpet, rang above the storm and the drunken shouting:

"Outwit God! Why, Mr. Evlyn Byrd, you cannot outwit me, who am the feeblest of His creatures!"

Chapter 15

The Concealed Path

It was night, and the first snow of October was in the air when my uncle got down from his horse before the door. The great stone house sat on a bench of the mountains. Behind it lay the forest, and below, the pasture land of the Hills.

After the disastrous failure of Prince Charles Edward Stuart to set up his kingdom in Scotland, more than one great Highland family had fled oversea to Virginia, and for a hundred years had maintained its customs. It was at the house of such a family that my uncle stopped.

There was the evidence of travel hard and long on my uncle and his horse. An old man bade him enter.

"Who is here?" said my uncle.

The servant replied with two foreign words, meaning "The Red Eagle" in the Gaelic tongue.

And he led my uncle through the hall into the dining-room. It was a scene laid back a hundred years in Skye that he came on. A big woman of middle age dined alone, in a long, beamed room, lighted with tallow candles. An ancient servant stood behind her chair.

Two features of the woman were conspicuous—her bowed nose and her coarse red hair.

She got up when she saw my uncle.

"Abner," she cried, "by the Blessed God I am glad to see you! Come in! Come in!"

My uncle entered, and she put him beyond her at the table.

"You ought to eat, Abner," she said; "for by all the tokens, you have traveled."

"A long way," replied my uncle.

"And did the ravens of Elijah send you to me?" said the woman. "For I need you."

"What need?" inquired my uncle, while he attacked the rib of beef and the baked potatoes, for the dinner, although set with some formality, was plain.

"Why, this need, Abner: For a witness whose name will stand against the world."

"A witness!" repeated my uncle.

"Aye, a witness," continued the woman. "The country holds me hard and dour, and given to impose my will. There will be a wedding in my house to-night, and I would have you see it, free of pressure. My niece, Margaret McDonald, has got her senses finally."

My uncle looked down at the cloth.

"Who is the man?" he said.

"Campbell," she answered, "and good man enough for a stupid woman."

For a moment my uncle did not move. His hands, his body, the very muscles in his eyelids, were for that moment inert as plaster. Then he went on with the potato and the rib of beef.

"Campbell is here, then?" he said.

"He came to-night," replied the woman, "and for once the creature has some spirit. He will have the girl to-night or never. He and my husband Allen Eliott, have driven their cattle out of the glades and on the way to Baltimore. Allen is with the cattle on the Cumberland road, and Campbell rode hard in here to take the girl or to leave her. And whether she goes or stays, he will not return. When the cattle are sold in Baltimore, he will take a ship out of the Chesapeake for Glasgow."

She paused and made a derisive gesture.

"The devil, Abner, or some witch trick, has made a man of Campbell. He used to be irresolute and sullen, but to-night he has the spirit of the men who lifted cattle in the lowlands. He is a Campbell of Glen Lion on this night. Believe me, Abner, the wavering beastie is now as hard as oak, and has the devil's courage. Wherefore is it that a man can change like that?"

"A man may hesitate between two masters," replied my uncle, "and be only weak, but when he finally makes his choice he will get what his master has to give him—the courage of heaven, if he go that way, or of hell, Madam, if he go that way."

"Man! Man!" she laughed. "If 'the one who is not to be named,' as we say, put his spirit into Campbell, he did a grand work. It is the wild old cattle-lifter of Glen Lion that he is the night!"

"Do you think," said my uncle, "that a McDonald of Glencoe ought to be mated with a Campbell of Glen Lion?"

The woman's face hardened.

"Did Lord Stair and the Campbells of Glen Lion massacre the McDonalds of Glencoe on yesterday at sunrise, or two hundred years back? Margaret—the fool!—said that before she got my final word."

"Is it not in an adage," said my uncle, "that the Highlander does not change?"

"But the world changes, Abner," replied the woman. "Campbell is not 'Bonnie Charlie'; he is at middle age, a dour man and silent, but he will have a sum of money from a half of the cattle, and he can take care of this girl."

Then she cried out in a sharper voice:

"And what is here in this mountain for her, will you tell me? We grow poor! The old men are to feed. Allen owes money that his half of the cattle will hardly pay. Even old MacPherson"—and she indicated the ancient man behind her chair—"has tried to tell her, in his wise-wife folderol, 'I see you in the direst peril that overtakes a lassie, and a big shouldered man to save you.' And it was no omen, Abner, but the vision of his common sense. Here are the lean years to dry out the fool's youth, and surely Campbell is big shouldered enough for any prophecy. And now, Abner, will you stay and be a witness?"

"I will be one witness," replied my uncle slowly, "if you will send for my brother Rufus to be another."

The woman looked at her guest in wonder.

"That would be twenty miles through the Hills," she said. "We could not get Rufus by the morn's morn."

"No," said Abner, "it would be three miles to Maxwell's Tavern. Rufus is there to-night."

The big-nosed, red-haired woman drummed on the cloth with the tips of her fingers, and one knew what she was thinking. Her relentless will was the common talk. What she wished she forced with no concern.

But the girl was afraid of Campbell. The man seemed evil to her. It was not evidenced in any act. It was instinct in the girl. She felt the nature of the man like some venomous thing pretending to be gentle until its hour. And this fear, dominant and compelling, gave her courage to resist the woman's will.

The long suit of Campbell for the girl was known to everybody, and the woman's favor of it and the girl's resistance. The woman foresaw what folk in the Hills would say, and she wished to forestall that gossip by the presence in her house of men whose word could not be gainsaid. If Abner and his brother Rufus were here, no report of pressure on the girl could gain belief.

She knew what reports her dominating personality set current. She, and not her husband, was the head of their affairs, and with an iron determination she held to every Highland custom, every form, every feudal detail that she could, against the detritus of democratic times and ridicule, and the gain upon her house of poverty, and lean years. She was alone at that heavy labor. Allen Eliott was a person without force. He was usually on his cattle range in the mountains, with his big partner Campbell, or in the great drive, as now, to Baltimore. And she had the world to face.

"That will be to wait," she said, "and Campbell is in haste, and the bride is being made ready by the women, and the minister is got . . . to Maxwell's Tavern!"

Then she arose.

"Well, I will make a bargain with you. I will send for Rufus, but you must gain Campbell over to the waiting. And you must gain him, Abner, by your own devices, for I will not tell him that I have sent out for a witness to the freedom of my niece in this affair. If you can make him wait, the thing shall wait until Rufus is come. But I will turn no hand to help.

"Is Campbell in the house?" said my uncle.

"Yes," she said, "and ready when the minister is come."

"Is he alone?" said Abner.

"Alone," she said, with a satirical smile, "as a bridegroom ought to be for his last reflections."

"Then," replied my uncle, "I will strike the bargain."

She laughed in a heavy chuckle, like a man.

"Hold him if you can. It will be a pretty undertaking, Abner, and practice for your wits. But by stealth it shall be. I will not have you bind the bridegroom like the strong man in the Scriptures." And the chuckle deepened. "And that, too, I think, might be no easier than the finesse you set at. He is a great man in the body, like yoursel'."

She stood up to go out, but before she went, she said another word.

"Abner," she said, "you will not blame me," and her voice was calm. "Somebody must think a little for these pretty fools. They are like the lilies of the field in their lack of wisdom; they will always bloom, and there is no winter! Why, man, they have no more brain than a haggis! And what are their little loves against the realities of life? And their tears, Abner, are like the rains in summer, showering from every cloud. And their heads crammed with folderol—a prince will come, and they cannot take a good man for that dream!" She paused and added:

"I will go and send for Rufus. And when you have finished with your dinner, MacPherson will take you in to Campbell."

The woman was hardly gone before the old man slipped over to Abner's chair.

"Mon," he whispered, "ha'e ye a wee drop?"

"No liquor, MacPherson," said my uncle.

The old man's bleared eyes blinked like a half-blinded owl's.

"It would be gran', a wee drop, the night," he said.

"For joy at the wedding," said my uncle.

"Na, mon, na, mon!" Then he looked swiftly around.

"The eagle ha beak and talons, and what ha the dove, mon?"

"What do you mean, MacPherson?" said my uncle.

The old creature peered across the table.

"Ye ha gran' shoulders, mon," he said.

My uncle put down his fork.

"MacPherson," he said, "what do you beat about?"

G*

"I wa borned," he replied, "wi a cowl, and I can see!"

"And what do you see?" inquired Abner.

"A vulture flying," said the old man, "but it is unco dark beneath him."

Again on this night every motion and every sign of motion disappeared from my uncle's body and his face. He remained for a moment like a figure cut in wood.

"A vulture!" he echoed.

"Aye, mon! What ha the dove to save it?"

"The vulture, it may be," said my uncle.

"The Red Eagle, and the foul vulture!" cried the old man. "Noo, mon, it is the bird of death!"

"A bird of death, but not a bird of prey." Then he got up.

"You may have a familiar spirit, MacPherson," he said coldly, "for all I know. Perhaps they live on after the Witch of Endor. It is a world of mystery. But I should not come to you to get up Samuel, and I see now why the Lord stamped out your practice. It was because you misled his people. If there is a vulture in this business, MacPherson, it is no symbol of your bridegroom. And now, will take me in to Campbell?"

The old man flung the door open, and Abner went out into the hall. As he crossed the sill, a girl, listening at the door, fled past him. She had been crouched down against it.

She was half-dressed, all in white, as though escaped for a moment out of the hands of tiring women. But she had the chalk face of a ghost, and eyes wide with fear.

My uncle went on as though he had passed nothing, and the old Scotchman before him only wagged his head, with the whispered comment, "It wa be gran', a wee drop, the night."

They came into a big room of the house with candles on a table, and a fire of chestnut logs. A man walking about stopped on the hearth. He was a huge figure of a man in middle life.

A fierce light leaped up in his face when he saw my uncle.

"Abner!" he cried. "Why does the devil bring you here?"

"It would be strange, Campbell," replied my uncle, "if the devil were against you. The devil has been much maligned. He is very nearly equal, the Scriptures tell us, to the King of Kings. He is no fool to mislead his people and to trap his servants. I find him always zealous in their interests, Campbell, fertile in devices, and holding hard with every trick to save them. I do not admire the devil, Mr. Campbell, but I do not find his vice to be a lack of interest in his own."

"Then," cried Campbell, "it is clear that I am not one of his own. For if the devil were on my side, Abner, he would have turned you away from this door to-night."

"Why, no," replied my uncle, with a reflective air, "that does not follow. I do not grant the devil a supreme control. There is One above him, and if he cannot always manage as his people wish, they shall not for that reason condemn him with a treasonable intent."

The man turned with a decisive gesture.

"Abner," he said, "let me understand this thing. Do you come here upon some idle gossip, to interfere with me in this marriage? Or by chance?"

"Neither the one nor the other," replied my uncle. "I went into the mountains to buy the cattle you and Eliott range there. I found you gone already, with the herd, toward Maryland. And so, as I returned, I rode in here to Eliott's house to rest and to feed my horse."

"Eliott is with the drove," said Campbell.

"No," replied my uncle, "Eliott is not with the drove. I overtook it on the Cheat River. The drivers said you hired them this morning, and rode away."

The man shifted his feet and looked down at my uncle.

"It is late in the season," he said. "One must go ahead to arrange for a field and for some shocks of fodder. Eliott is ahead."

"He is not on the road ahead," returned Abner. "Arnold and his drovers came that way from Maryland, and they had not seen him."

"He did not go the road," said Campbell; "he took a path through the mountains.".

My uncle remained silent for some moments.

"Campbell," said my uncle, "the Scriptures tell us that there is a path which the vulture's eye hath not seen. Did Eliott take that path?"

The man changed his posture.

"Now, Abner," he said, "I cannot answer a fool thing like that."

"Well, Campbell," replied my uncle, "I can answer it for you: Eliott did not take that path."

The man took out a big silver watch and opened the case with his thumb-nail.

"The woman ought to be ready," he said.

My uncle looked up at him.

"Campbell," he said, "put off this marriage."

The man turned about.

"Why should I put it off?" he said.

"Well, for one reason, Campbell," replied my uncle, "the omens are not propitious."

"I do not believe in signs," said the man.

"The Scriptures are full of signs," returned Abner. "There was the sign to Joshua and the sign to Ahaz, and there is the sign to you."

The man turned with an oath.

"What accursed thing do you hint about, Abner?"

"Campbell," replied my uncle, "I accept the word; accursed is the word."

"Say the thing out plain! What omen? What sign?"

"Why, this sign," replied Abner: "MacPherson, who was born with a cowl, has seen a vulture flying."

"Damme, man!" cried Campbell. "Do you hang on such a piece of foolery. MacPherson sees his visions in a tin cup —raw corn liquor would set flying beasts of Patmos. Do you tell me, Abner, that you believe in what MacPherson sees?"

"I believe in what I see myself," replied my uncle.

"And what have you seen?" said the man.

"I have seen the vulture!" replied my uncle. "And I was born clean and have no taste for liquor."

"Abner," said Campbell, "you move about in the dark, and I have no time to grope after you. The woman should be ready."

"But are you ready?" said my uncle.

"Man! Man!" cried Campbell. "Will you be forever in a fog? Well, travel on to Satan in it! I am ready, and here are the women!"

But it was not the bride. It was MacPherson to inquire if the bride should come.

My uncle got up then.

"Campbell," he said, in his deep, level voice, "if the bride is ready, you are not."

The man was at the limit of forbearance.

"The devil take you!" he cried. "If you mean anything, say what it is!"

"Campbell," replied my uncle, "it is the custom to inquire if any man knows a reason why a marriage should not go on. Shall I stand up before the company and give the reason, while the marriage waits? Or shall I give it to you here while the marriage waits?"

The man divined something behind my uncle's menace.

"Bid them wait," he said to MacPherson.

Then he closed the door and turned back on my uncle—his shoulders thrown forward, his fingers clenched, his words prefaced by an oath.

"Now, sir,"—and the oath returned,—"what is it?"

My uncle got up, took something from his pocket, and put it down on the table. It was a piece of lint, twisted together, as though one had rolled it firmly between the palms of one's hands.

"Campbell," he said, "as I rode the trail on your cattle range, in the mountains, this morning, a bit of white thing caught my eye. I got down and picked up this fragment of lint on the hard ground. It puzzled me. How came it thus rolled? I began to search the ground, riding slowly in an ever-widening circle. Presently I found a second bit, and then a third, rolled hard together like the first. Then I observed a significant thing: these bits were in line and leading from your trail down the slope of the cattle range to the border of the forest. I went back to the trail, and there on the baked earth, in line with these bits of lint, I found a spot where a bucket of water had been poured out."

Campbell was standing beyond him, staring at the bit of lint. He looked up without disturbing the crouch of his shoulders.

"Go on," he said.

"It occurred to me," continued my uncle, "that perhaps these bits of lint might be found above the trail, as I had found them below it, and so I rode straight on up the hill to a rail fence. I found no fragment of twisted stuff, but I found another thing, Campbell: I found the weeds trampled on the other side of the fence. I got down and looked closely. On the upper surface of a flat rail, immediately before the trampled weeds, there was an impression as though a square bar of iron had been laid across it."

My uncle stopped. And Campbell said:

"Go on."

Abner remained a moment, his eyes on the man; then he continued:

"The impression was in a direct line toward the point on the trail where the water had been poured out. I was puzzled. I got into the saddle and rode back across the trail and down the line of the fragments of lint. At the edge of the forest I found where a log-heap had been burned. I got down again and walked back along the line of the twisted lint. I looked closely, and I saw that the fragments of dried grass, and now and then a rag-weed, had been pressed down, as though by something moving down the hillside from the trail to the burned log-heap.

"Now, Campbell," he said, "what happened on that hillside?"

Campbell stood up and looked my uncle in the face. "What do you think happened?" he said.

"I think," replied Abner, "that some one sat in the weeds behind the fence with a half-stocked, square-barreled rifle laid on the flat rail, and from that ambush shot something passing on the trail, and then dragged it down the hillside to the log-heap. I think that poured-out water was to wash away the blood where the thing fell. I do not know where the bits of lint came from, but I think they were rolled there under the weight of the heavy body. Do I think correctly, eh, Campbell?"

"You do," said the man.

My uncle was astonished, for Campbell faced him, his aspect grim, determined, like one who at any hazard will have the whole of a menace out. "Abner," he said, "you have trailed this thing with some theory behind it. In plain words, what is that theory?"

My uncle was amazed.

"Campbell," he replied, "since you wish the thing said plain, I will not obscure it. Two men own a great herd of cattle between them. The herd is to be driven over the mountains to Baltimore and sold. If one of the partners is shot out of his saddle and the crime concealed, may not the other partner sell the entire drove for his own and put the whole sum in his pocket?

"And if this surviving partner, Campbell, were a man taken with the devil's resolution, I think he might try to make one great stroke of this business. I think he might hire men to drive his cattle, giving out that his partner had gone on ahead, and then turn back for the woman he wanted, take her to Baltimore, put her on the ship, sell the cattle, and with the woman and money sail out of the Chesapeake for the Scotch Highlands he came from! Who could say what became of the missing partner, or that he did not receive his half of the money and meet robbery and murder on his way home?"

My uncle stopped. And Campbell broke out into a great ironical laugh.

"Now, let this thing be a lesson to you, Abner. Your little deductions are correct, but your great conclusion is folly.

"We had a wild heifer that would not drive, so we butchered the beast. I had great trouble to shoot her, but I finally managed it from behind the fence."

"But the bits of lint," said my uncle, "and the washed spot?"

"Abner," cried the man, "do you handle cattle for a lifetime and do not know how blood disturbs them? We did not want them in commotion, so we drenched the place where the heifer fell. And your bits of lint! I will discover the mystery there. To keep the blood off we put an old quilt under the yearling and dragged her down the hill on that. The bits of lint were from the quilt, and rolled thus under the weight of the heifer."

Then he added: "That was weeks ago, but there has been no rain for a month, and these signs of crime, Abner, were providentially preserved against your coming!"

"And the log-heap," said my uncle, like one who would have the whole of an explanation, "why was it burned?"

"Now, Abner," continued the man, "after your keen deductions, would you ask me a thing like that? To get rid of the offal from the butchered beast. We would not wash out the blood-stains and leave that to set our cattle mad."

His laugh changed to a note of victory.

"And now, Abner," he cried, "will you stay and see me married, who have come hoping to see me hanged?"

My uncle had moved over to the window. While Campbell spoke, he seemed to listen, not so much to the man as to sounds outside. Now far off on a covered wooden bridge of the road there was the faint sound of horses. And with a grim smile Abner turned about.

"I will stay," he said, "and see which it is."

It was the very strangest wedding—the big, determined woman like a Fate, the tattered servants with candles in their hands, the minister, and the bride covered and hidden in her veil, like a wooden figure counterfeiting life.

The thing began. There was an atmosphere of silence. My uncle went over to the window. The snow on the road deadened the sounds of the advancing horses, until the iron shoes rang on the stones before the door. Then, suddenly, as though he waited for the sound, he cried out with a great voice against the marriage. The big-nosed, red-haired woman turned on him:

"Why do you object, who have no concern in this thing?"

"I object," said Abner, "because Campbell has sent Eliott on the wrong path!"

"The wrong path!" cried the woman.

"Aye," said Abner, "on the wrong path. There is a path which the vulture's eye hath not seen, Job tells us. But the path Campbell sent Eliott on, the vulture did see."

He advanced with great strides into the room.

"Campbell," he cried, "before I left your accursed pasture, I saw a buzzard descend into the forest beyond your log-heap. I went in, and there, shot through the heart, was the naked body of Allen Eliott. Your log-heap, Campbell, was to burn the quilt and the dead man's clothes. You trusted to the vultures, for the rest, and the vultures, Campbell, over-reached you."

My uncle's voice rose and deepened.

"I sent word to my brother Rufus to raise a *posse comitatus* and bring it to Maxwell's Tavern. Then I rode in here to rest and to feed my horse. I found you, Campbell, on the second line of your hell-planned venture!

"I got Mrs. Eliott to send for Rufus to be a witness with me to your accursed marriage. And I undertook to delay it until he came."

He raised his great arm, the clenched bronze fingers big like the coupling pins of a cart.

"I would have stopped it with my own hand," he said, "but I wanted the men of the Hills to hang you. . . . And they are here."

There was a great sound of tramping feet in the hall outside.

And while the men entered, big, grim, determined men, Abner called out their names:

"Arnold, Randolph, Stuart, Elnathan Stone and my brother Rufus!"

Chapter 16

The Edge of the Shadow

IT WAS A LAND of strange varieties of courage. But, even in the great hills, I never saw a man like Cyrus Mansfield. He was old and dying when this ghastly adventure happened; but, even in the extremity of life, with its terrors on him, he met the thing with his pagan notions of the public welfare, and it is for his own gods to judge him.

It was a long afternoon of autumn. The dead man lay in the whitewashed cabin staring up at the cobwebbed ceiling. His left cheek below the eye was burned with the brand of a pistol shot. The track of a bullet ran along the eyebrow, plowing into the skull above the ear. His grizzled hair stood up like a brush, and the fanaticism of his face was exaggerated by the strained postures of death.

A tall, gaunt woman sat by the door in the sun. She had a lapful of honey locust, and she worked at that, putting the pieces together in a sort of wreath. The branches were full of thorns, and the inside of the woman's hand was torn and wounded upon the balls of the fingers and the palm, but she plaited the thorns together, giving no heed to her injured hand.

She did not get up when my Uncle Abner and Squire Randolph entered. She sat over her work with imperturbable stoicism.

The man and woman were strangers in the land, preëmpting one of Mansfield's cabins. Their mission was a mystery for conjecture. And now the man's death was a mystery beyond it.

When Randolph inquired how the man had met his death, the woman got up, without a word, went to a cupboard in the wall, took out a dueling pistol, and handed it to him. Then, she spoke in a dreary voice:

213

"He was mad. 'The cause,' he said, 'must have a sacrifice of blood.' "

She looked steadily at the dead man.

"Ah, yes," she added, "he was mad!"

Then she turned about and went back to her chair in the sun before the door.

Randolph and Abner examined the weapon. It was a handsome dueling pistol, with an inlaid silver stock and a long, octagon barrel of hard, sharp-edged steel. It had been lately fired, for the exploded percussion cap was still on the nipple.

"He was a poor shot," said Randolph; "he very nearly missed."

My uncle looked closely at the dead man's wound and the burned cheek beneath it. He turned the weapon slowly in his hand, but Randolph was impatient.

"Well, Abner," he said, "did the pistol kill him, or was it the finger of God?"

"The pistol killed him," replied my uncle.

"And shall we believe the woman, eh, Abner?"

"I am willing to believe her," replied my uncle.

They looked about the cabin. There was blood on the floor and flecked against the wall, and stains on the barrel of the pistol, as though the man had staggered about, stunned by the bullet, before he died. And so the wound looked—not mortal on the instant, but one from which, after some time, a man might die.

Randolph wrote down his memorandum, and the two went out into the road.

It was an afternoon of Paradise. The road ran in a long endless ribbon westward toward the Ohio. Negroes in the wide bottom land were harvesting the corn and setting it up in great bulging shocks tied with grapevine. Beyond on a high wooded knoll, stood a mansion-house with white pillars.

My uncle took the duelling pistol out of his pocket and handed it to the Justice of the Peace.

"Randolph," he said, "these weapons were made in pairs; there should be another. And," he added, "there is a crest on the butt plate."

"Virginia is full of such folderols," replied the Justice, "and bought and sold, pledged and traded. It would not serve to identify the dead man. And besides, Abner, why do we care? He is dead by his own hand; his rights and his injuries touch no other; let him lie with his secrets."

He made a little circling gesture upward with his index finger.

" 'Duncan is dead,' " he quoted. " 'After life's fitful fever he sleeps well.' Shall we pay our respects to Mansfield before we ride away?"

And he indicated the house like a white cornice on the high cliff above them.

They had been standing with their backs to the cabin door. Now the woman passed them. She wore a calico sunbonnet, and carried a little bundle tied up in a cotton handkerchief. She set out westward along the road toward the Ohio. She walked slowly, like one bound on an interminable journey.

Moved by some impulse they looked in at the cabin door. The dead man lay as he had been, his face turned toward the ceiling, his hands grotesquely crossed, his body rigid. But now the sprigs of honey locust, at which the woman worked, were pressed down on his unkempt grizzled hair. The sun lay on the floor, and there was silence.

They left the cabin with no word and climbed the long path to the mansion on the hill.

Mansfield sat in a great chair on the pillared porch. It was wide and cool, paved with colored tiles carried over from England in a sailing ship.

He was the strangest man I have ever seen. He was old and dying then, but he had a spirit in him that no event could bludgeon into servility. He sat with a gray shawl pinned around his shoulders. The lights and shadows of the afternoon fell on his jaw like a plowshare, on his big, crooked, bony nose, on his hard gray eyes, bringing them into relief against the lines and furrows of his face.

"Mansfield," cried Randolph, "how do you do?"

"I still live," replied the old man, "but at any hour I may be ejected out of life."

"We all live, Mansfield," said my uncle, "as long as God wills."

"Now, Abner," cried the old man, "you repeat the jargon of the churches. The will of man is the only power in the universe, so far as we can find out, that is able to direct the movings of events. Nothing else that exists can make the most trivial thing happen or cease to happen. No imagined god or demon in all the history of the race has ever influenced the order of events as much as the feeblest human creature in an hour of life. Sit down, Abner, and let me tell you the truth before I cease to exist, as the beasts of the field cease."

He indicated the great carved oak chairs about him, and the two visitors sat down.

Randolph loved the vanities of argument, and he thrust in:

"I am afraid, Mansfield," he said, "you will never enjoy the pleasures of Paradise."

The old man made a contemptuous gesture.

"Pleasure, Randolph," he said, "is the happiness of little men; big men are after something more. They are after the satisfaction that comes from directing events. This is the only happiness: to crush out every other authority—to be the one dominating authority—to make events take the avenue one likes. This is the happiness of the god of the universe, if there is any god of the universe."

He moved in his chair, his elbows out, his fingers extended, his bony face uplifted.

"Abner," he cried, "I am willing for you to endure life as you find it and say it is the will of God, but, as for me, I will not be cowed into submission. I will not be held back from laying hold of the lever of the great engine merely because the rumble of the machinery fills other men with terror."

"Mansfield," replied my uncle, in his deep, level voice, "the fear of God is the beginning of wisdom."

The old man moved his extended arms with a powerful threshing motion, like a vulture beating the air with its great wings.

"Fear!" he cried. "Why, Abner, fear is the last clutch of the animal clinging to the intelligence of man as it emerges from the instinct of the beast. The first man thought the monsters about him were gods. Our fathers thought the elements were gods, and we think the impulse moving the machinery of the

world is the will of some divine authority. And always the
only thing in the universe that was superior to these things
has been afraid to assert itself. The human will that can change
things, that can do as it likes, has been afraid of phantasms
that never yet met with anything they could turn aside."

He clenched his hands, contracted his elbows, and brought
them down with an abrupt derisive gesture.

"I do not understand," he said, "but I am not afraid. I will
not be beaten into submission by vague, inherited terrors. I
will not be subservient to things that have a lesser power than
I have. I will not yield the control of events to elements that
are dead, to laws that are unthinking, or to an influence that
cannot change.

"Not all the gods that man has ever worshiped can make
things happen to-morrow, but I can make them happen;
therefore, I am a god above them. And how shall a god that is
greater than these gods give over the dominion of events into
their hands?"

"And so, Mansfield," said Abner, "you have been acting
just now upon this belief?"

The old man turned his bony face sharply on my uncle.

"Now, Abner," he said, "what do you mean by this Delphic
sentence?"

For reply, my uncle extended his arms toward the white-
washed cabin.

"Who is the dead man down there?"

"Randolph can tell you that," said Mansfield.

"I never saw the man until to-day," replied the Justice.

"Eh, Randolph," cried the old man, "do you administer the
law and have a memory like that? In midsummer the justices
sat at the county seat. Have you forgot that inquisition?"

"I have not," said the Justice. "It was a fool's inquiry. One
of Nixon's Negro women reported a slave plot to poison the
wells and attack the people with a curious weapon. She got the
description of the weapon out of some preacher's sermon—a
kind of spear. If she had named some implement of modern
warfare, we could have better credited her story."

"Well, Randolph," cried the old man, "for all the wisdom of
your justices, she spoke the truth. They were pikes the woman

saw, and not the spears of the horsemen of Israel. Did you notice a stranger who remained in a corner of the courtroom while the justices were sitting? He disappeared after the trial. But did you mark him, Randolph? He lies dead down yonder in my Negro cabin."

A light came into the face of the Justice.

"By the Eternal," he cried, "an abolitionist!"

He flipped the gold seals on his watch fob; then he added, with that little circling gesture of his finger:

"Well, he has taken himself away with his own hands."

"He is dead," said Mansfield, thrusting out his plowshare jaw, "as all such vermin ought to be. We are too careless in the South of these vicious reptiles. We ought to stamp them out of life whenever we find them. They are a menace to the peace of the land. They incite the slaves to arson and to murder. They are beyond the law, as the panther and the wolf are. We ought to have the courage to destroy the creatures.

"The destiny of this republic," he added, "is in our hands."

My Uncle Abner spoke then:

"It is in God's hands," he said.

"God!" cried Mansfield. "I would not give house room to such a god! When we dawdle, Abner, the Yankees always beat us. Why, man, if this thing runs on, it will wind up in a lawsuit. We shall be stripped of our property by a court's writ. And instead of imposing our will on this republic, we shall be answering a little New England lawyer with rejoinders and rebuttals."

"Would the bayonet be a better answer?" said my uncle.

"Now, Abner," said Mansfield, "you amuse me. These Yankees have no stomach for the bayonet. They are traders, Abner; they handle the shares and the steel-yard."

My uncle looked steadily at the man.

"Virginia held that opinion of New England when the King's troops landed," he said. "It was a common belief. Why, sir, even Washington riding north to the command of the Colonial army, when he heard of the battle of Bunker Hill, did not ask who had won; his only inquiry was, 'Did the militia of Massachusetts fight? It did fight, Mansfield, with immortal courage."

My Uncle Abner lifted his face and looked out over the great valley, mellow with its ripened corn. His voice fell into a reflective note.

"The situation in this republic," he said, "is grave, and I am full of fear. In God's hands the thing would finally adjust itself. In God's slow, devious way it would finally come out all right. But neither you, Mansfield, nor the abolitionist, will leave the thing to God. You will rush in and settle it with violence. You will find a short cut of your own through God's deliberate way, and I tremble before the horror of blood that you would plunge us into."

He paused again, and his big, bronzed features had the serenity of some vast belief.

"To be fair," he said, "everywhere in this republic, to enforce the law everywhere, to put down violence, to try every man who takes the law in his own hand, fairly in the courts, and, if he is guilty, punish him without fear or favor, according to the letter of the statute, to keep everywhere a public sentiment of fair dealing, by an administration of justice above all public clamor—in this time of heat, this is our only hope of peace!"

He spoke in his deep, level voice, and the words seemed to be concrete things having dimensions and weight.

"Shall a fanatic who stirs up our slaves to murder," said Mansfield, "be tried like a gentleman before a jury?"

"Aye, Mansfield," replied my uncle, "like a gentleman, and before a jury! If the fanatic murders the citizen, I would hang him, and if the citizen murders the fanatic, I would hang him too, without one finger's weight of difference in the method of procedure. I would show New England that the justice of Virginia is even-eyed. And she would emulate that fairness, and all over the land the law would hold against the unrestraint that is gathering."

"Abner," cried Mansfield, "you are a dawdler like your god. I know a swifter way."

"I am ready to believe it," replied my uncle. "Who killed the mad abolitionist down yonder?"

"Who cares," said the old man, "since the beast is dead?"

"I care," replied Abner.

"Then, find it out, Abner, if you care," said the old man, snapping his jaws.

"I have found it out," said my uncle, "and it has happened in so strange a way, and with so curious an intervention, that I cannot save the State from shame."

"It happened in the simplest way imaginable," said Randolph. "The fool killed himself."

It was not an unthinkable conclusion. The whole land was wrought up to the highest tension. Men were beginning to hold their properties and their lives as of little account in this tremendous issue. The country was ready to flare up in a war, and to fire it the life of one man would be nothing. A thousand madmen were ready to make that sacrifice of life. That a fanatic would shoot himself in Virginia with the idea that the slave owners would be charged by the country with his murder and so the war brought on, was not a thing improbable in that day's extremity of passion. To the madman it would be only the slight sacrifice of his life for the immortal gain of a holy war.

My uncle looked at the Justice with a curious smile.

"I think Mansfield will hardly believe that," he said.

The old man laughed.

"It is a pretty explanation, Randolph," he said, "and I commend it to all men, but I do not believe it."

"Not believe it!" cried the Justice, looking first at my uncle and then at the old man. "Why, Abner, you said the woman spoke the truth!"

"She did speak it," replied my uncle.

"Damme, man!" cried the Justice. "Why do you beat about? If you believe the woman, why do you gentlemen disbelieve my conclusion on her words?"

"I disbelieve it, Randolph," replied my uncle, "for the convincing reason that I know who killed him."

"And I," cried Mansfield, "disbelieve it for an equally convincing reason—for the most convincing reason in the world, Randolph,"—and his big voice laughed in among the pillars and rafters of his porch—"because I killed him myself!"

Abner sat unmoving, and Randolph like a man past belief. The Justice fumbled with the pistol in his pocket, got it out, and laid it on the flat arm on his chair, but he did not speak. The confession overwhelmed him.

The old man stood up, and the voice in his time-shaken body was Homeric:

"Ho! Ho!" he cried. "And so you thought I would be afraid, Randolph, and dodge about like your little men, shaken and overcome by fear." And he huddled in his shawl with a dramatic gesture.

"Fear!" And his laugh burst out again in a high staccato. "Even the devils in Abner's Christian hell lack that! I shot the creature, Randolph! Do you hear the awful words? And do you tremble for me, lest I hang and go to Abner's hell?"

The mock terror in the old man's voice and manner was compelling drama. He indicated the pistol on the chair arm.

"Yes," he said, "it is mine. Abner should have known it by the Mansfield arms."

"I did know it," replied my uncle.

The old man looked at the Justice with a queer ironical smile; then he went into the house.

"Await me, Randolph," he said. "I would produce the evidence and make out your case."

And prodded by the words, Randolph cursed bitterly.

"By the Eternal," he cried, "I am as little afraid as any of God's creatures, but the man confounds me!"

And he spoke the truth. He was a justice of the peace in Virginia when only gentlemen could hold that office. He lacked the balance and the ability of his pioneer ancestors, and he was given over to the vanity and the extravagance of words, but fear and all the manifestations of fear were alien to him.

He turned when the old man came out with a rosewood box in his hand, and faced him calmly.

"Mansfield," he said, "I warn you. I represent the law, and if you have done a murder, I will get you hanged."

The old man paused, and looked at Randolph with his maddening ironical smile.

"Fear again, eh, Randolph!" he said. "Is it by fear that you would always restrain me? Shall I be plucked back from the gibbet and Abner's hell only by this fear? It is a menace I have too long disregarded. You must give me a better reason."

Mansfield opened the rosewood box and took out a pistol like the one on the arm of Randolph's chair. He held the weapon lightly in his hand.

"The creature came here to harangue me," he said, "and like the genie in the copper pot, I gave him his choice of deaths."

He laughed, for the fancy pleased him.

"In the swirl of his heroics, Abner, I carried him the pistol yonder, to the steps of my portico where he stood, and with this other and my father's watch, I sat down here. 'After three minutes, sir,' I said, 'I shall shoot you down. It is my price for hearing your oration. Fire before that time is up. I shall call out the minutes for your convenience.'

"And so, I sat here, Abner, with my father's watch, while the creature ranted with my pistol in his hand.

"I called out the time, and he harangued me: 'The black of the Negro shall be washed white with blood!' And I answered him: 'One minute, sir!'

" 'The Lord will make Virginia a possession for the bittern!' was his second climax, and I replied, 'Two minutes of your time are up!'

" 'The South is one great brothel,' he shouted, and I answered, 'Three minutes, my fine fellow,' and shot him as I had promised! He leaped off into the darkness with my un-fired pistol and fled to the cabin where you found him."

There was a moment's silence, and my uncle put out his arm and pointed down across the long meadow to a grim out-line traveling far off on the road.

"Mansfield," he said, "you have lighted the powder train that God, at His leisure, would have dampened. You have broken the faith of the world in our sincerity. Virginia will be credited with this man's death, and we cannot hang you for it!"

"And why not?" cried Randolph, standing up. He had been prodded into unmanageable anger. "The Commonwealth has granted no letters of marque; it has proclaimed no outlawry. Neither Mansfield nor any other has a patent to do murder. I shall get him hanged!"

My uncle shook his head.

"No, Randolph," he said, "you cannot hang him."

"And why not?" cried the Justice of the Peace, aroused now, and defiant. "Is Mansfield above the law? If he kills this madman, shall he have a writ of exemption for it?"

"But he did not kill him!" replied my uncle.

Randolph was amazed. And Mansfield shook his head slowly, his face retaining its ironical smile.

"No, Abner," he said, "let Randolph have his case. I shot him."

Then he put out his hand, as though in courtesy, to my uncle. "Be at peace," he said. "If I were moved by fear, there is a greater near me than Randolph's gibbet. I shall be dead and buried before his grand jury can hold its inquisition."

"Mansfield," replied my uncle, "be yourself at peace, for you did not kill him."

"Not kill him!" cried the man. "I shot him thus!"

He sat down in his chair and taking the pistol out of the rosewood box, leveled it at an imaginary figure across the portico. The man's hand was steady and the sun glinted on the steel barrel.

"And because you shot thus," said Abner, "you did not kill him. Listen, Mansfield: the pistol that killed the Abolitionist was held upside down and close. The brand on the dead man's face is under the bullet hole. If the pistol had been held as usual, the brand would have been above it. It is a law of pistol wounds: as you turn the weapon, so will the brand follow. Held upside down, the brand was below the wound."

A deepening wonder came into the old man's ironical face.

"How did the creature die, then, if I missed him?"

Abner took up the weapon on the arm of Randolph's chair.

"The dead man did not shoot in Mansfield's fantastic duel," he said. "Nevertheless this pistol has been fired. And observe there is a smeared bloodstain on the sharp edges of the barrel. I think I know what happened..

"The madman with his pistol, overwrought, struggled in the cabin yonder to make himself a 'sacrifice of blood' and so bring on this war. Someone resisted his mad act—someone who seized the barrel of the pistol and in the struggle also got a wounded hand. Who in that cabin had a wounded hand, Randolph?"

"By the living God!" cried the Justice of the Peace. "The woman who plaited thorns! It was a blind to cover her injured hand!"

Abner looked out across the great meadows at a tiny figure far off, fading into the twilight of the distant road that led toward the Ohio.

"To cover her injured hand," he echoed, "and also, perhaps, who knows, to symbolize the dead man's mission, as she knew she saw it! The heart of a woman is the deepest of all God's riddles!"

Chapter 17

The Adopted Daughter

"Isn't she a beauty—eh, Randolph?"

Vespatian Flornoy had a tumbler of French brandy. He sucked in a mouthful. Then he put it on the table.

The house was the strangest in Virginia. It was of some foreign model. The whole second floor on the side lying toward the east was in two spacious chambers lighted with great casement windows to the ceiling. Outside, on this brilliant morning, the world was yellow and dried-up, sere and baked. But the sun was thin and the autumn air hard and vital.

My uncle, Squire Randolph, the old country doctor, Storm, and the host, Vespatian Flornoy, were in one of these enormous rooms. They sat about a table, a long mahogany piece made in England and brought over in a sailing ship. There were a squat bottle of French brandy and some tumblers. Flornoy drank and recovered his spirit of abandon.

Now he leered at Randolph, and at the girl that he had just called in.

He was a man one would have traveled far to see—yesterday or the day ahead of that. He had a figure out of Athens, a face cast in some forgotten foundry by the Arno, thick-curled mahogany-colored hair, and eyes like the velvet hull of an Italian chestnut. These excellencies the heavenly workman had turned out, and now by some sorcery of the pit they were changed into abominations.

Hell-charms, one thought of, when one looked the creature in the face. Drops of some potent liquor, and devil-words had done it, on yesterday or the day ahead of yesterday. Surely not the things that really had done it—time and the iniquities of Gomorrah. His stock and his fine ruffled shirt were soiled. His satin waistcoat was stained with liquor.

"A daughter of a French marquis, eh!" he went on. "Sold into slavery by a jest of the gods—stolen out of the garden of a convent! It's the fabled history of every octoroon in New Orleans!"

Fabled or not, the girl might have been the thing he said. The contour of the face came to a point at the chin, and the skin was a soft Oriental olive. She was the perfect expression of a type. One never could wish to change a line of her figure or a feature of her face. She stood now in the room before the door in the morning sun, in the quaint, alluring costume of a young girl of the time—a young girl of degree, stolen out of the garden of a convent! She had entered at Flornoy's drunken call, and there was the aspect of terror on her.

The man went on in his thick, abominable voice:

"My brother Sheppard, coming north to an inspection of our joint estate, presents her as his adopted daughter. But when he dropped dead in this room last night and I went about the preparation of his body for your inquisition—eh, what, my gentlemen! I find a bill of sale running back ten years, for the dainty baggage!

"French, and noble, stolen from the garden of a convent, perhaps! Perhaps! but not by my brother Sheppard. His adopted daughter—sentimentally, perhaps! Perhaps! But legally a piece of property, I think, descending to his heirs. Eh, Randolph!"

And he thrust a folded yellow paper across the table.

The Justice put down his glass with the almost untasted liquor in it, and examined the bill of sale.

"It is in form!" he said. "And you interpret it correctly, Flornoy, by the law's letter. But you will not wish to enforce it, I imagine!"

"And why not, Randolph?" cried the man.

The Justice looked him firmly in the face.

"You take enough by chance, sir. You and your brother Sheppard held the estate jointly at your father's death, and now at your brother's death you hold it as sole heir. You will not wish, also, to hold his adopted daughter."

Then he added:

"This bill of sale would hold in the courts against any un-indentured purpose, not accompanied by an intention expressed in some overt act. It would also fix the status of the girl against any pretended or legendary exemption of birth. The judges might believe that your brother Sheppard was convinced of this pretension when he rescued the child by purchase, and made his informal adoption at a tender age. But they would hold the paper, like a deed, irrevocable, and not to be disturbed by this conjecture."

"It will hold," cried the man, "and I will hold! You make an easy disclaimer of the rights of other men."

Then his face took on the aspect of a satyr's.

"Give her up, eh! to be a lady! Why Randolph, I would have given Sheppard five hundred golden eagles for this little beauty—five hundred golden eagles in his hand! Look at her, Randolph. You are not too old to forget the points—the trim ankle, the slender body, the snap of a thoroughbred. There's the blood of the French marquis, on my honor! A drop of black won't curdle it."

And he laughed, snapping his fingers at his wit.

"It only makes the noble lady merchandise! And perhaps, as you say, perhaps it isn't there, in fact. Egad! old man, I would have bid a thousand eagles if Sheppard had put her up. A thousand eagles! and I get her for nothing! He falls dead in my house, and I take her by inheritance."

It was the living truth. The two men, Vespatian Flornoy and his brother Sheppard, took their father's estate jointly at his death. They were unmarried, and now at the death of Sheppard, the surviving brother Vespatian was sole heir, under the law, to the dead man's properties: houses and lands and slaves. The bill of sale put the girl an item in the inventory of the dead man's estate, to descend with the manor-house and lands.

The thing had happened, as fortune is predisposed to change, in a moment, as by the turning of dice.

At daybreak on this morning Vespatian Flornoy had sent a Negro at a gallop, to summon the old country doctor, Storm, Squire Randolph and my Uncle Abner. At midnight, in this

H

chamber where they now sat, Sheppard as he got on his feet, with his candle, fell and died, Vespatian said, before he could reach his body. He lay now shaven and clothed for burial in the great chamber that adjoined.

Old Storm had stripped the body and found no mark. The man was dead with no scratch or bruise.

He could not say what vital organ had suddenly played out —perhaps a string of the heart had snapped. At any rate, the dead man had not gone out by any sort of violence, nor by any poison. Every drug or herb that killed left its stamp and superscription, old Storm said, and one could see it, if one had the eye, as one could see the slash of a knife or the bruise of an assassin's fingers.

It was plain death "by the Providence of God," was Randolph's verdict. So the Justice and old Storm summed up the thing and they represented the inquiry and the requirements of the law.

My uncle Abner made no comment on this conclusion. He came and looked and was silent. He demurred to the "Providence of God" in Randolph's verdict, with a great gesture of rejection. He disliked this term in any human horror. "By the abandonment of God," he said, these verdicts ought rather to be written. But he gave no sign that his objection was of any special tenor. He seemed profoundly puzzled.

When the girl came in, at Vespatian's command, to this appraisal, he continued silent. At the man's speech, and evident intent, his features and his great jaw hardened, as though under the sunburned skin the bony structure of the face were metal.

He sat in his chair, a little way out beyond the table, as he sat on a Sunday before the pulpit, on a bench, motionless, in some deep concern.

Randolph and Vespatian Flornoy were in this dialogue. Old Storm sat with his arms folded across his chest, his head down. His interest in the matter had departed with his inspection of the dead man, or remained in the adjoining chamber where the body lay, the eyelids closed forever on the land of living men, shut up tight like the shutters of a window in a house of mystery. He only glanced at the girl with no interest, as at a bauble.

And now while the dialogue went on and Storm looked down his nose, the girl, silent and in terror, appealed to my uncle in a furtive glance, swift, charged with horror, and like a flash of shadow. The great table had a broad board connecting the carved legs beneath, a sort of shelf raised a little from the floor. In her glance, swift and fearful, she directed my uncle's attention to this board.

It was a long piece of veneered mahogany, making a shelf down the whole length of the table. On it my uncle saw a big folded cloth of squares white and black, and set a huge ivory chess-men. The cloth was made to spread across the top of the table, and the chess-men were of unusual size in proportion to the squares; the round knobs on the heads of the pawns were as big as marbles. Beside these things was a rosewood box for dueling-pistols, after the fashion of the time.

My uncle stooped over, took up these articles and set them on the table.

"And so, Flornoy," he said, "you played at chess with your brother Sheppard."

The man turned swiftly; then he paused and drank his glass of liquor.

"I entertained my brother," he said, "as I could; there is no coffee-house to enter, nor any dancing women to please the eye, in the mountains of Virginia."

"For what stake?" said my uncle.

"I have forgotten, Abner," replied the man, "—some trifle."

"And who won?" said my uncle.

"I won," replied the man. He spoke promptly.

"You won," said my uncle, "and you remember that; but what you won, you have forgotten! Reflect a little on it, Flornoy."

The man cursed, his face in anger.

"Does it matter, Abner, a thing great or small? It is all mine to-day!"

"But it was not all yours last night," said my uncle.

"What I won was mine," replied the man.

"Now, there," replied my uncle, "lies a point that I would amplify. One might win, but might not receive the thing one played for. One might claim it for one's own, and the loser might deny it. If the stake were great, the loser might undertake to repudiate the bargain. And how would one enforce it?"

The man put down his glass, leaned over and looked steadily at my uncle.

Abner slipped the silver hooks on the rosewood box, slowly, with his thumb and finger.

"I think," he said, "that if the gentleman you have in mind won, and were met with a refusal, he would undertake to enforce his claim, not in the courts or by any legal writ, but by the methods which gentlemen such as you have in mind are accustomed to invoke."

He opened the box and took out two pistols of the time. Then his face clouded with perplexity. Both weapons were clean and loaded.

The man, propping his wonderful face in the hollow of his hand, laughed. He had the face and the laughter of the angels cast out with Satan, when in a moment of some gain over the hosts of Michael they forgot the pit.

"Abner," he cried, "you are hag-ridden by a habit, and it leads you into the wildest fancies!"

His laughter chuckled and gurgled in his throat.

"Let me put your theory together. It is a very pretty theory, lacking in some trifles, but spirited and packed with dramatic tension. Let me sketch it out as it stands before your eye. . . . Have no fear, I shall not mar it by any delicate concern for the cunning villain, or any suppression of his evil nature. I shall uncover the base creature amid his deeds of darkness!"

He paused, and mocked the tragedy of actors.

"It is the hour of yawning graveyards—midnight in this house. Vespatian Flornoy sits at this table with his good brother Sheppard. He has the covetousness of David the son of Jesse, in his evil heart. He would possess the noble daughter of the Latin marquis, by a sardonic fate sold at childhood into slavery, but by the ever watchful Providence of God, for such cases made and provided, purchased by the good brother Sheppard and adopted for his daughter!

"Mark, Abner, how beautifully it falls into the formula of the tragic poets!

"The wicked Vespatian Flornoy, foiled in every scheme of purchase, moved by the instigation of the Devil, and with no fear of God before his eyes, plays at chess with his good brother Sheppard, wins his interest in the manor-house and lands, and his last gold-piece—taunts and seduces him into a final game with everything staked against this Iphigenia. The evil one rises invisible but sulphurous to Vespatian's aid. He wins. In terror, appalled, aghast at the realization of his folly, the good brother Sheppard repudiates the bargain. They duel across the table, and Vespatian, being the better shot, kills his good brother Sheppard!

"Why, Abner, it is the plan of the 'Poetics.' It lacks no element of completeness. It is joined and fitted for the diction of Euripides!"

The man declaimed, his wonderful fouled face, his Adonis head with its thick curled hair, virile and spirited with the liquor and the momentum of his words. Old Storm gave no attention. Randolph listened as to the periods of an oration. And my uncle sat, puzzled, before the articles on the table. The girl now and then, when the speaker's eyes were on my uncle, by slight indicatory signs affirmed the speech, and continued strongly to indicate the chessmen.

My uncle began to turn the pieces over under the protection of his hand, idly, like one who fingers about a table in abstraction. Presently he stopped and covered one of the pieces with his hand. It was a pawn, large, like the other chessmen, but the round ivory knob at the top of it was gone. It had been sawed off!

The man Flornoy, consumed with his idea, failed to mark the incident, and moved by the tenor of his speech, went on:

"This is the Greek plan for a tragedy. It is the plan of Athens in the fifth century. It is the plan of Sophocles and Æschylus. Mark how it turns upon the Hellenic idea of a dominating Fate: a Fate in control over the affairs of men, pagan and not good. The innocent and virtuous have no gain above the shrewd and wicked. The good Sheppard dies, and the evil Vespatian takes his daughter, his goods and lands to enjoy in a gilded life, long and happy!"

He thought the deep reflection in my uncle's face was confusion at his wit.

"That ending would not please you, Abner. Luther and Calvin and John Wesley have lived after Aristotle assembled this formula in his 'Poetics.' And they will have the evil punished—a dagger in the wicked Vespatian's heart, and the virgin slave, by the interposition of the will of Heaven, preserved in her virginity. And so you come, like the Providence of God, to set the thing in order!"

My uncle looked up at the man, his hand covering the mutilated pawn, his face calm in its profound reflection.

"You quote the tragic poets, with much pedantry," he said. "Well, I will quote them too: 'Ofttimes, to win us to our harm, the instruments of darkness tell us truth!' How much truth, in all this discourse, have you told us?"

"Now, Abner," cried the man, "if it is truth you seek, and not the imaginations of a theory, how much could there be in it? If it were not for the granite ledges of reality, one might blow iris-colored bubbles of the fancy and watch them, in their beauty, journey to the stars! But alas, they collide with the hard edges of a fact and puff out.

"To begin with, the pistols have not been fired!"

"One could reload a pistol," replied my uncle.

"But one could not shoot a man, Abner, and leave no mark of the bullet on his body!"

He paused and addressed the old doctor.

"I sent for Storm, when I sent for Randolph, to rid me of every innuendo of a gossip. Ask him if there is a mark of violence on my brother's body."

The old man lifted his lined, withered face.

"There is no mark on him!" he said.

Vespatian Flornoy leaned across the table.

"Are you sure?" he said. "Perhaps you might be mistaken."

The words were in the taunting note of Elijah to the priests of Baal.

The old man made a decisive gesture. "*Voilà!*" he said, "I have handled a thousand dead men! I am not mistaken!"

Vespatian Flornoy put up his hands as in a great, hopeless gesture.

"Alas, Abner," he said, "we must give up this pretty theory. It does honor to your creative instinct, and save for this trifle, we might commend it to all men. But you see, Abner, Storm and the world will unreasonably insist that a bullet leaves a mark. I do not think we can persuade them against their experience in that belief. I am sorry for you, Abner. You have a reputation in Virginia to keep up. Let us think; perhaps there is a way around this disconcerting fact."

And he put his extended palm across his forehead, in mock reflection.

It was at this moment, when for an instant the man's face was covered, that the girl standing before the door made a strange indicatory signal to my Uncle Abner.

Vespatian Flornoy, removing his hand, caught a glimpse of the girl's after-expression. And he burst out in a great laugh, striking the table with his clenched hand.

"Egad!" he cried. "By the soul of Satan! the coy little baggage is winking at Abner!"

He saw only the final composition of the girl's face. He did not see the stress and vigor of the indicatory sign. He roared in a pretension of jealous anger.

"I will not have my property ogle another in my house. You shall answer for this, Abner, on the field of honor. And I warn you, sir: I have the surest eye and the steadiest hand in the mountains of Virginia."

It was the truth. The man was the wonder of the countryside. He could cut a string with a pistol at ten paces; he could drive in a carpet-tack with his bullet, across the room. With the weapon of the time, the creature was sure, accurate to a hair, and deadly.

"No man," he cried, "shall carry off this dainty baggage. Select your weapon, Abner; let us duel over this seduction!"

He spoke in the flippancies of jest. But my uncle's face was now alight with some great comprehensive purpose. It was like the face of one who begins to see the bulk and outlines of a thing that before this hour, in spite of every scrutiny, was formless.

And to Flornoy's surprise and wonder, my uncle put out his hand, took up one of the pistols and suddenly fired it into the wood of the mantelpiece beyond the table. He got up and looked at the mark. The bullet was hardly bedded in the veneer.

"You use a light charge of powder, Flornoy," said my uncle.

The man was puzzled at this act, but he answered at once.

"Abner," he said, "that is a secret I have learned. A pistol pivots on the grip. In firing, there are two things to avoid: a jerk on the trigger, and the tendency of the muzzle to jump up, caused by the recoil of the charge. No man can control his weapon with a heavy charge of powder behind the bullet. If one would shoot true to a hair, one must load light."

It seemed a considerable explanation. And not one of the men who heard it ever knew whether it was, in fact, the controlling cause, or whether another and more subtle thing inspired it.

"But, Flornoy," said my uncle, "if to kill were the object of a duelist, such a charge of powder might defeat the purpose."

"You are mistaken, Abner," he said. "The body of a man is soft. If one avoids the bony structure, a trifling charge of powder will carry one's bullet into a vital organ. There is no gain in shooting through a man as though one were going to string him on a thread. Powder enough to lodge the bullet in the vital organ is sufficient."

"There might be a point in not shooting through him," said Abner.

The man looked calmly at my uncle; then he made an irrelevant gesture.

"No object, Abner, but no use. The whole point is to shoot to a hair, to lodge the bullet precisely in the point selected. Look how a light charge of powder does it."

And taking up the other pistol, he steadied it a moment in his hand, and fired at Abner's bullet-hole. No mark appeared on the mantel board. One would have believed that the bullet, if the barrel held one, had wholly vanished. But when they looked closely, it was seen that my uncle's bullet, struck precisely, was driven a little deeper into the wood. It was amazing accuracy. No wonder the man's skill was a byword in the land.

My uncle made a single comment.

"You shoot like the slingers of Benjamin!" he said.

Then he came back to the table and stood looking down at the man. He held the mutilated ivory pawn in his closed left hand. The girl, like an appraised article, was in the doorway; Storm and Randolph looked on, like men before the blind moving of events.

"Flornoy," said Abner, "you have told us more truth than you intended us to believe. How did your brother Sheppard die?"

The man's face changed. His fingers tightened on the pistol. His eyes became determined and alert.

"Damme, man," he cried, "do you return to that! Sheppard fell and died, where you stand, beside the table in this room. I am no surgeon to say what disorder killed him. I sent for Storm to determine that."

My uncle turned to the old eccentric doctor.

"Storm," he said, "how did Sheppard Flornoy die?"

The old man shrugged his shoulders and put out his nervous hands.

"I do not know," he said, "the heart, maybe. There is no mark on him."

And here Randolph interrupted.

"Abner," he said, "you put a question that no man can answer: something snaps within the body, and we die. We have no hint at the cause of Sheppard's death."

"Why yes," replied my uncle, "I think we have."

"What hint?" said Randolph.

"The hint," said Abner, "that the eloquent Vespatian gave us just now in his discourse. I think he set out the cause in his apt recollection from the Book of Samuel."

He paused and looked down at the man.

Vespatian Flornoy got on his feet. His face and manner changed. There was now decision and menace in his voice.

H*

"Abner," he said, "there shall be an end to this. I have turned your ugly hint with pleasantry, and met it squarely with indisputable facts. I shall not go any further on this way. I shall clear myself now, after the manner of a gentleman."

My uncle looked steadily at the man.

"Flornoy," he said, "if you would test your innocence by a device of the Middle Ages, I would suggest a simpler and swifter method of that time. Wager of battle is outlawed in Virginia. It is prohibited by statute, and we cannot use it. But the test I offer in its place is equally medieval. It is based on the same belief, old and persistent, that the Providence of God will indicate the guilty. And it is not against the law."

He paused.

"The same generation of men who believed in Wager of Battle, in the Morsel of Execration, in the red-hot plowshares, as a test of the guilt of murder, also believed that if the assassin touched his victim, the body of the murdered man would bleed!

"Flornoy," he said, "if you would have recourse to one of those medieval devices, let it be the last. . . . Go in with me and touch the body of your brother Sheppard, and I give you my word of honor that I will accept the decision of the test."

It was impossible to believe that my Uncle Abner trifled, and yet the thing was beyond the soundings of all sense.

Storm and Randolph, and even the girl standing in the door, regarded him in wonder.

Vespatian Flornoy was amazed.

"Damme, man!" he cried, "superstitions have unhinged your mind. Would you believe in a thing like that?"

"I would rather believe it," replied my uncle, "than to believe that in a duel God would direct the assassin's bullet."

Then he added, with weight and decision in his voice:

"If you would be clear of my suspicion, if you would be free to take and enjoy the lands and properties that you inherit, go in before these witnesses and touch the dead body of your brother Sheppard. There is no mark appearing on him. Storm has found no wound to bleed. You are innocent of any measure in his death, you tell us. There's no peril to you, and I shall ride away to assure every man that Sheppard

Flornoy died, as Randolph has written, by the 'Providence of God.' "

He extended his arm toward the adjacent chamber, and across the table he looked Flornoy in the face.

"Go in before us and touch the dead man."

"By the soul of Satan!" cried the man, "if you hang on such a piece of foolery, you shall have it. The curse of superstition sticks in your fleece, Abner, like a burr."

He turned and flung open the door behind him and went in. The others followed—Storm and Randolph behind the man, the girl, shaken and fearful, and my Uncle Abner.

Sheppard Flornoy lay prepared for burial in the center of the room. The morning sun entering through the long windows flooded him with light; his features were sharply outlined in the mask of death, his eyelids closed.

They stood about the dead man, at peace in this glorious shroud of sun, and the living brother was about to touch him when my uncle put out his hand.

"Flornoy," he said, "the dead man ought to see who comes to touch him. I will open his eyes."

And at the words, for no cause or reason conceivable to the two men looking on, Vespatian Flornoy shouted with an oath, and ran in on my uncle.

He was big and mad with terror. But even in his youth and fury he was not a match for my Uncle Abner. Liquor and excess failed before wind and sun and the clean life of the hills. The man went down under my uncle's clenched hand, like an ox polled with a hammer.

It was Randolph who cried out, while the others crowded around the dead man and his brother unconscious on the floor.

"Abner, Abner," he said, "what is the answer to this ghastly riddle?"

For reply my uncle drew back the eyelids of the dead man. And stooping over, Randolph and old Storm saw that Sheppard Flornoy had been shot through the eye, and that the head of the ivory pawn had been forced into the bullet-hole to round out the damaged eyeball under the closed lid.

The girl sobbed, clinging to my uncle's arm. Randolph tore

the bill of sale into indistinguishable bits. And the old doctor Storm made a great gesture with his hands extended and crooked.

"Mon Dieu!" he cried, in a consuming revulsion of disgust. "My father was surgeon in the field for Napoleon, I was raised with dead men, and a drunken assassin fools me in the mountains of Virginia!"

Chapter 18

Naboth's Vineyard

ONE HEARS a good deal about the sovereignty of the people in this republic; and many persons imagine it a sort of fiction, and wonder where it lies, who are the guardians of it, and how they would exercise it if the forms and agents of the law were removed. I am not one of those who speculate upon this mystery, for I have seen this primal ultimate authority naked at its work. And, having seen it, I know how mighty and how dread a thing it is. And I know where it lies, and who are the guardians of it, and how they exercise it when the need arises.

There was a great crowd, for the whole country was in the courtroom. It was a notorious trial.

Elihu Marsh had been shot down in his house. He had been found lying in a room, with a hole through his body that one could put his thumb in. He was an irascible old man, the last of his family, and so, lived alone. He had rich lands, but only a life estate in them, the remainder was to some foreign heirs. A girl from a neighboring farm came now and then to bake and put his house in order, and he kept a farm hand about the premises.

Nothing had been disturbed in the house when the neighbors found Marsh; no robbery had been attempted, for the man's money, a considerable sum, remained on him.

There was not much mystery about the thing, because the farm hand had disappeared. This man was a stranger in the hills. He had come from over the mountains some months before, and gone to work for Marsh. He was a big blond man, young and good looking; of better blood, one would say, than the average laborer. He gave his name as Taylor, but he was not communicative, and little else about him was known.

239

The country was raised, and this man was overtaken in the foothills of the mountains. He had his clothes tied into a bundle, and a long-barreled fowling-piece on his shoulder. The story he told was that he and Marsh had settled that morning, and he had left the house at noon, but that he had forgotten his gun and had gone back for it; had reached the house about four o'clock, gone into the kitchen, got his gun down from the dogwood forks over the chimney, and at once left the house. He had not seen Marsh, and did not know where he was.

He admitted that this gun had been loaded with a single huge lead bullet. He had so loaded it to kill a dog that sometimes approached the house, but not close enough to be reached with a load of shot. He affected surprise when it was pointed out that the gun had been discharged. He said that he had not fired it, and had not, until then, noticed that it was empty. When asked why he had so suddenly determined to leave the country, he was silent.

He was carried back and confined in the county jail, and now, he was on trial at the September term of the circuit court.

The court sat early. Although the judge, Simon Kilrail, was a landowner and lived on his estate in the country some half dozen miles away, he rode to the courthouse in the morning, and home at night, with his legal papers in his saddle-pockets. It was only when the court sat that he was a lawyer. At other times he harvested his hay and grazed his cattle, and tried to add to his lands like any other man in the hills, and he was as hard in a trade and as hungry for an acre as any.

It was the sign and insignia of distinction in Virginia to own land. Mr. Jefferson had annulled the titles that George the Third had granted, and the land alone remained as a patent of nobility. The Judge wished to be one of these landed gentry, and he had gone a good way to accomplish it. But when the court convened he became a lawyer and sat upon the bench with no heart in him, and a cruel tongue like the English judges.

I think everybody was at this trial. My Uncle Abner and the strange old doctor, Storm, sat on a bench near the center aisle of the court-room, and I sat behind them, for I was a

half-grown lad, and permitted to witness the terrors and
severities of the law.

The prisoner was the center of interest. He sat with a stolid
countenance like a man careless of the issues of life. But not
everybody was concerned with him, for my Uncle Abner and
Storm watched the girl who had been accustomed to bake for
Marsh and red up his house.

She was a beauty of her type; dark haired and dark eyed
like a gypsy, and with an April nature of storm and sun.
She sat among the witnesses with a little handkerchief clutched
in her hands. She was nervous to the point of hysteria, and
I thought that was the reason the old doctor watched her.
She would be taken with a gust of tears, and then throw up
her head with a fine defiance; and she kneaded and knotted
and worked the handkerchief in her fingers. It was a time
of stress and many witnesses were unnerved, and I think I
should not have noticed this girl but for the whispering of
Storm and my Uncle Abner.

The trial went forward, and it became certain that the
prisoner would hang. His stubborn refusal to give any reason
for his hurried departure had but one meaning, and the circumstantial evidence was conclusive. The motive, only, remained in doubt, and the Judge had charged on this with so
many cases in point, and with so heavy a hand, that any
virtue in it was removed. The Judge was hard against this
man, and indeed there was little sympathy anywhere, for it
was a foul killing—the victim an old man and no hot blood
to excuse it.

In all trials of great public interest, where the evidences of
guilt overwhelmingly assemble against a prisoner, there comes
a moment when all the people in the court-room, as one man,
and without a sign of the common purpose, agree upon a
verdict; there is no outward or visible evidence of this decision, but one feels it, and it is a moment of the tensest stress.

The trial of Taylor had reached this point, and there lay
a moment of deep silence, when this girl sitting among the
witnesses suddenly burst into a very hysteria of tears. She
stood up shaking with sobs, her voice choking in her throat,
and the tears gushing through her fingers.

What she said was not heard at the time by the audience in the court-room, but it brought the Judge to his feet and the jury crowding about her, and it broke down the silence of the prisoner, and threw him into a perfect fury of denials. We could hear his voice rise above the confusion, and we could see him struggling to get to the girl and stop her. But what she said was presently known to everybody, for it was taken down and signed; and it put the case against Taylor, to use a lawyer's term, out of court.

The girl had killed Marsh herself. And this was the manner and the reason of it: She and Taylor were sweethearts and were to be married. But they had quarreled the night before Marsh's death and the following morning Taylor had left the country. The point of the quarrel was some remark that Marsh had made to Taylor touching the girl's reputation. She had come to the house in the afternoon, and finding her lover gone, and maddened at the sight of the one who had robbed her of him, had taken the gun down from the chimney and killed Marsh. She had then put the gun back into its place and left the house. This was about two o'clock in the afternoon, and about an hour before Taylor returned for his gun.

There was a great veer of public feeling with a profound sense of having come at last upon the truth, for the story not only fitted to the circumstantial evidence against Taylor, but it fitted also to his story and it disclosed the motive for the killing. It explained, too, why he had refused to give the reason for his disappearance. That Taylor denied what the girl said and tried to stop her in her declaration, meant nothing except that the prisoner was a man, and would not have the woman he loved make such a sacrifice for him.

I cannot give all the forms of legal procedure with which the closing hours of the court were taken up, but nothing happened to shake the girl's confession. Whatever the law required was speedily got ready, and she was remanded to the care of the sheriff in order that she might come before the court in the morning.

Taylor was not released, but was also held in custody, although the case against him seemed utterly broken down. The Judge refused to permit the prisoner's counsel to take a verdict. He said that he would withdraw a juror and continue the case. But he seemed unwilling to release any clutch of the law until some one was punished for this crime.

It was on our way, and we rode out with the Judge that night. He talked with Abner and Storm about the pastures and the price of cattle, but not about the trial, as I hoped he would do, except once only, and then it was to inquire why the prosecuting attorney had not called either of them as witnesses, since they were the first to find Marsh, and Storm had been among the doctors who examined him. And Storm had explained how he had mortally offended the prosecutor in his canvass, by his remark that only a gentleman should hold office. He did but quote Mr. Hamilton, Storm said, but the man had received it as a deadly insult, and thereby proved the truth of Mr. Hamilton's expression, Storm added. And Abner said that as no circumstance about Marsh's death was questioned, and others arriving about the same time had been called, the prosecutor doubtless considered further testimony unnecessary.

The Judge nodded, and the conversation turned to other questions. At the gate, after the common formal courtesy of the country, the Judge asked us to ride in, and, to my astonishment, Abner and Storm accepted his invitation. I could see that the man was surprised, and I thought annoyed, but he took us into his library.

I could not understand why Abner and Storm had stopped here, until I remembered how from the first they had been considering the girl, and it occurred to me that they thus sought the Judge in the hope of getting some word to him in her favor. A great sentiment had leaped up for this girl. She had made a staggering sacrifice, and with a headlong courage, and it was like these men to help her if they could.

And it was to speak of the woman that they came, but not in her favor. And while Simon Kilrail listened, they told this extraordinary story: They had been of the opinion that Taylor was not guilty when the trial began, but they had suffered it to proceed in order to see what might develop. The reason was that there were certain circumstantial evidences, overlooked by the prosecutor, indicating the guilt of the woman and the innocence of Taylor. When Storm examined the body of Marsh he discovered that the man had been killed by poison, and was dead when the bullet was fired into his body. This meant that the shooting was a fabricated evidence to direct suspicion against Taylor. The woman had baked for Marsh on this morning, and the poison was in the bread which he had eaten at noon.

Abner was going on to explain something further, when a servant entered and asked the Judge what time it was. The man had been greatly impressed, and he now sat in a profound reflection. He took his watch out of his pocket and held it in his hand, then he seemed to realize the question and replied that his watch had run down. Abner gave the hour, and said that perhaps his key would wind the watch. The Judge gave it to him, and he wound it and laid it on the table. Storm observed my Uncle with, what I thought, a curious interest, but the Judge paid no attention. He was deep in his reflection and oblivious to everything. Finally he roused himself and made his comment.

"This clears the matter up," he said. "The woman killed Marsh from the motive which she gave in her confession, and she created this false evidence against Taylor because he had abandoned her. She thereby avenged herself desperately in two directions. . . . It would be like a woman to do this, and then regret it and confess."

He then asked my uncle if he had anything further to tell him, and although I was sure that Abner was going on to say something further when the servant entered, he replied now that he had not, and asked for the horses. The Judge went out to have the horses brought, and we remained in silence. My uncle was calm, as with some consuming idea, but Storm was as nervous as a cat. He was out of his chair when the door was closed, and hopping about the room looking at the law books standing on the shelves in their leather covers. Suddenly he stopped and plucked out a little volume. He whipped through it with his forefinger, smothered a great oath, and shot it into his pocket, then he crooked his finger to my uncle, and they talked together in a recess of the window until the Judge returned.

We rode away. I was sure that they intended to say something to the Judge in the woman's favor, for, guilty or not, it was a fine thing she had done to stand up and confess. But something in the interview had changed their purpose. Perhaps when they had heard the Judge's comment they saw it would be of no use. They talked closely together as they rode, but they kept before me and I could not hear. It was of the woman they spoke, however, for I caught a fragment.

"But where is the motive?" said Storm.

And my uncle answered, "In the twenty-first chapter of the Book of Kings."

We were early at the county seat, and it was a good thing for us, because the court-room was crowded to the doors. My uncle had got a big record book out of the county clerk's office as he came in, and I was glad of it, for he gave it to me to sit on, and it raised me up so I could see. Storm was there, too, and, in fact, every man of any standing in the county.

The sheriff opened the court, the prisoners were brought in, and the Judge took his seat on the bench. He looked haggard like a man who had not slept, as, in fact, one could hardly have done who had so cruel a duty before him. Here was every human feeling pressing to save a woman, and the law to hang her. But for all his hag-ridden face, when he came to act, the man was adamant.

He ordered the confession read, and directed the girl to stand up. Taylor tried again to protest, but he was forced down into his chair. The girl stood up bravely, but she was white as plaster, and her eyes dilated. She was asked if she still adhered to the confession and understood the consequences of it, and, although she trembled from head to toe, she spoke out distinctly. There was a moment of silence and the Judge was about to speak, when another voice filled the court-room. I turned about on my book to find my head against my Uncle Abner's legs.

"I challenge the confession!" he said.

The whole court-room moved. Every eye was on the two tragic figures standing up: the slim, pale girl and the big, somber figure of my uncle. The Judge was astounded.

"On what ground?" he said.

"On the ground," replied my uncle, "that the confession is a lie!"

One could have heard a pin fall anywhere in the whole room. The girl caught her breath in a little gasp, and the prisoner, Taylor, half rose and then sat down as though his knees were too weak to bear him. The Judge's mouth opened, but for a moment or two he did not speak, and I could understand his amazement. Here was Abner assailing a confession which he himself had supported before the Judge, and speaking for the innocence of a woman whom he himself had shown to be guilty and taking one position privately, and another publicly. What did the man mean? And I was not surprised that the Judge's voice was stern when he spoke.

"This is irregular," he said. "It may be that this woman killed Marsh, or it may be that Taylor killed him, and there is some collusion between these persons, as you appear to suggest. And you may know something to throw light on the matter, or you may not. However that may be, this is not the time for me to hear you. You will have ample opportunity to speak when I come to try the case."

"But you will never try this case!" said Abner.

I cannot undertake to describe the desperate interest that lay on the people in the courtroom. They were breathlessly silent; one could hear the voices from the village outside, and the sounds of men and horses that came up through the open windows. No one knew what hidden thing Abner drove at. But he was a man who meant what he said, and the people knew it.

The Judge turned on him with a terrible face.

"What do you mean?" he said.

"I mean," replied Abner, and it was in his deep, hard voice, "that you must come down from the bench."

The Judge was in a heat of fury.

"You are in contempt," he roared. "I order your arrest. Sheriff!" he called.

But Abner did not move. He looked the man calmly in the face.

"You threaten me," he said, "but God Almighty threatens you." And he turned about to the audience. "The authority of the law," he said, "is in the hands of the electors of this county. Will they stand up?"

I shall never forget what happened then, for I have never in my life seen anything so deliberate and impressive. Slowly, in silence, and without passion, as though they were in a church of God, men began to get up in the courtroom.

Randolph was the first. He was a justice of the peace, vain and pompous, proud of the abilities of an ancestry that he did not inherit. And his superficialities were the annoyance of my Uncle Abner's life. But whatever I may have to say of him hereafter I want to say this thing of him here, that his bigotry and his vanities were builded on the foundations of a man. He stood up as though he stood alone, with no glance about him to see what other men would do, and he faced the Judge calmly above his great black stock. And I learned then that a man may be a blusterer and a lion.

Hiram Arnold got up, and Rockford, and Armstrong, and Alkire, and Coopman, and Monroe, and Elnathan Stone, and my father, Lewis, and Dayton and Ward, and Madison from beyond the mountains. And it seemed to me that the very hills and valleys were standing up.

It was a strange and instructive thing to see. The loud-mouthed and the reckless were in that courtroom, men who would have shouted in a political convention, or run howling with a mob, but they were not the persons who stood up when Abner called upon the authority of the people to appear. Men rose whom one would not have looked to see—the blacksmith, the saddler, and old Asa Divers. And I saw that law and order and all the structure that civilization had builded up, rested on the sense of justice that certain men carried in their breasts, and that those who possessed it not, in the crisis of necessity, did not count.

Father Donovan stood up; he had a little flock beyond the valley river, and he was as poor, and almost as humble as his Master, but he was not afraid; and Bronson, who preached Calvin, and Adam Rider, who traveled a Methodist circuit.

No one of them believed in what the other taught; but they all believed in justice, and when the line was drawn, there was but one side for them all.

The last man up was Nathaniel Davisson, but the reason was that he was very old, and he had to wait for his sons to help him. He had been time and again in the Assembly of Virginia, at a time when only a gentleman and landowner could sit there. He was a just man, and honorable and unafraid.

The Judge, his face purple, made a desperate effort to enforce his authority. He pounded on his desk and ordered the sheriff to clear the courtroom. But the sheriff remained standing apart. He did not lack for courage, and I think he would have faced the people if his duty had been that way. His attitude was firm, and one could mark no uncertainty upon him, but he took no step to obey what the Judge commanded.

The Judge cried out at him in a terrible voice.

"I am the representative of the law here. Go on!"

The sheriff was a plain man, and unacquainted with the nice expressions of Mr. Jefferson, but his answer could not have been better if that gentleman had written it out for him.

"I would obey the representative of the law," he said, "if I were not in the presence of the law itself!"

The Judge rose. "This is revolution," he said; "I will send to the Governor for the militia."

It was Nathaniel Davisson who spoke then. He was very old and the tremors of dissolution were on him, but his voice was steady.

"Sit down, your Honor," he said, "there is no revolution here, and you do not require troops to support your authority. We are here to support it if it ought to be lawfully enforced. But the people have elevated you to the Bench because they believed in your integrity, and if they have been mistaken they would know it." He paused, as though to collect his strength, and then went on. "The presumptions of right are all with your Honor. You administer the law upon our authority and we stand behind you. Be assured that we will not suffer our authority to be insulted in your person." His voice grew deep and resolute. "It is a grave thing to call us up against you, and not lightly, nor for a trivial reason shall any man dare to do it." Then he turned about. "Now, Abner," he said, "what is this thing?"

Young as I was, I felt that the old man spoke for the people standing in the courtroom, with their voice and their authority, and I began to fear that the measure which my uncle had taken was high handed. But he stood there like the shadow of a great rock.

"I charge him," he said, "with the murder of Elihu Marsh! And I call upon him to vacate the Bench."

When I think about this extraordinary event now, I wonder at the calmness with which Simon Kilrail met this blow, until I reflect that he had seen it on its way, and had got ready to meet it. But even with that preparation, it took a man of iron nerve to face an assault like that and keep every muscle in its place. He had tried violence and had failed with it, and he had recourse now to the attitudes and mannerisms of a judicial dignity. He sat with his elbows on the table, and his clenched fingers propping up his jaw. He looked coldly at Abner, but he did not speak, and there was silence until Nathaniel Davisson spoke for him. His face and his voice were like iron.

"No, Abner," he said, "he shall not vacate the Bench for that, nor upon the accusation of any man. We will have your proofs, if you please."

The Judge turned his cold face from Abner to Nathaniel Davisson, and then he looked over the men standing in the courtroom.

"I am not going to remain here," he said, "to be tried by a mob, upon the *viva voce* indictment of a bystander. You may nullify your court, if you like, and suspend the forms of law for yourselves, but you cannot nullify the constitution of Virginia, nor suspend my right as a citizen of that commonwealth.

"And now," he said, rising, "if you will kindly make way, I will vacate this courtroom, which your violence has converted into a chamber of sedition."

The man spoke in a cold, even voice, and I thought he

had presented a difficulty that could not be met. How could these men before him understand to keep the peace of this frontier, and force its lawless elements to submit to the forms of law for trial, and deny any letter of those formalities to this man? Was the grand jury, and the formal indictment, and all the right and privilege of an orderly procedure for one, and not for another?

It was Nathaniel Davisson who met this dangerous problem.

"We are not concerned," he said, "at this moment with your rights as a citizen; the rights of private citizenship are inviolate, and they remain to you, when you return to it. But you are not a private citizen. You are our agent. We have selected you to administer the law for us, and your right to act has been challenged. Well, as the authority behind you, we appear and would know the reason."

The Judge retained his imperturbable calm.

"Do you hold me a prisoner here?" he said.

"We hold you an official in your office," replied Davisson, "not only do we refuse to permit you to leave the courtroom, but we refuse to permit you to leave the Bench. This court shall remain as we have set it up until it is our will to re-adjust it. And it shall not be changed at the pleasure or demand of any man but by us only, and for a sufficient cause shown to us."

And again I was anxious for my uncle, for I saw how grave a thing it was to interfere with the authority of the people as manifested in the forms and agencies of the law. Abner must be very sure of the ground under him.

And he was sure. He spoke now, with no introductory expressions, but directly and in the simplest words.

"These two persons," he said, indicating Taylor and the girl, "have each been willing to die in order to save the other. Neither is guilty of this crime. Taylor has kept silent, and the girl has lied, to the same end. This is the truth: There was a lovers' quarrel, and Taylor left the country precisely as he told us, except the motive, which he would not tell lest the girl be involved. And the woman, to save him, confesses to a crime that she did not commit.

"Who did commit it?" He paused and included Storm with

a gesture. "We suspected this woman because Marsh had been killed by poison in his bread, and afterwards mutilated with a shot. Yesterday we rode out with the Judge to put those facts before him." Again he paused. "An incident occurring in that interview indicated that we were wrong; a second incident assured us, and still later, a third convinced us. These incidents were, first, that the Judge's watch had run down; second, that we found in his library a book with all the leaves in it uncut, except at one certain page; and, third, that we found in the county clerk's office an unindexed record in an old deed book." There was deep quiet and he went on:

"In addition to the theory of Taylor's guilt or this woman's, there was still a third; but it had only a single incident to support it, and we feared to suggest it until the others had been explained. This theory was that some one, to benefit by Marsh's death, had planned to kill him in such a manner as to throw suspicion on this woman who baked his bread, and finding Taylor gone, and the gun above the mantel, yielded to an afterthought to create a further false evidence. It was overdone!

"The trigger guard of the gun in the recoil caught in the chain of the assassin's watch and jerked it out of his pocket; he replaced the watch, but not the key which fell to the floor, and which I picked up beside the body of the dead man."

Abner turned toward the judge.

"And so," he said, "I charge Simon Kilrail with this murder; because the key winds his watch; because the record in the old deed book is a conveyance by the heirs of Marsh's lands to him at the life tenant's death; and because the book we found in his library is a book on poisons with the leaves uncut, except at the very page describing that identical poison with which Elihu Marsh was murdered."

The strained silence that followed Abner's words was broken by a voice that thundered in the courtroom. It was Randolph's.

"Come down!" he said.

And this time Nathaniel Davisson was silent.

The Judge got slowly on his feet, a resolution was forming in his face, and it advanced swiftly.

"I will give you my answer in a moment," he said.

Then he turned about and went into his room behind the Bench. There was but one door, and that opening into the court, and the people waited.

The windows were open and we could see the green fields, and the sun, and the far-off mountains, and the peace and quiet and serenity of autumn entered. The Judge did not appear. Presently there was the sound of a shot from behind the closed door. The sheriff threw it open, and upon the floor, sprawling in a smear of blood, lay Simon Kilrail, with a dueling pistol in his hand.

TOM STACEY REPRINTS

This series makes available again some of the best books by the best authors of our time, priced at £1.80 each except where otherwise stated. Already published are:

Michael Arlen
    THESE CHARMING PEOPLE
H. C. Bailey
    THE SULLEN SKY MYSTERY
Francis Beeding
    THE LEAGUE OF DISCONTENT
Hilaire Belloc
    THE FOUR MEN
Earl Derr Biggers
    CHARLIE CHAN CARRIES ON
    THE CHINESE PARROT
Max Brand
    SILVERTIP
Edgar Rice Burroughs
    AT THE EARTH'S CORE
    PELLUCIDAR
    TARZAN'S QUEST
Robert W. Chambers
    THE SLAYER OF SOULS
Richard Dalby
    THE SORCERESS IN STAINED GLASS   (£2.00)
Clemence Dane & Helen Simpson
    ENTER SIR JOHN
Carter Dickson
    THE JUDAS WINDOW
    MURDER IN THE SUBMARINE ZONE
    THE TEN TEACUPS
Edna Ferber
    CIMARRON
    SHOW BOAT
Peter Fleming
    THE SIEGE AT PEKING
Francis Gérard
    SECRET SCEPTRE
David Graeme
    MONSIEUR BLACKSHIRT
    THE VENGEANCE OF MONSIEUR BLACKSHIRT
H. Rider Haggard
    THE ANCIENT ALLAN
    THE GHOST KINGS
    RED EVE
Macdonald Hastings
    CORK ON THE WATER
Anthony Hope
    THE HEART OF PRINCESS OSRA
Ronald Kirkbride
    THE KING OF THE VIA VENETO
John Lambourne
    THE KINGDOM THAT WAS

C. A. Lejeune
THANK YOU FOR HAVING ME
Helen McCloy
TWO-THIRDS OF A GHOST
John P. Marquand
STOPOVER: TOKYO
A. E. W. Mason
CLEMENTINA
FIRE OVER ENGLAND
A. Merritt
BURN WITCH BURN
Gladys Mitchell
THE RISING OF THE MOON
Clarence E. Mulford
BAR-20
HOPALONG CASSIDY
Clayton Rawson
DEATH FROM A TOP HAT
Sax Rohmer
BROOD OF THE WITCH-QUEEN
THE YELLOW CLAW
R. C. Sherriff
THE FORTNIGHT IN SEPTEMBER
G. B. Stern
THE YOUNG MATRIARCH   (£2.50)
Rex Stout
RED THREADS
SOME BURIED CASEAR
WHERE THERE'S A WILL
Angela Thirkell
THE HEADMISTRESS
S. S. Van Dine
THE BENSON MURDER CASE
Edgar Wallace
SANDI THE KING-MAKER
Alec Waugh
JILL SOMERSET   (£2.00)
P. C. Wren
ACTION AND PASSION   (£2.25)
Philip Yordan
MAN OF THE WEST

CHILDREN'S BOOKS
Frances Hodgson Burnett
RACKETTY-PACKETTY HOUSE   (£1.30)
Thornton W. Burgess
OLD MOTHER WEST WIND   (£1.70)
MOTHER WEST WIND'S CHILDREN   (£1.70)
Austin Clare
THE CARVED CARTOON   (£1.80)
Howard Pyle
THE MERRY ADVENTURES OF ROBIN HOOD   (£2.25)

Tom Stacey Reprints Ltd.
28–29 Maiden Lane, London WC2E J7P